The
Condimental
Op

cocktail'd stories served on a bent

paper platter

The Condimental Op

cocktail'd stories served on a bent
paper platter

Andrez Bergen

PERFECT
EDGE
BOOKS

Winchester, UK
Washington, USA

First published by Perfect Edge Books, 2013
Perfect Edge Books is an imprint of John Hunt Publishing Ltd., Laurel House, Station Approach,
Alresford, Hants, SO24 9JH, UK
office1@jhpbooks.net
www.johnhuntpublishing.com
www.perfectedgebooks.com

For distributor details and how to order please visit the 'Ordering' section on our website.

Text copyright: Andrez Bergen 2013

ISBN: 978 1 78279 189 8

A CIP catalogue record for this book is available from the British Library.

Design: Stuart Davies

Printed and bound by CPI Group (UK) Ltd, Croydon, CR0 4YY

We operate a distinctive and ethical publishing philosophy in all areas of our business, from our global network of authors to production and worldwide distribution.

CONTENTS

THE CONDIMENTAL OP:

cocktail'd stories served on a bent paper platter

SHORT YARNS, OFF-CUTS, IDEAS, COMICS, REJECT MATÉRIEL, SUBTITLING & IRREGULAR ARTICLES 1989—2013

COVER ARTWORK BY COCOA BERGEN
ARTWORK, ABOVE, BY ANDREW CHIU
ARTWORK, PAGE 10, BY NICOLAS GOMES
ARTWORK, PAGE 41, BY MAAN HOUSE
ARTWORK, PAGE 103, BY SCOTT CAMPBELL
ARTWORK, PAGES 146 TO 149, BY MARCOS VERGARA
ARTWORK, PAGES 161 TO 164, BY ANDREZ BERGEN
X-RAY, PAGE 261, BY THE DOC

Also by the same author:

TOBACCO-STAINED MOUNTAIN GOAT
ONE HUNDRED YEARS OF VICISSITUDE
WHO IS KILLING THE GREAT CAPES OF HEROPA?

'ONE HUNDRED YEARS OF VICISSITUDE' (2012)

"Charles Dickens collides with Haruki Murakami in a pulsating tale of history, redemption and revenge." FANTASY BOOK REVIEW

"A wildly enchanting journey down the rabbit hole." ELIZABETH A. WHITE

"A cracking great story." BRITISH FANTASY SOCIETY

"Dreamlike and bewitchingly evocative." THE FLAWED MIND

"A unique, memorable story — indescribable, exhilarating." FORCES OF GEEK

"Quirky, poignant, and utterly brilliant." DRYING INK

"Hard-boiled and entertaining." ZOUCH MAGAZINE

"*One Hundred Years of Vicissitude* reaffirms a postmodern dexterity of Cirque du Soleil proportions." FARRAGO MAGAZINE

"Breathtakingly detailed. I defy you to read this book." STEAMPUNK MAGAZINE

"Exquisite, incredibly touching and devastating in its beauty." I MEANT TO READ THAT

"A terrific book!" BARE*BONES

"Crime, geisha, time travel; masterfully balances these things and turns its nose up at pretentious literature."
INSOMNIA PRESS

"A wonderful tale... This is what good literary fiction reads like." ALWAYSUNMENDED

"A witty voyage of ideas, history, pop culture, style, characters and scenes that are unforgettable." RAYMOND EMBRACK

"A strange mixture of science fiction, fantasy, and literary fiction." A FANTASTICAL LIBRARIAN

"I love this. The narrator is fascinating — as are his two unlikely companions." LITREACTOR

"Told in the author's inimitable narrative style — Bergen relishes wacky tangents and dives head-first into philosophical dialogues that prove to be some of the most satisfying parts of his books." DEATH BY KILLING

'TOBACCO-STAINED MOUNTAIN GOAT'
(2011)

"Andrez Bergen put science fiction, noir, Australia and Japan into a literary hadron collider, and *Tobacco-Stained Mountain Goat* came out." THE THOUSANDS MAGAZINE

"*Tobacco-Stained Mountain Goat* is an incredible novel, completely unexpected and with such a wonderfully rich and unique style that is simply mesmerizing, unmissable." SF BOOK REVIEWS

"Such an engrossing and visual read — with gorgeous, subtle moments in there as well." LIP MAGAZINE

"Original and unforgettable." DARK WOLF'S FANTASY REVIEWS

"At the heart of Bergen's novel is the love affair our author has with popular culture. This book is bursting with nods and homages to everything from Humphrey Bogart to *Mobile Suit Gundam*." VERBICIDE MAGAZINE

"A wonderful ambush of a novel. It leads you down a well-tread path and then jumps from the brush and drags you to uncharted lands. It has been a while since I had this childlike joy at turning the page. It's an insane, hard-boiled future shocker. Wow." JOSH STALLINGS, *author of* Beautiful, Naked & Dead

"Flows effortlessly; smart, mesmerizingly dark and difficult to put down." VICE MAGAZINE

"Andrez wears his pop-culture influences on his sleeve, and the result is a compote that mashes up a plethora of fictional frame-

works into a believable, seamless whole. Floyd Maquina is ruggedly handsome and generally ruined; witty, self-destructive and self-effacing with his air of gracious defeat."
THE FLAWED MIND

"I can say without qualification that not only is *Tobacco-Stained Mountain Goat* one of my Top 5 reads of 2011, it is one of the most creative and engaging books I've ever read. Period. My mind is completely blown." ELIZABETH A. WHITE

"A post-modern mélange that is the most intriguing of novels — hardboiled and playful at the same time."
AUSTRALIAN SPECULATIVE FICTION IN FOCUS

"Terrific stuff, truly unique. One of my favourite books of 2011."
HEATH LOWRANCE, *author of* The Bastard Hand

"*Tobacco-Stained Mountain Goat* is a retro pop culturalist's dream come true — and entertaining to boot." PERMISSION TO KILL for Cocoa and Yoko

INTRO

This grubby medley of written stuff is something I started nutting out last year, in between writing two novels (*One Hundred Years of Vicissitude* and *Who is Killing the Great Capes of Heropa?*) at the same time that I cobbled together an anthology called *The Tobacco-Stained Sky*, worked a full-time job teaching English here in Tokyo, and tried to keep enough spare change time-wise to entertain my young daughter — thereby (hopefully) not ignoring her too much.

2012 was that kind of fun-filled fiasco.

To start off this new year in similar 'style' I finished putting together the collection resting either (a) in your hands, or (b) on-screen, depending on your preference. Luckily, *One Hundred Years of Vicissitude*, which I published via Perfect Edge Books last October, somehow climbed to #1 at Amazon — giving me the churlish freedom to push this project through.

You'll find nips, tucks and evasive moments here that refer directly or indirectly to characters and situations in my three novels (especially my first, *Tobacco-Stained Mountain Goat*),

I

hopefully without needing to consult any of these in the full — but a reading might just enhance the dubious experience and help top up the precariously empty coffers of my wallet.

Additionally I've lobbed in some unrelated stuff: recent(ish) short stories and articles I penned for *Geek* magazine in the US, *Impact* in the UK, and *Zebra* back in Melbourne, along with a few pages of dodgy prose pieces written for a coffee-table tome of fancy photos in 1989.

For most of the yarns I've added a precursory waffle, in italics, which is more insider-trading in case you've read my other material. These do contain spoilers, so skip them if you want to read each story fresh.

On a personal level, enormous gratitude must go to my wife Yoko, who has so patiently understood my need to spend great wads of time daydreaming, writing, editing and promotion. And I love the fact that this particular book comes with cover art done by Cocoa last year, at age six, since it also contains an article I wrote for *VICE* magazine in 2005 — immediately prior to her birth and about same. Cocoa, more than any individual, is responsible for my rediscovery of the act of story-telling.

Finally, the title of this book is a silly riff on Dashiell Hammett's famous detective the Continental Op, whose real name is never mentioned in any outing.

I used it previously for a chapter in *Tobacco-Stained Mountain Goat* and a twelve-inch Little Nobody record I put out through IF? Records in 2010 (with remixes by Detroit's Aux 88 and K. Alexi Shelby in Chicago).

Hopefully Dashiell doesn't writhe in his coffin over at Arlington National Cemetery. Then again, I'm far enough away not to mind.

Andrez, February 2013

PART 1: OTHER BITS

All things start somewhere; so let's begin here with one of my more recent short stories.

I wrote **Sugar & Spice** *for Chris Rhatigan's crime/hardboiled anthology* **All Due Respect** *(published via Full Dark City Press) and luckily he dug the story. I was going to throw in the pun 'respected' but think I'll leave the shallow laughs till later in the tome, when you're punch-drunk and less critical.*

"Crime and postmodernism go together like peanut butter and jelly," Chris emailed me back from India (really). "Gleefully maniacal stuff." Fiona Johnston, a fellow contributor, wrote in her review: "The teenagers who attempt the heist haven't the common sense to work out that the rare copy they've spotted displayed might not be all it seems and they pay dearly for this mistake. Yet again, Bergen gives a master-class in short story writing." (ta, matey)

The **All Due Respect** *collection brings together some wild people like Fiona, Joe Clifford, Patti Abbott, Nigel Bird, Tom Pitts, CJ Edwards, Chris Leek, Richard Godwin, Mike Monson, Matthew C. Funk, Ron T. Brown and David Cranmer — so hunt it down if you can.*

This particular inclusion was put together in October 2012, while I had my head deeply buried in my third novel **Who is Killing the Great Capes of Heropa?** *— which is all about comicbook lore and superhero culture, mixed up with noir.*

No real surprise, then, that I decided to have two high-school kids knock over a comicbook store in a more contemporary Melbourne.

The comic shop in question is based on the one I used to hang out at while in high school. Minotaur now is a huge, highly successful institution in Melbourne, but back in the '80s it was a small shop down a minor arcade in the city.

Off Bourke Street.

Incidentally, these kids hop on the train at South Yarra, the nearest station to my old high school Melbourne High, they have their fingers in the till at the school tuck-shop (sounds familiar) and the bicycle of choice is a classic '70s Malvern Star chopper... same as mine when I was that age.

Sugar & Spice

Rankine lifted his head off the floor and peered at his gut, at the blood pumping out of the big hole in his shirtfront, running down the sides and creating a huge puddle on the carpet.

"Crap," he muttered. "That's going to be a bugger to patch."

Wasn't supposed to be like this, no way. Three days ago Mitch reckoned it'd be a blow-over, easy street romp — if not exactly sugar and spice and everything nice, then something marginally sweet.

The shop was down an unpopular arcade, in the city on Bourke Street, not much pedestrian traffic, and the nearest cop house three blocks away.

Basics, security-wise: a camera that probably didn't work, just for show to scare the amateurs, and a newly installed magnetic tag security detector straddling the doorway. Probably bought on eBay, but they heard it go off when some kid tried something, so they knew that baby was no Trojan Horse.

The bloke behind the counter seemed to actually be two people sharing the same beard, receding hairline and dress-sense (bordering on offensive suburban hippy).

There were no nametags to double-check who was who and they were always too busy reading shit to pay attention to customers' questions — which Mitch said worked to their advantage since they wouldn't know what was going on till it was too late.

The big attraction? This was no diamond merchant, not a bank, nor a service station/convenience store. It wasn't even a dodgy school kiosk, their usual port-of-criminal-call.

This was a comicbook store, a minor affair specializing in new releases from America and a wad of collectibles. No manga at all, which was one of the reasons Rankine had never heard of the place.

The thing was, they had a copy of *Action Comics* #1 up on the wall.

This meant nothing to Rankine, who coveted an early, uncensored printing of Katsura Masakazu's *Video Girl Ai* manga, since later printings changed the art to cover up the nudity.

Mitch courteously filled in the massive gaps in his American comic knowhow: the issue that gave Superman his big break, published in the U.S. in 1938 for just ten cents. Over seventy years later a rare copy was sold online for $2.16m.

"You know Nick Ratatouille?" Mitch went on.

"Maybe." Rankine had been out front of the folks' place, sitting on his bum on the nature-strip fixing an elusive puncture on the tyre of his painstakingly rebuilt 1974 Malvern Star chopper, trying not to get tangled up in Mitch's plans.

Mitch had a tendency to lead partners astray — namely arrest or injury, or both — even if he always got off scot-free. Still, this was one question Rankine believed he could tackle without a lure or a slap. "Isn't he the muscle for Occitan and the boys over on Catalan Crescent?"

"Right on. He heard from a mate who heard from another mate that it was sold by Nicolas Cage."

"You reckon the comic in that shop is the same one once owned by him?"

"No, you moron — but if that one got two mill, there's every chance the one on the wall in this dive will get half that, at least. A million, R, that we can split down the middle. You could get your bloody Malvern Star gold-plated if you want."

That'd been the clincher. Not the gold plating but the swandooly.

Rankine went along with it all, even forking out the dosh for the ski masks from an army disposals shop on Elizabeth Street and a couple of BB-guns he got FedEx'd from Japan that were replica full-scale Enfield revolvers.

Knocking over a comicbook store would be a breeze. Nothing could go wrong.

So they'd skipped out on high school on a Monday — he'd forged the letters from their mums as usual — and got out of their uniforms in the toilets at South Yarra Station before heading into town on a Frankston Line train at 2:10 p.m.

Got off at Flinders Street before three, after typical bloody delays, and waltzed straight to the arcade. Flicked through some brand new Marvel comics that bored Rankine silly, waiting till no one else was in the shop, and then pulled on the balaclavas and pointed their faux firearms at the bird behind the counter.

"Give us the fucking comic, dickhead!" Mitch screamed in too loud a voice.

"Sure, kid, sure, don't get your knickers in a knot," old Beard-and-Bald assured him, hands clutching air. "Which one?"

"Clark Kent up there, on the wall." Mitch waved the gun in a general direction over the clerk's head. "Move it!"

"You mean... Are you talking about this?" The man pointed to *Action Comics* #1, a primitive-looking Superman lifting a green car above his head and smashing it.

"Sure. Hand-pass it over."

"You boys do realize it's a repro?"

Rankine leaned forward. "A what?"

"Reproduction. This isn't the real thing — why on earth would we have it sitting right here in our shop? That'd be lunacy."

Rankine couldn't be sure, but he sussed the old hippy was lying. Mitch, however, was in a rage, shoving his popgun forward.

"Bullshit!" he shouted, so incensed he lost control of his drool.

Rankine observed this spittle traveling across air from his partner's mouth; saw it settle down on the desktop and sit there, bubbly and offensive.

That was when Beard-and-Bald got angry. He stared at the saliva, and then dropped his right hand —

Fretting some, Mitch waggled his toy. "Don't move!"

— And the man stood up straight with an Uzi submachine gun stuck in his mitt. Rankine had a sneaking suspicion this baby hadn't been purchased via mail order from Tokyo; conjecture confirmed when the thing start dishing out real 9mm bullets.

"Nobody spits in my shop! No fucker steals my comics!" Beard-and-Bald raved as he raked the small area, destroying much of the merchandise before he found his real targets.

Mitch, Rankine could see from his place spreadeagled on his back, was dead as a dodo, folded up against the wall with brains wallpapering a bunch of DC comics in a rack.

He returned attention to his stomach, felt dizzy, tried to pull together the flaps of skin there — same technique as sticking together the flaps of rubber with the puncture the other day.

Now, if only he had his tyre-sealant glue.

The next story was done for a 2012 anthology assembled by Luca Veste and Paul D. Brazill.

It was called Off the Record 2, *included forty-six other writers, and was put together to raise money for two children's literacy charities in the U.S. and the U.K.*

The guidelines? A story based around a classic film title. Given I'm a movie journalist, this was a Heaven-sent request.

I decided to use the Blake Edwards cross-dressing romp Victor Victoria *(1982), which starred Julie Andrews and James Garner — but I've never seen it. Can't say why. I'm not the biggest fan of Julie Andrews.* The Sound of Music *makes me writhe, but I do tend to like Blake's movies from the '60s.*

When I wrote the piece I also wasn't sure about the title and was leaning toward Howard Hughes' Hell's Angels, *since that's all about World War I, biplanes, dog-fighting and big dirigibles. Same as my story. The reason I went with* Victor Victoria, *I think, is because — although the time frame is just after the Edwardian era — there's something Victorian about the yarn, possibly resulting from the inclusion of Britannia.*

I decided to go for a relatively flippant version of Captain W. E. Johns' classic Biggles *romps. You know, the books about the ace pilot and adventurer written from the 1930s. I'm also poking fun at racial stereotypes: the German officer, Wilhelm Klink, is based on Colonel Klink from* Hogan's Heroes *and other sham "German" characters I've seen on the telly.*

So it's an adventure, hopefully amusing, and also a convoluted love story. With a god.

As it turned out I dug the Britannia character so much I morphed her into Pretty Amazonia (a super-powered, seven-foot human being) in Who is Killing the Great Capes of Heropa?, *which was written straight after this.*

Wilks I liked too, since he's snatched from a fairly two-dimensional, minor character in the Biggles stories (in which he developed a friendly rivalry with James Bigglesworth during First World War air combat, and destroyed his own pyjamas with a machine gun). I've thought about doing more with this debonair cad.

Oh, and I tagged-on the chestnut following this one (An Octopus's Grotto is His Castle) since they were written round the same period and I just noticed they have very, very similar opening lines. Weird. That one was written for the suave Solarcide anthology Nova Parade (check out solarcide.com).

Yes, it lovingly takes the piss out of big-ocean-beastie literature from the 19th century (Herman Melville's Moby-Dick, Jules Verne's Twenty Thousand Leagues Under the Sea, Victor Hugo's Toilers of the Sea, Lewis Carroll's The Walrus and the Carpenter) and their mid-20th century Hollywood spin-offs.

"Read the story earlier and I'd definitely like to take that one off you for the collection," Solarcide's Martin Garrity said in an email dated April 29, 2012. "Good stuff, man, good stuff indeed. It's completely different in style to any of the other stories we have so far and that rocks."

I'm not sure what the fixation was with octopuses. Cocoa and I sure were eating a lot of them (with lemon juice — yum) at the time.

Anyway, thought I'd set off the flavour of this old-school section of the book with a lovely picture of a bi-plane, courtesy of French designer Nicolas Gomes.

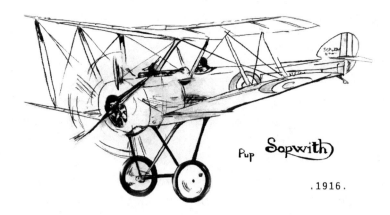

Pup Sopwith)

.1916.

Victor Victoria

I do believe my first bona fide blunder of the war was when I shot a goddess between the eyes.

Unforced error number two came into play the moment I took note of said mistake. Having yanked up my goggles, I perched in the seat of my plane, stunned. With my head turned around, searching for her descent, I obviously wasn't looking where I was going, and the next thing I knew I'd collided slap-bang up the arse end of a 530-foot dirigible.

The propeller of my Sopwith Pup punctured the rubberized cotton fabric, the nose went in, the biplane shuddered, and then we hung there, conjoined in the clouds several thousand feet up. The name *L.19* was written in big gothic letters on a ripped flap that waved above my head, and beneath that "Kaiserliche Marine".

I'd buggered a bloody zeppelin.

Hence, it wasn't long before the Huns on board started taking pot shots at me, having positioned themselves on an iron trellis built into the rear-engine gondola. They were so close I could see the rifles poking out — standard issue 7.92 mm Mauser Gewehr 98s — but the dunderheads were such poor marksmen that I continued to sit there, strapped into my open cockpit, unharmed and reasonably unfussed.

Eventually I got tired of the fun, games and projectiles. I unholstered my Webley Mk IV revolver to fire off three rounds in return. The soldiers ducked for cover. Then I glanced around, wondering what the devil I should do.

"You know, that hurt."

I peered over the side of my aeroplane, past the words "Sea's Shame" that my batman McPherson had stenciled onto the canvas fuselage, to the jutting-out wooden wheel frame beneath my Pup. What I discovered alarmed me far more than the pointy-headed fools only yards distant.

Winged Victory, or whomsoever this was, hung there one-handed. In her other hand, the left one, the woman was armed with a trident and shield, and on top of her head she wore a centurion's helmet that was at an accidentally jaunty angle — probably because it had a couple of dents in it, courtesy of my machine gun. Golden hair poked out from under the hard hat, and this fluttered in the breeze. Her ocean-blue eyes, however, remained fixed on mine. They were anything but flighty.

"So, are you going to offer assistance? Or would you prefer to sit there and gawk while those men continue shooting?"

"Can't you fly?"

"Do I look like I have wings?"

She had a point. There was nary a feather on her body.

"She's younger than me, too."

"Who is younger?"

"Your Winged Victory."

I certainly hadn't expected things to turn out in this squalid manner — they'd started out innocuously enough. There had been heavy fog the evening before, when a fleet of zeppelins took advantage of the cover to bomb a string of inconsequential towns in the West Midlands.

The next afternoon — today — one of the intruders was spotted over the North Sea, which explained away my current mission flying a spot of reconnaissance. Having flown out from Freiston Airfield in Lincolnshire and spent the past frigid, unproductive hour in empty skies, I'd decided to return home to a jolly good cup of warm cocoa, with a shot of Dalmore whisky, when directly ahead in my flight path — in the midst of a bank of clouds and silhouetted by the setting sun — I spied Winged Victory.

Before I could think, I was triggering my Vickers machine gun, the woman tumbled, and I crashed. This surely smacked of something of a feat.

"I do wish you would desist with the Winged Victory nonsense," called out my unwilling passenger, as I unstrapped and leaned over to give her a hand. "She's Greek," that voice nattered on, "and, dare I say it, has no arms and lacks a head."

A bullet whizzed close by my ear. "Would you stop that?" I yelled, directing my words at a stout sergeant in a greatcoat and a rather dangerous Pickelhaube spiked helmet. "Can't you see I'm busy?"

The man lowered his rifle to act sheepish. "Es tut mir leid!"

"Not a problem. Be a good fellow and go fetch your commanding officer."

At least the gunplay ceased. I encircled the woman's wrist with my gloved fingers and proceeded to haul, although I had a bugger of a time. I barely managed the exercise, what with the heavy armoured trinkets and her Amazonian stature — at about six feet, she was at least as tall as me, and had broader shoulders.

Finally, she propped herself up behind the cockpit, powerful, stark naked legs straddling the canvas for balance. While I'm hardly one to gush, the woman's face was something precious — chiseled, athletic, magnificently bewitching.

"Is there a way down?" she asked, while I rudely stared.

"You mean to terra firma?"

"No, I mean the moon."

"Ahh, you're joking."

"Bravo." She breathed out in loud, overdramatic fashion, apparently annoyed. I suppose I would be too, if I were god-like and recently gunned down by an overzealous aerialist. "Now, about getting off..."

"I think we're stuck until this zeppelin lands. I heard the Huns have introduced a device called a parachute, but we haven't anything like that in the Royal Flying Corps. I suppose you could jump. You are, I take it, some kind of deity?"

The young lady held up a majestic chin. "I am. I have been worshipped by people since the Pritani, well before the Romans invaded Britain two thousand years ago, and in all that time nobody ever shot at me before."

"Hold on. If you really were some kind of patron saint-cum-goddess, why didn't you kick the Spigs back to Italy?"

"We choose not to interfere in human affairs."

"Well, that's bloody convenient. Why, then, do you bother lugging about the military gear, and what's the story with the Roman helmet?"

"It belonged to Julius Caesar. I liked Gaius. After he invaded, he named the island after me, Britannia. Claudius I loathed — he had no respect for foreign figureheads — but Hadrian was marginally better."

"Oh, I see. Britannia. Of course. I do apologize for the Winged Victory bon mot. I'm known as Wilks. Might I call you Brit?"

Since I was leaning out of the cockpit, I felt something tap my buttocks.

"Are you forgetting the trident?" the woman reminded me. Thank Heavens; she resisted using the sharp bits. "Britannia shall do nicely. If you're searching for something earthier, you may call me Frances. I prefer Britannia."

"Speaking of earth — given that you're a god, well, I would

venture to guess that jumping will not be a problem."

She looked down through the clouds and I would swear I saw a grimace. "How high are we?"

"About three or four thousand feet, the last time I checked."

"Then it's a problem."

"You have height restrictions?"

"Something of the sort." Britannia shivered. No wonder, since she was wearing only a light shift of linen material that barely came down to her thighs, and the woman had a lot of cold metal pressing against her.

After I took off my leather coat, I reached across to place it on her shoulders.

"What are you doing?"

"Attempting to be a gentleman."

"Well, stop it. I reside on a completely different plane. I don't feel the chill. Put the blasted thing back on."

"Right you are." It was my turn to play annoyed as I buttoned up the coat. "Anyway, I thought Britannia was a nymph of some kind."

"Hardly."

"And aren't you supposed to have a lion? What were you doing, prancing about on top of a zeppelin?"

"Trying to help — you looked like you were going to fly straight past, so I decided to intervene."

"Against your better nature?"

"I do that sometimes. These people dropped bombs on my native soil. I was cross." She smiled. "I left my lion at home." Touché.

I resisted a spot of laughter, and again instead looked over the side of the aeroplane. I decided the sea was closer than it had been only a quarter of an hour before. "We're losing altitude."

"Quite possibly it has something to do with the giant hole you ripped in their side. Gas must be escaping."

"True — which means we'll end up in the drink in the North

Sea, not the best idea in February. It's probably around forty degrees Fahrenheit this time of year."

I heard somebody discreetly cough nearby.

There was a new addition to the open window of the gondola. With the monocle, a Luger 9mm in his hand, the soft hat and pencil-thin moustache, this man was a stiff-necked caricature of the German officer class.

"I say, Englander, my name is Kapitänleutnant Wilhelm Klink."

"Charmed, I'm sure. Flying Officer 'Wilks' Wilkinson, 287 Squadron, RFC, commanded by Major William E. Johns."

I heard him click unseen heels as he bowed. "We are currently throwing excess baggage into the sea in order that we might gain some height and make it to the continent. Your blasted *flugzüg* — your aeroplane — is not helping matters, Herr Wilkinson."

"Sorry, Herr Klink, but the crate is here to stay. Your men shooting at me has not been much fun — it makes it difficult to come up with a viable plan."

"Well, you *are* the enemy."

"There is that. But tell you what; I have a woman here with me."

Klink adjusted his monocle. "Ja. Quite the *fräulein*."

"Eyes off, Fritz."

"My apologies." While he inclined his head, Klink's stare remained affixed to my hitchhiker. The man was incorrigible. "You know, I always envied you English your Britannia. The Americans have Columbia, even the Italians have their mundane Italia Turrita, but we Germans... ahhh, we are sadly lacking in the allegorical personifications."

"Er...yes." I frowned. "Once the balloon— "

"Zeppelin. This is a zeppelin, not a balloon."

"All right. Well, once the zeppelin gets lower, Britannia and I will bail out, jumping into the sea and thereby lightening the load up to two hundred and eighty pounds."

"I beg your pardon," the girl behind me grouched, "just how chubby do you presume me to be?"

"Well, you are six feet and wearing all that armour."

"Pfft."

Klink rubbed his chin. "To tell the truth, I am more concerned with the aircraft — not that I do not appreciate the gesture."

"Every little bit helps, am I correct, Kapitänleutnant?"

"*Ja, Ja,* in getting my crew safely home."

"Then we have a deal? Toss me a lifesaver, there's a good fellow."

I hadn't counted on Klink lobbing the contraption so damned hard, and I can't fault the officer for accuracy — the lifesaver struck me on the forehead and, being unstrapped, I fell straight out of the plane.

I recall nothing thereafter, until I came to in darkness in the shallow water of a cove. I was saturated, half-drowned and mostly frozen. Flashes of memory — a flapping dirigible, the burlesque German officer, Britannia in a dimpled helmet and very little else — played a merry jig across my mind and I deduced that an aeroplane crash and a bump on the skull must have conjured up the whole fiasco. Since I had no plane, I could only assume I'd ditched at sea.

Turned out, I was on the coast of northern France.

A helpful farmwoman named Marianne, who carried a rowdy rooster tucked under her arm, got me safely to British lines. While she spoke no English, this woman was remarkable for her height — she towered over me in her Phrygian cap — and an impressive stamina, since she never tired once during our ninety-mile hike.

Two weeks later I discovered myself back in Blighty, at company HQ. I was informed by my commanding officer, Major Johns, that a zeppelin earmarked *L.19* had in fact gone down in the North Sea, with a loss of all hands, and he was putting the kill on my record sheet.

"Jolly good show, old chap," the major decided as he shook my hand.

So. There was a balloon. But what about the balance of the featherbrained dream? I returned to my quarters and allowed McPherson to mix up a drink. I continued seeing the girl's face in the sights of my Vickers, right before I pulled the trigger, as I stood first in front of the fireplace and then wandered over to a bay window. It was dusk outside.

"Restless, sir?" McPherson inquired as he handed me a tumbler.

"Vaguely." I bowed my head. Was she dead too? Or was she some figment of an overactive, semi-concussed imagination? "I think I'll hit the sack, old man," I decided. "Take the evening off. Sally forth and enjoy yourself."

I trudged slowly up the staircase with the drink between my fingers. I felt inconceivably dismal. Probably, it had to do with touching God — or, in this case, a goddess — and losing her. Never good form to do that kind of thing. One might as well try manhandling the sun.

When I entered my room I switched on a lamp, and straight away noticed the Corinthian helmet on the desk. It had been hammered back into shape. Next to it — slouched unmajestically on my favourite leather armchair, with her feet up, sans armour, and showing far too much leg — was someone I recognized.

"You."

"Me." She straightened up, stretched her back, and smiled. "You recall that that my name is not Winged Victory?"

"I do seem to remember that. It was a Victorian fancy — and, to be honest, I thought you didn't exist. That you were only up here." I tapped my right temple, but this acted as the woman's cue to stand up and slip out of the miserly frock she wore.

"Perhaps you should put down your glass?"

I realized I was spilling the drink, and did as suggested.

Britannia stood before me, without even her shield, her head at an angle, blue eyes close, golden hair framing her face, and I realized she pipped my height by two inches.

"I like you."

"Where's your trident?" I responded. I had no intention of accidentally sitting on the bugger.

"It was on extended loan — now returned to its rightful owner." I could feel her cool breath on my neck.

"Shield?"

"Beneath the bed. You're stalling."

"Not at all. I believe you said you didn't interfere in human affairs."

"Nobody ever shot at me before. C'mere."

An Octopus's Grotto is His Castle

And I presume my big mistake was messing with the witch.

Admittedly, at the time I didn't know she was a bona fide, card-carrying sort, though such types of people aren't going to advertise. It's the charlatans that put up signage and practice hocus pocus to dazzle the masses.

The real ones go about their business incognito, or — as in this case — operate from a brothel house.

Anyhow, it's never good to piss off a real witch. They tend to go in for things like petty vengeance. It happens in all the fairy tales, am I right?

This particular tale began on a chilly day at the beginning of November 1872. I was biding my time in New York City, looking for a ride to the Mother Country. I'm a sailor by profession — not a particularly good one, though you wouldn't know that from my references, most of which are forged.

Call me Chris Mael.

I'm a man of few talents. In fact, the only one I can think of is the ability that's bolstered my purse on odd occasion: I have the knack of holding my breath underwater for over four minutes. The first time I truly appreciated the talent was when a furious skipper had me keel-hauled for attempted mutiny.

I had an appointment to keep with an old shipmate turned actor/playwright, name of Bertie Aiken — or Albert, as he now preferred to be known. Bertie was a debonair ladies' man that the ladies would never have, a bully trap, black hair brushed back and a wily moustache planted above a lip that curled often.

He had on a revival of one of his plays, *The Witches of New York,* that I went to see at the Bowery Theatre. After lights out, we decided to go on a bender, accompanied by Bertie's mate Tommy Nast.

A cartoonist by trade, Tommy spoke with a tiny German inflection and had his dark hair parted from the left with a sensuous wave. He was a little plump and wore a Colonel Custer beard. Tommy was prob'ly Bertie's new mandrake, though I declined to ask.

We found a vacant table without chairs at a quaint drinking establishment called The Tituba, and did the perpendicular for the next few hours.

I do recall a discussion about that champion of women's suffrage, Victoria Woodhull, who was running for U.S. president — and who'd been arrested the same day for publishing a supposedly obscene newspaper.

"Ahh, 'tis bollocks," Bertie announced over a cigar. "The woman is a self-righteous pain, but I respect her dedication, and the men of this fair city are running scared. They spread outrageous rumours that she's having affairs and is a witch, and even portray her as Mrs. Satan."

"Actually, that last one was mine, in *Harper's Weekly,*" Nast said in his thinly guttural accent. "I thought the bat wings and goat horns suited her. But otherwise she has a sultry look in the caricature I did. I'd bed the woman."

Bertie allowed a dark look to cross his face. "Then why the

slander?"

"They paid me a pretty penny."

"Slut."

"Indeed!"

There was other bosh too, gossip about the recent visit to America of Grand Duke Alexei Alexandrovich of Russia and a witch trial in France I heard about when we stopped over in Calais. Also, griping about the third placed New York Mutuals, a baseball team Bertie and Tommy adored.

To be honest, I couldn't give a flying fig.

I was more interested in the currently touring all-amateur English cricket team, and a certain prolific batsman named William Gilbert Grace — I'd hoped to con my way into one of the matches while I was in the 'States, but no such luck. Not that I was overly fond of English cricket — I had in mind dissemination of the team for future bets. There was talk of our colonial team playing the English in a few years' time, and nobody liked a studied whirl like me.

Drink followed drink, and it wasn't long before I couldn't see a hole in a ladder. Everything switched to blurry, and instead of Bertie and Tommy, I found myself beside some young saucebox with blonde curls hanging onto my ear, in a buggy behind a very fast horse.

I ended up at a dilapidated double-storey gaff on Manhattan's extreme East Side, near the river and below East 14th Street.

I vaguely recall a circus or show too vulgar and degrading to describe here. More meaningful, I switched my blonde for Marie, a Creole woman with colour, all laminated dark skin, oiled midnight hair, and an outrageous Louisiana accent. She was twice my age. On the door of her room was a painted black circle, with outwardly reaching crescent moons to either side. There was an eight-spoked wagon wheel on the wall.

I have flashes of memory of the night thereafter: I woke up bewildered when the woman plucked a few hairs out of my scalp, and sometime later I looked over and saw her flicking through the book I kept in my pockets, then carefully tore free a page. I passed out before I could complain. Still later, I'm sure she was wrestling with a black rooster, but that could have been a drunken fancy.

Next day, I ought to have crept out silently and licked my wounds. Instead, I made a ruckus, woke her up, announced she was hideous, and strode from the house onto the cobblestones, my chin held high. Lord knows why — she was apparently precisely my style when I was maggoted.

I approached the Battery and gazed out at all the sailed ships in the harbour, colours flapping in a light breeze and tiny individuals working the decks like busy ants. Suckers. Then I made my way down to the employment wharf. Any ship heading Britain-way would do me fine.

I signed up with a two-masted brigantine, the *Marie Céleste*, one hundred feet from bow to stern. Although it had a French name it was in fact an American vessel. They had a crew of six, but were desperate for a seventh, especially with my kind of 'experience'. They asked no questions and offered good terms.

I decided to get a morsel to eat before we sailed, but as I folded up the freshly signed contract a grim-looking beggar right there accosted me on the street.

"Morning to ye, shipmate, morning!"

"Hardly your shipmate — shipmate." I smiled nastily.

"Anything down there about your soul?" he asked, foul breath trailing my way, as he pointed at the papers I'd tucked into my breast pocket.

I wasn't in the mood. My head was swimming still. "Push off, mate."

"Oh, perhaps you hav'n't got any."

"Prob'ly not."

"Well, well, what's signed, is signed; and what's to be, will be; and then again, perhaps it won't be, after all."

"Whatever." The man was talking in inane circles.

"Anyhow, it's all fixed and arranged a'ready by that witch o' yours."

"Right you are." I was gazing out at the ships. What a peaceful, glorious sight.

"May the ineffable heavens bless ye; I'm sorry I stopped ye, but take this." The man pressed something cold into my hand. "Old Elijah will see you through. As I say to ye, what's to be, will be; and then again, perhaps it won't be, after all."

God, he was doing my head in — but with that last bit, he stumped away, making a hell of a racket on the flagstones. I hadn't noticed the ivory peg leg before now. I looked at the object I held in my fingers: a fisherman's knife, the word *Gilliat* scratched into its surface with a childish hand.

Not a bad piece of work, and I'd misplaced mine the week before in some alley thief's belly. It would need a decent scrub, though, to remove the stench of the man who'd left it with me.

The ship departed the next morning. We had passengers, the captain's wife and child, and an old seadog member of the crew did the usual song-and-dance about women on board being bad luck.

For a week we sailed the Atlantic while I found ways to avoid actual work. Early one morning, when a storm haunted the horizon, the captain — who'd started to suspect my true nature — sent me up the mast to the narrow crow's nest. Perfect. I settled in there for a read.

I had an 1871 copy of *Vingt mille lieues sous les mers* in my coat pocket, the book that Creole ladybird had been handling, with illustrations by Édouard Riou and Alphonse de Neuville. My favourite part was when the octopus attacks the Nautilus and scoffs down a crewmember.

In the English versions, it's misleadingly translated as a giant squid, but in the original French version of Jules Verne's *Twenty Thousand Leagues Under the Sea*, it's definitely "poulpe", or octopus.

I spoke a fair portion of the lingo — put that down to a season employed on a French trawler in the Caribbean — and I'd nicked the book from the boson. I figured it'd fetch a coin or two, but had become attached to the tome over the past few months. It was my sole long-term possession aside from my hat and a lucky ducat with which I refused to part.

The picture by Neuville, of Nemo, arms crossed at the huge oval observation window, staring out at the giant octopus — well, that page was missing. Curious. It must've been what the Creole scrag tore out.

What with the gentle swaying up there on my perch and the warm sunlight, I presume I fell asleep. When I woke, it was late afternoon. The silence below forewarned me. The ship was deserted — the captain's woman and child were also gone — and a lifeboat was missing. God knows what had happened. I could've weighed anchor or gone looking, but that'd be too much effort for a solitary crewmember like me.

Never one to put off taking advantage of the moment, I broke open a keg of rum, found some limes and mint sprigs in the galley, and made a succession of mojitos. At least I wouldn't be getting scurvy.

I grabbed a bag of coins, a pistol and the ship's papers from the captain's cabin and began putting together differently constructed paper aircraft, tossing them into the headwind to see which design was most effective.

When I ran out of papers, I accidentally knocked over the compass and it broke on the deck. In my drunkenness I believed I could repair it — all I needed was a key component from the clock. Instead of fixing the compass, the clock stopped working.

I was drunk as a skunk and singing a sea shanty — "Cape Cod boys don't got no sleds/Haul away, haul away (yip!)/They slide down hills on codfish heads/And we're bound away for Australia," along with much humming of the lines I'd forgotten

— so I tied a rope, the peak halyard, around my waist, just in case. I didn't trust my sea legs in this state.

Neither should I have trusted my sea fingers, since the moment I fell overboard the knot came unravelled and I plummeted into the dark water unhindered.

The keel of a ship slices overhead — always a portent of bother — and then, after the keel passes, something falls into the sea.

For a moment there are a million bubbles and the water is too disturbed to make out the object. A sneaking suspicion crosses my mind that this may be a net, so I hang back.

But instead of coils of rope assembled by overburdened fishermen's wives, I discover the under-half of a human form. The legs dance a merry caper, and they're sorely tempting ones at that. Easy enough to reach out, embrace, squeeze a little, and then yank. Holding onto said conquest, swimming down into the ebony depths — a blackness aided and abetted by my ink sac — to a place of privacy, perhaps under an outcrop of coral, there to snack.

I am feeling rather peckish after my evening constitutional.

Oh, for heaven's sake, what do you expect? That I'll stick to a steady diet of vegetarian fodder like seaweed? And while I'm fond of my animal protein, I'm sick to death of clams, worms, prawns and crabs. As for sea snails, otherwise known as the popcorn of the deep sea, I'll slap (eight times) anyone who again offers up this treat — regardless of added-extra condiments.

I sometimes discover an ailing gull or aged albatross floating about above, but they're either chewy or a little off.

This individual splashing about before me looks to be in his prime.

And, to be completely honest, I'm in the mood for a bit of grandstanding. Let's see those pesky squid and cuttlefish carry off someone this large with equal finesse.

I feel the rapid beat of three hearts. I'm excited, and it's been an age since I felt this way. At least three months, not that I'm counting. Well, actually, I am. When you have a life expectancy guaranteed to make most self-aware species fret — the oldest octopus I ever met reached five years of age before she carked it — you tend to do a bit of repetitive calculating in groups of eight, with two eyes firmly held on a blinkered future. Right now I'm sitting on four years.

Anyhow, back to the matter overhead. I manoeuvre into opportune position and expel a jet of water to begin my ascent. While I bide my time, I'm not about to let this delicacy off the hook, so to speak.

One of my eyes dips above the surface. The ship is far away now, but I see the name *Marie Céleste* on the rear end of her. Then I get my bearings.

There's a thick fog, yet I can make out mangroves not so far away, leading to hills covered in lush tropical trees. Either British or French Guiana, I'm not certain which — all these steamy, inhospitable islands look the same. I decide it is the former one, for convenience's sake.

I turn my eye to the swimmer. The proximity to that coast means he's probably a local. I loathe British food. But, given the ship's moniker, he might be from France — indeed I hope so. I do love my French cuisine.

The man hasn't seen me. He's staring all about, like he's looking for something, but the ship is gone and he's all alone. He's not a bad-looking thing — bearing a certain harsh attractiveness to him that reminds me of a German actor I also enjoyed named Andrews Engelmann. This man, however, is overacting. He's panicking and splashing about and it's exhausting to observe.

Let's cut the struggles short, shall we?

I unfurl one of my legs, since I deduce this is all it will take.

I direct the leg to coil itself around the man's right thigh and calf, and he freezes for an instant before the panic truly begins.

This doesn't matter. I have a superb grip and propel myself to the shallow seabed with my prize. The man writhes and twists with a vigour that's tiring. This forces me to employ a second arm, and then a third, and it's difficult to swim with the remaining five. Somehow his hand pulls a little gun free but that's not going to work down here, and anyhow he drops it. Silly boy. His fortitude is on the decline and the antics vanish as we pass the wreckage of a large ship with the faded moniker *Preussen* painted on its stern.

There's a cave ahead, full of dark shadows. Perfect. A grotto it is for some gourmet grub.

Months pass.

I've come to call the cave home, and if I had opposable thumbs I might make a tapestry that reads "Home, Sweet Home", or "An Octopus' Grotto is his Castle", or some such nonsense. Perhaps I could train the chromatophores in my skin to do the signage for me, instead of bothering with trivial workings like camouflage.

On one of my morning jaunts I spy someone diving, poking about in a recent wreck.

I have the taste for fine food in my belly as I ramble closer. I think I'm there with an epicurean's intent to inspect the goods, but the craving overwhelms my aged senses. Within moments I have the man in my embrace, I'm tearing off the mask, looking at features that strike me as very Rock Hudson. It's important to feast on attractive things and I'm enamoured.

I gather up this prince and pull him along to the grotto, my castle, where the first thing he sees is the polished-up skeleton of my last big meal, the swimmer, sitting cross-legged next to a sack of gold coins and a knife said meal had been carrying.

Rock Hudson's face, sans diving mask, grimaces, and before I know it he has scooped up the knife and he turns on me. What I do observe in that brief transition from attacker to victim is that the blade has a serrated edge and the name *Gilliat* inscribed across its shiny silver surface.

Right then and there, like some absurd epiphany, I realize the jig is up. Am I going to perish? Well, are Dover's cliffs still white? Seconds before he lashes out with the knife I have time to address a few points. At least the man isn't Japanese — he'll just kill me and be done with it. Europeans in these parts didn't indulge in eating octopus flesh. In the Greek islands, in all likelihood, I'd be pegged up on a clothesline to dry out in the sun, while in Japan I'd end up still squirming on a plate, to be eaten with shabby disposable wooden chopsticks.

Embarrassing stuff.

Here, I'll have a more peaceful requiem.

I don't even bother hitting him with the ink.

Zigzag is a story I fiddled over for some time, and in an early incarnation last year I worked with comicbook artist Drezz Rodriguez to make it into a five-page visual yarn that's to be published in the Tobacco-Stained Sky *anthology.*

My favourite handgun (the British Webley-Fosbery) is involved, the same pistol that killed Sam Spade's partner Miles Archer in The Maltese Falcon, *and the one that's so pivotal in both* Tobacco-Stained Mountain Goat *and* One Hundred Years of Vicissitude. *If you want to see what it looks like, check out the comic included herein* (Get Busy).

After working with Drezz I buried the written version.

This year I decided to revive it, gave it a major overhaul, and submitted it to the Slit Your Wrists (SYW!) crew for their baptismal anthology Shock & Appall.

Zigzag

While I whistle Cole Porter's *Who Wants to be a Millionaire*, pitch wandering between Frank Sinatra's version and Bill Oddie's, I'm cleaning this bastard like there's neither tomorrow nor the day after. Mind you, it's not the song I try to scour — that's accidental — but the babe in my grip.

She's ancient, older even than the Porter ditty (scribbled down in 1956 for some Hollywood musical), and likely hasn't been used in fifty-odd years. Maybe more.

There are better, more functional gats that've been churned out on rotating industrial sushi belts since this one first reflected the light of day, or night-time luminous-tube signage, on the metallic surface of her skin. She's an oddball piece that should be in a bloody museum, collecting dust in temperature-controlled bliss — preferably to be seen rather than heard.

Yet here she was, a little the worse for wear, in the ongoing process of being debased by the elements, and I was doing a spit and polish minus the saliva.

Don't ask how many minutes had passed, but I'd started out

with a cloth soaked in sewing-machine oil that I lobbed over my shoulder once it turned a disturbing combination of black and rust-red, a gritty feeling to the touch.

Next up I used a fat pipe-cleaner, pumping this in and out and then a wee bit more for good measure, twisting and turning, doing ninety-degree rotations with what began as deft flicks of the wrist but degenerated into something akin to a rheumatic swirl. I wasn't sure it was the best tool — surely there were more professional ones — but the pipe-cleaner served its nefarious purpose and the old girl was looking dolled-up by the moment.

Then I swabbed a fresh rag with more of that machine oil and wiped down the exterior surfaces, giving them the kind of love and attention I'd never wasted on any flesh-and-blood woman.

"She's looking spic-and-span, I'll give you that much," I hear his voice praise from the direction of the couch, on the other side of the coffee table from where I'm seated. Focused on my task as I am, I don't bother with a glance or time-waster like that. The job before me is all that matters. I'm busy caressing the zigzag grooves on the cylinder.

The voice circles me now, a warm, gravelly purr joined at the hip to a lazy stroll, footsteps followed by the sound of ice beating a futile attempt to escape its glass.

"Colonel Fosbery would be proud of you. Yes, he would. See how she shines?" There's a sip, a slow exhale, and a chuckle. "Who'd've countenanced a journey of one hundred years, just so she could wind up here?"

I don't want to listen, but do anyway, multi-tasking when I least appreciate the skill. The barrel is something special. I use a silicone cloth to wipe off fingerprints after all the manhandling.

The figure is opposite me, back on the sofa, a vague silhouette in the corner of my eye that leans forward and says, patiently, "I think you can about call it a wrap now — why don't you set her up for me as well, there's a good chap."

She might've been ancient, but the gat is dead easy to suss out.

She's cocked by simply shoving the cylinder-barrel assembly back as far as it'll go, and in doing so I make out the sound of an internal spring that holds it in position.

I don't know when I notice I've stopped whistling. Cole Porter doesn't ring right for what's about to happen, despite the gun now flashing and myself no more than a flunkey.

I pass him the gun, grip-first — it's the polite thing to do.

Placing an empty glass on the table, the man accepts the prize. He examines her in the light from the overhead fluorescent and finally I look at his face. Pleased seems to be the emotion that passes across it, although I can't really be sure. I hardly know the gent.

"Are you ready now?" he inquires of the Webley-Fosbery as she settles herself into his left hand, barrel pointed in my direction.

I doubt the question was intended for me, but I nod anyway. 'Cos all I want is you.

This next fantasy 'potboiler' was something I concocted in April 2012 — immediately after destroying my brain finishing off my second novel One Hundred Years of Vicissitude. *I remember I was all at sea, and decided to try my hand at an offbeat, God-hopefully-comic adventure/fantasy romp.*

I was probably re-reading Roy Thomas' classic retake (with artist Barry Windsor-Smith) of Robert E. Howard's Conan the Barbarian, *which he did at Marvel Comics in the early '70s. I tend to flick through it often on the loo.*

The twist here (for me) was a tough, sardonic female protagonist who left my male leads for dead. While the thing was fun to write and I'd love to try my hand at this again, at the time I felt it lacked something special to motivate further work. Still do. I eventually shelved the greater concept (this may change, depending on time).

I did pitch it about to some swords 'n' sandals 'n' sorcery mags and anthologies, but the standard response was like this one: "Thank you for sending us A Woman of Some Sense. *This is a perfectly good story, but it doesn't quite have the feel I want for Sword & Sorceress. Try this on another market."*

The people at Beneath Ceaseless Skies wrote back in June 2012 that "The narrator is entertaining, but I found I never got quite enough grounding in the setting, and the story didn't have quite enough substance to it to completely win me over." Quite.

In the end, it was published via the very nice people at Big Pulp.

Looking back, I think I had a hankering to stick a character in a story with the lord-someone-or-other moniker, I always had a soft spot for cliffhanger scenes, and I do kind of dig the silly repartee — though at times this needs to be reined in and/or ditched completely.

The story could do with some love, a more solid sense of jocularity and an overhaul, but I decided to place it in, warts 'n' all, possibly to fill out some space.

A Woman of Some Sense

How I got here was not important.

The way in which I removed myself mattered, especially given my position — hanging upside down from a leather strap that was loosely coiled around the shin of my left leg, the other end snagged in a two-inch-thick scrub plant that grew out of a cliff face. The cliff continued in a straight line down to rocky terrain about a hundred and fifty feet away. So, while extraction was my principle concern, I also had to hang docile and move as little as possible. The ring-in bonsai up there could snap at any moment, and then it'd be sayonara Valeria.

Thank somebody for the belly dancing lessons. A couple of years ago I wouldn't have been able to do what I now did — lift up my torso, using my stomach and back muscles alone — so that the world flipped the right way round, and my eyes were parallel with my knees. The belly dancing had been done to sneak into a palace and steal a treasure. I hadn't expected fringe benefits.

That was precisely when the bonsai shook and dirt tumbled

down. I froze, not an easy thing when you've bent yourself up into a U-shape and every fibre of your body squabbles for release. This is the kind of moment when how you got here does become important, and in my case it was the fault of a man. Always was; always would be.

This man's name was Lord Ervin of Brownwood.

"That's nowhere near Redwood, is it?" I quipped, when I first encountered the effete, rake-thin uppercruster in an arranged meeting at an inn.

Ervin frowned and wobbled his unattractive head. "I haven't the woolliest."

In case you haven't figured it out, I was more enamoured with this man's hefty purse than any screaming loud physical attributes. He had none. But his moneybag — ahhh, his moneybag.

"I hear tell that you are rather the good swordswoman."

"Swordsman," I said. "I'm better than any man, other woman or diabolical pell you might decide to match me up with."

Ervin, several inches shorter and with that shimmying skull, walked slowly around me there in the yard of the inn. "Tall, full-bosomed—"

"Excuse me?" My sword was out of its scabbard and at his narrow throat in less time than it took for him to finish his irritating appraisal.

"—Err... devilishly fast with a blade, I'll give you that. Kudos, my dear. Also large-limbed, compact shoulders — yet still overtly feminine."

"So I do have charms." I slotted the sword home. "Ta. What's the ruckus?"

"Ruckus?"

"You know, racket. Swindle."

"I have no idea what you are talking about."

"The job."

"Oh! Oh, yes, I see. Well, I want you to be my wife."

I laughed when I heard this. The other option was bringing out my blade again and sticking the fellow for real, but he did tickle my funny bone.

"Laugh away," Lord Ervin muttered in an annoyed fashion. He dusted down a log and sat there. "I don't mean a bona fide bride, just someone to pretend being one."

After my chuckles subsided, I felt sorry for the loser and sat next to him. "Why?"

"I need a bodyguard for a trip from this town to my villa."

"What kind of bodyguarding are we talking?"

"Really, now."

"How far is it?"

"The villa? A day's ride."

"You're expecting trouble?"

"I will be carrying a shipment of jewels. Word has leaked out and about."

"Iffy."

"I suppose."

"And the sham spouse?"

"I believe a 'wife' would be a wonderful disguise. No one would suspect."

"Well, I think some might, given your personality and habits."

"How dare you!" After a momentary head sway, Ervin slapped me with his glove. I'd have said it hurt, just to make the fellow feel better, but it merely tingled and I wasn't in the mood for fabrications to make a potential employer feel better. That cost extra.

"Look, how much are you prepared to pay?"

This man's vitriol was a quick-burning beast. The rage vanished, and he was suddenly counting out gold doubloons into both my hands.

"Enough?"

"With this, I'd marry you for real."

"Oh, no need." The blueblood's frigid gaze washed over me. "Of course, we will have to get you a change of clothes. Breeches, boots, a scabbard and a shirt better worn by pirates of ill-repute are not appropriate."

"Aren't all pirates people of ill-repute?"

"Even so, this wardrobe is hardly becoming for the spouse of someone as important as me — or even some low-ranking fool, for that matter."

"Keep the compliments coming," I sighed. "I feel like we're married already."

Which was why, the next day, I was embalmed with an extremely tight bodice — stiffened with whalebone — that cut off half my blood circulation, and my legs smothered beneath three different voluminous skirts that dragged on the ground when I dared walking. My hair was braided and twisted up into a top-knot beneath a silk veil that hampered my peripheral vision, and I ended up riding my horse far more than usual if only to avoid accidents.

"You look a vision," Lord Ervin was gushing as he cantered beside me on a road beside a high bluff. His noggin wobbled more than usual.

"I look like an upscale dimwit."

"Like me?" He had a minor smirk.

I smiled back. "Like you."

In the midst of the sweet nothings — which were what these words truly meant — the ambush took place. Think ruffians swinging down from trees to our left and jumping out of bushes and from behind trunks. The place was full of the fiends. I counted at least twenty as I clutched for the rapier that was hidden somewhere in my skirts, but this took too long — and then I was knocked from the horse. Five men surrounded me with an assortment of dangerous instruments, ranging from a primitive garden hoe to an overdone mace.

I finally got out my sword, dealt with the five, and was

straight after leaning against my horse — breathless, dizzy and wheezing. I had to get the corset off. Hacking at the strings, I ripped it free and tossed the garment as I swung around to face another dozen fiends. I couldn't see Ervin or his mare anywhere close by — perhaps he'd scarpered. Good for him.

Another four men dropped before I misjudged my place on the edge of the cliff, tripped on my skirts, and took an unhealthy plunge.

Which was how I wound up here, upside down in a tricky situation.

A lucky one, I'll give you that — I should have ended up on the rocks far below, where the bodice I'd cut off even now lay. The problem was how to untangle myself from the leather strap, get a decent grip on the vertical rock, and climb the six feet to stable terra firma.

"May I give you a hand, fair maiden?"

I spied Ervin gazing over the edge, a large grin on his face.

"Fair maiden, my foot. You know your disguise very nearly killed me?"

"That was the plan."

I stared up at him. I figured the smile wasn't so friendly after all. "Go on. You have a captive audience down here."

"Why, that's very kind of you."

"I've learned how much the villains of the piece like to wax boring."

"Well said."

"Not particularly. Anyhow — what's afoot?"

Ervin pouted in a triumphant kind of way. I noted that his head had stopped bouncing. "I spread the rumour around these parts that my new bride would be carrying all my worth, given to her as a sign of my absolute devotion. When those cretins attacked, they went straight for you, and I was able to slip away. I knew either you would kill them or vice versa, and to be honest I didn't care which outcome transpired. I could ride home safely with my fortune."

"You took a risk coming back, then, to see what happened."

"I was going to lie," he chuckled, "but in this position I see there's no need."

"Wrong."

While we'd been indulging in honeymoon talk, I'd got a decent grip on the rocks, untied the leather strap, and tethered it to a strip of cloth from my dress. This I had fashioned into a rough lasso and I swung it around and up, over the man's narrow shoulders, before his lordship knew what to expect. Then I pulled — hard.

"You won't be needing this," I muttered, tearing the purse from Lord Ervin's belt as he flew past. He certainly screamed like a girl. It was embarrassing.

After I heard the crunch of bones far below, I focused on climbing the rock face, inch by precarious inch. It took me half an hour to reach the top. When I got there, I flopped over onto my back and looked up at a beautiful blue sky I hadn't noticed before now.

"God, I'm sick of men. Always doing the wrong bloody thing." I sat back up, laughed, and shook my hair free of the veil. Then I lobbed it and focused on the silk bag of coins on the ground beside me. "Oh, well. Time to go shopping."

The next two pieces were never written or intended as stand-alone short stories.

While my first pair of novels were an homage to sci-fi/dystopia with noir undertones and classic hardboiled cinema (Tobacco-Stained Mountain Goat) *and surreal, slipstream fantasy* (One Hundred Years of Vicissitude), *the latest pays respect to two things I love the most — one of them being 1930s-40s noir detective stories.*

In particular that written by Raymond Chandler (The Big Sleep, The Long Goodbye) *and Dashiell Hammett* (The Maltese Falcon, The Thin Man) *and the film adaptations by rather brilliant directors like John Huston, Robert Altman and Howard Hawks.*

But I have a confession to make to anyone who'll listen — I also adore 1960s comicbooks and occasionally obsess over comic artist Jack 'King' Kirby. His work for Marvel in the '60s, the so-called Silver Age or pop-art era, remains mind-boggling for me 50 years after it was first drafted.

So, anyway, back to the next two stories you'll find here. They're dual prologue pieces I had in my original manuscript for the novel Who is Killing the Great Capes of Heropa?, *a noir/superhero homage I wrote in the second half of 2012.*

The first one, The Kármán Line, *I ended up keeping and I'm inserting it as a teaser.*

The second, here called Icing on the Cape, *outlined the death of superhero Sir Omphalos (a.k.a. the Big O), which is a pivotal point through the novel.*

I was fortunate enough to have a character design for him drawn by Maan House in Uruguay (see previous page) this January, a collaborative combination of ideas that included an unused design for Captain America by Jack Kirby, the Equalizers' logo on the belt buckle, and the cape design for Captain America's short-time alias Nomad created by Sal Buscema and Gil Kane in 1974.

Funnily enough, I abandoned this particular prologue by the time of tweaking the final manuscript in the September-December rewrite, because the thing didn't want to click.

The Celsius/Fahrenheit riff was dead in the water no matter how much I really wanted to work with it, and without the riff the scene was just plain bland.

And keeping the Big O's actual death "unknown", aside from basic information, adds to the man's mystique.

So, I've added this short, deleted aside in here for your very own verdict, whether or not you've read the novel.

The Kármán Line

"Aer—t," the radio receiver squawks inside her helmet. "Aeri—st, re—ng me?"

"Hello, you've called the Aerialist," the Cape says in response. "She's not home at the moment, too busy falling from a ridiculous height. Please leave a message after the tone so the girl can get back to you — you know, after all the king's horses and all the king's men put her together again. Beep."

God knows if anyone hears the quip. The only feedback coming through loud and clear is shrill static.

The Aerialist was aware of risks, but sabotage — someone cutting a hole in her jetpack to siphon out the fuel — had not been one of the hazards people bothered to mention.

Fifteen seconds pass and the drop is only one thousand, nine hundred feet shorter, according to the instrumentation on her wrist. Three hundred and twenty-six thousand of the imperial buggers to go.

The Aerialist is slap-bang in freefall, somewhere marginally past the Kármán line — in plain English about a hundred kilometres to impact on earth. Unless, of course, she hits something higher like Mount Everest (shaving off nine kilometres) or the top of the Empire State, four hundred and forty metres above terra firma.

Not that either place is optional here.

Flame-on! she quips, laughing for just a moment.

Inferring she's alit does, however, exaggerate the case. Objects light up when they fall at tens of miles a second, whereas her rate of descent clocks in around a few hundred miles per hour. Maybe seven hundred. Slower than a lead balloon.

That doesn't stop her brain racing, conjuring up the insane, expecting fire to lick up on the outside the pressure suit. This suit takes the brunt of buffeting as she tumbles arse over tit. No hope. Nothing. Just falling till she hits the ground.

Never thought it'd end via such a lame whimper, she further mulls, dizzy now. *Maybe I should've packed a parachute?*

Icing on the Cape

From out of the west with not quite the speed of light and a hearty 'Hi-yo' he comes, soaring thirty metres above a meadow on the outskirts of town. It's taken the Cape half an hour's flying time to reach this point. There's an azure blue sky and the temperature hovers around twenty-three degrees Celsius — or seventy-three point four in the old Fahrenheit system.

One wondered if German physicist Daniel Gabriel Fahrenheit would have resented younger contemporary Anders Celsius had he only known that the Swede's temperature scale would gut Fahrenheit over the ensuing three centuries.

Then the Cape purges the notion.

You and your over-analyzing, Gypsie-Ann would likely grumble — ironic, given her penchant for the same pursuit.

So, instead, the masked man resolves to enjoy the moment and the beauty of all about him. Pristine weather and gorgeous country houses; the white-picket fences below that nipped and tucked rolling green lawns and flowers of multiple colours.

Ahead there are boys playing cricket on an oval, clad in white uniforms with green, baggy caps, and they wave as he crosses overhead. One boy whoops and runs in the same direction, spinning his hat in the air.

The Cape smiles and salutes.

His path takes him along a quiet country highway framed by trees with spring blossoms, a lake on the right, and gently sloping fields of wheat with the odd golden haystack to the left. It's difficult to imagine anywhere more beautiful.

Down on the road, cruising at slower speed is a shiny burgundy-coloured jalopy without a roof. The couple on the front bench seat smile contentedly at one another as the Cape overtakes, sight unseen, only a few feet above. Their four-year-old daughter in the back, clutching a teddy bear, is more observant. She notices his passing shadow, looks heavenward, and beams. Then she's also waving frantically.

God, he loves these people.

There's a loud crack from somewhere nearby, followed rapidly by two more, and the noise strikes him as familiar — gunshots! — just as his cape rips. This throws out its carefully tuned aerodynamics, and before he knows it the masked man is spiralling across space, anorak awry.

Panic is pointless. He understands this.

He calms his mind, which goes some way toward smothering the nausea of the spin. *What would Celsius, the winner, do in a situation like this?* he asks himself.

Straight after, the Cape realizes he's fated to follow in Fahrenheit's footsteps — the loser's. His tumble is hardly manageable, and there's now an obstacle to consider: a huge roadside billboard, the only one for miles, straight ahead of this errant flight path.

Impact will occur in just seconds, no matter what manoeuvre he attempts, and at this speed there can be only one outcome.

There's a massive face he knows all too well, plastered up there on the twenty foot by sixty foot advertisement, and he's headed right for a big 'O' on the forehead.

No choice, the Cape decides quickly and fires off "Cool McCool" — to zero effect. One second before he rams the billboard, the masked man has time for one more word: "Shit."

This is another prologue, the one I did use to commence my novel One Hundred Years of Vicissitude. *It was a late inclusion, since the book was supposed to open with Chapter 1 (Wolram's wandering around the no-man's land that is the apparent afterlife), but I felt the novel needed a swift kick to open proceedings — and grabbed a spot I liked (involving murder) later on in the story.*

Swing Time

It's swing time, and Fred Astaire and Ginger Rogers must be cooling their heels elsewhere.

In all honesty, I can't distinguish swing from boogie-woogie— styles my grandparents would be better equipped to judge. Though not wearing a tuxedo to match the music, I am blessed with a suave smoking jacket.

Anyhow, this jazz-inflected number continues to blare, doing seventy-eight rpm on brittle shellac, something warbled in Japanese about people having fun just by singing the zany song.

The whole package is strung together in a crackly, mono din that originates from a gramophone, housed in a lacquered wooden casket on the other side of the room.

Splayed on the floor before the music box lays a half-naked man, inert.

You'll find me propped up on the bed. It boasts a hard, uncomfortable mattress and the quilts are awry, but who would fret, seated next to a young, exquisite geisha?

Not that she doesn't have flaws.

This girl bears smudged makeup, a vivid red streak (blood) on one white cheek, and she's wrapped in a twisted, half-open kimono that's fallen off her shoulder.

I glimpse an ample amount of small, pale breast, as I reach over to light the cigarette she has pinioned between her teeth. Eyes off, you ancient rotter.

It's damnably humid in this small, Spartan closet, and both of us are sweating. The temperature is something I doubt the fellow on the floor needs to concern himself with.

'He's dead?' I pipe up, in a blustering voice that startles me.

'As a doornail,' the woman says, unruffled, and then she exhales a plume of smoke toward the ceiling.

'So. What shall we do now?'

'I have no idea about you, but I'm enjoying the song and this cigarette.'

'You don't mind sharing them with a man you just murdered?'

'Well, I'd say he's far more functional in this state.'

She places her bare feet on the corpse's back, wriggles her toes, and then leans back to relax. There's a smirk on her cherubic mouth.

'That's better. Who needs a footstool?'

PART 2: ROY & SUZIE

Just so we're straight, Roy Scherer is a smidgeon me. And not. Straight enough?

The guy is far more gung-ho and proactive in diabolical situations, ones in which I'd probably curl up in a corner and cry. We share a certain amount of cynicism, though he takes his to extremes, and I'm a lot nicer than Roy. I like to think I am, anyway.

Where we meet is in a lack of love for zombies.

I don't know what it is, but I never managed a soft spot for brain-eating fiends lurching about above ground. When it came to horror, I much prefer my terrifying aliens — The Thing from Another World *still gets to me — and vampires, so long as these babies are free of the vices of Anne Rice and Stephenie Meyer.*

Which is one of the reasons that I approached the zombie genre when Nigel Bird and Chris Rhatigan invited me early on in 2012 to pen my first published "horror" story for their anthology Pulp Ink 2.

At the time I was researching the great Peter Lorre, an idea I had for a character that is part homage in my novel One Hundred Years of Vicissitude *— which I was writing at the time — and otherwise because Lorre reminds me of a Polish mate of mine, Mateusz Sikora, an artist with whom I started a record label (IF?) years ago.*

Lorre, for me, is one of the highlights in John Huston's The Maltese Falcon, *and he rocks his brief scenes in* Casablanca.

Understandably there is a fair amount of cross-pollination between this story and One Hundred Years, *but wasn't I talking up zombies?*

In retrospect, the yarn is a cop out. The solitary zombie in my Pulp Ink 2 *story ends up not being a zombie at all, but someone suffering from Lazarus syndrome — actually a real enigma; look it up on Wikipedia.*

For the story I decided to conjure up two new characters, the hard-bitten, grouchy Roy Scherer I've already mentioned, and his younger, bookish-yet-dizzy partner in supermundane investigations, Suzie Miller.

They came out of some recess of my brain that'd lapped up odd-couple interaction from the likes of, well, The Odd Couple, *along with* the '70s Rock Hudson/Susan Saint James *vehicle* McMillan & Wife *(I even pinched their real birth-names for the characters — shhh) and more obvious recent telly offerings* Moonlighting *and* Remington Steele. *I'd be remiss not to add that the champagne bubbles of* The Thin Man *are tossed about in there as well.*

Obviously Roy and Suzie clicked for me—straight after the Pulp Ink 2 *story, I wrote two others (and a prequel) featuring the bickering, constantly irritated duo. I'm thinking more.*

Lazarus Slept

"A zombie. I hate zombies."

I leaned back against the barn wall. This job was going to be the death of me. The job, or my partner, Suzie, and I use the term in its loosest sense.

"Actually, I don't think he qualifies as a zombie, per se."

There she was, on tiptoes, right in my ear. Why on earth she had to tag along, I never understood. I operated better alone — her old man knew that. Why couldn't this blonde busybody get the message? I glanced at her. "What?"

"More a relative of Lazarus, you know? The guy that was reanimated by Jesus Christ."

"No, I don't know. Are you going to give me another diatribe in the middle of a scene?"

"Well, I think it's important in our business to be accurate. If we went around claiming succubae were incubae, or silver bullets stopped vampires, well, we wouldn't be in business all that long, y'know?"

"Our business? My business."

"*Er* — who pays the bills, Roy?"

I could feel the acid steeping in my gut. The stuff was brewing down there in oak barrels aplenty. "Not now, okay? Timing." I pushed both index fingers in my ears.

It was right then that our new playmate Lazarus decided to round the corner, so I unplugged, settled my Smith & Wesson Model 10 in the crook of the guy's neck, and fired off a single shot. I didn't want to waste bullets — no need to be further still in Suzie's clutching debt. The man reeled backwards and lay on the ground, inert.

"Too easy. Lazarus didn't rise twice, did he?"

"Don't think so. Then again, I've never actually read the book, I just heard about it."

"You're feeding me second-hand yarns? So much for accuracy. Jeez." I stepped slowly over to the body. Even in the crap half-light, just before dawn, I could see it was twitching. "Fuckit. He's not dead."

"Oh, Christ!"

"Will you stop bringing him into it?"

"All right, all right. What should we do? Do you think we should drive a stake through his heart just in case?"

"He's not Bela Lugosi. What is this fixation with vampires?"

The man groaned down there on the ground, and then slowly sat up, clutching his throat, and placing his wobbly head between his knees. I considered popping off another round, but then decided otherwise. Suzie and I stood awkwardly, waiting for something.

"You all right, mister?" Suzie finally asked.

"Look what you did to my neck," the man cried out between splayed legs. I was impressed he could talk at all. Definitely wasn't a zombie. "You...you bungled it! You and your stupid attempt to kill me!"

Suzie shifted from one sneaker to another. "Not me," my rock-solid partner assured him.

"Coward," I muttered.

She frowned over the rim of her bookish glasses, but the expression had little room to stand on such a damnably young face. "Haven't you caused enough trouble? I stick my neck out for nobody. Sorry, no offence."

"None taken," Lazarus said in a rasping treble.

"That's right, blame me." I blew out loudly. "Look, sorry, but we're here because we got a job to do, a client to make happy."

"Who—?"

"Well, now, that wouldn't be very professional, handing out names like speeding tickets. Anyway, this client of ours — who'll stay nameless — reported a fiend mutilating his flock. Local police reckoned it was a feral dog or cat, but said farmer suspected otherwise, and then he spotted someone on two legs. Given it's the middle of the night and you just stuffed your face with some defenceless lamb, we'd be excused for thinking you were the culprit." The speech was a longer one than I usually made. It exhausted me.

At that, Lazarus cried.

Yes, he bawled. Suzie and I looked at one another. Aside from his blubbering there was an ungainly silence. The girl handed him a tissue, but I broke the peace first.

"Well, this is comical. What now?"

"Apologize?" my partner asked. Of course.

"Apologize?"

"You could try. I'm not sure I can stand much more of this. It's all a bit pathetic, really."

"The devil, you say? I'm not going to apologize — don't you remember why we're here and what this guy just did? You're the stickler for professionalism. What do we tell our client? 'We found your bogeyman, and we shot the bastard, but then he sobbed a lot, we had a change of mind, and we kissed and made up'?"

"Well, that's a no-brainer. Who's going to hire people who

sympathize with their cases?"

Lazarus held up his hand. "Will you two be quiet? You're giving me a splitting headache, and I'm already in enough pain."

"Sorry, I haven't domesticated her yet."

"Fat chance." The girl crossed her arms and looked away.

"Who are you people?"

On cue, like she'd been desperately awaiting the invitation, Suzie's body unravelled and she handed him the baby blue business card. "Scherer and Miller, Investigators of the Paranormal and Supermundane," she said by rote.

Lazarus looked up. It was tough to mark his age — late fifties? — before he died. His face was a bloated, partially fermented stew that looked to me a lot like dead actor Peter Lorre, but put that down to too many late nights with a bottle of rye and a fistful of American International flicks for company.

"Who's Scherer?" he inquired, in goddamned polite fashion.

"That would be me," I said.

"So you're Miller?"

"Er, no. That would be — was — my dad. I'm Suzie"

Lazarus leaned over and vomited up a pool of gunk, most of it blood, but I also spotted bits and pieces of sheep.

"You do know raw lamb is prone to parasites?" Suzie admonished him. "You ought to be more careful."

"I'm sorry. I can't help myself," Lazarus bawled. He was blubbering again, a grown ghoul shedding tears. This was ridiculous.

"Well, next time. Just for the record, are you craving brains?" Suzie pushed the frames back up her maddeningly cute button nose, and then conjured up a pad and pencil. "I want to be sure we're dealing here with Lazarus syndrome, or if it's localized zombiefication."

"What the hell does it matter? Ever since I woke up in that awful, awful morgue, somehow alive again, I've been ravenous, craving meat, hungry, desperate, mad, frantic—"

One more point-blank thirty-eight special, this time in his left eye, killed that appetite. "My, my, my! Such a lot of guts around town and so few brains."

"Ew," Suzie said.

"I think we can mark down this case as closed."

"My dad would've been more prudent about it."

"Your old man's dead."

"Even so, you don't think that was bit gung-ho? Maybe we could've helped out the poor man, y'know?"

"We're not in the business of helping these spooks. Count your blessings — at least we didn't have to waste any silverware. Can we go back to the office now? I'm dying for something to eat."

The title of Adam's Ribs *was oddly inspired by a childhood memory from one episode of M*A*S*H (according to Wikipedia it's the eleventh in the third season, and fifty-ninth overall) in which Hawkeye is craving ribs from a restaurant of the same name back in Chicago.*

I don't know what this has to do with vampires, the theme of the story, but I guess it was a six-degrees-of-separation moment: vampire, stake, point at ribcage, clutch for something interesting as a title from the recesses of the rancid brain, conjure up M*A*S*H. Et voilà.

This one was put together in 2012 for Andrew Hudson's horror-related anthology Somewhere in the Shadows, *and was the second outing for Roy & Suzie.*

Adam's Ribs

Now for the messy part, the part where I usually end up with splinters or a blister from gripping the bugger too hard.

I placed the stake on the chest just so, where the heart's supposed to be. In the early days I used to bring an anatomy diagram with me, just to make sure I got it right. You really don't want to get it wrong. These spooks wake up grumpy, and they're likely to take out their crankiness on the nearest bystander — that's right, you with the silly wooden tent peg in your hand.

Having positioned the thing, I lifted up the mallet, prepared to strike, and—

"Wait! Wait a moment!"

—Missed the stake completely. I heard a couple of ribs break instead. Shit.

Suzie stuck her head into my point of view, between me and the corpse with the busted-up bones. "Are you one hundred percent positive this guy is a vampire?" she asked me in that cloying, up-and-down tone of hers that drives me to distraction. It's like conversing with a verbal yoyo.

"Suzie, move. Now. No time for safety checks."

"Well, I don't know, I think we ought to create the time, y'know, just to be sure? Lawsuits and all. We don't want to do this, and then find out after that we nailed the wrong man. Cadaver. Vampire... *er* — you know what I mean."

"I do. And I think we can skip the litmus test, thanks to you."

"Really?" The giddy girl actually looked happy. "Why?"

A pair of hands rounded her neck from behind, and started to squeeze — hard. Something I'd dreamed about doing over the past six months. Suzie's glasses fell to the floor as she went in the other direction, up in the air. She was gasping, wheezing, and still trying to talk. God, shut up.

For dramatic effect, the ghoul lifted her further — which was when Suzie gripped the chandelier.

That's the problem with vampires.

They live so long they get grand notions about themselves, move from holes in the ground into crypts with marble slabs, and on into houses, and then — if they live a few centuries like this boy — migrate up to mansions with crystal chandeliers stuck to the ceiling.

The same very thing Suzie was hanging onto now for dear life, frustrating the vampire, since he was still holding her aloft and couldn't exactly lob her across the room when she had a half-decent grip on something.

Meanwhile, he looked straight down at me with my stick, a wide-open space between us inviting another go at his heart.

Not such a bright boy, this one. He should've just let the girl go. Instead, he stood there with his hands in the air, his mouth wide open with surprise. I should've guessed this'd be an easy round — the vampire dressed in duds from the '80s, he still owned a CD collection, and I could imagine he indulged in moonwalking across dance floors in front of horrified clubbers.

"Roy!" I heard Suzie shout.

Damn — I thought the vampire was still arresting her vocal

cords. "You can hold her tighter," I hissed at the ghoul in a low voice. "Help me out here."

"What?" The vampire looked more confused than ever. Definitely well-past his use-by date.

"Roy, any time you're ready."

"I don't know, Suze," I said, holding the vampire's eyes with mine. "Are we one hundred percent sure this bozo qualifies?"

"Actually, I'd say one or two percent above that. Only just."

"What is wrong with you people?" the vampire fumed, and I could see he'd made the prolonged decision to let the girl go. Playtime was over.

I plunged the stake into his stomach first. "That was for fun," I said, as the spook shrieked with pain. I pulled the tool out and stuck it right where the heart was supposed to be, behind a couple of fractured ribs. "And that's for offensive fashion."

There was no exploding, no accelerated decrepitude, not even a decent yodel. The vampire fell backwards onto his bed, holding the stake, and lay there stiff. Cue lacklustre applause. Fall of shabby curtain. Blah, blah.

Suzie was still hanging from the chandelier above me, her high-heels a few inches from my nose.

"Did we win?" she asked.

"Yeah, yeah. Don't we always?"

"You'll catch me?"

I thought hard about that one.

Revert to Type *was the third story I wrote in 2012 that featured my new duo Roy and Suzie, Investigators of the Paranormal and Supermundane, and the one I had the most problems getting accepted.*

Then again, the process isn't so bad when you receive nice rejections like this one from Mike Chinn in June 2012, who was putting together The Alchemy Press Book of Pulp Heroes: *"Although I enjoyed* Revert to Type *I'm afraid that it didn't make the final cut — but don't imagine that's because it was a bad story or I didn't enjoy your writing. I'm sure you'll have no trouble placing it elsewhere."*

When I pitched it to fellow writer (and mate) Liam José @ Crime Factory in Australia — for their Horror Factory *anthology — he suggested as follows:*

"Love the characters and the banter, but...it just feels like there is no weight to it, there aren't clear enough stakes, and no real feeling of conflict. I love the fun breezy tone, so I'm not suggesting that the first three quarters be changed, but I think it should have a slightly darker ending. Just an idea, but have you considered the typewriter landing on someone when it is struck out the window? The idea is already seeded in there, and it would tie everything together, make the piece feel stronger, and would be really effective in contrast with the light feel. It would almost undercut that slightly self-assured cockiness that Roy possesses."

Liam was spot-on.

I nipped and tucked the end along these lines, and the tactic works better, methinks. This also empowers Suzie a fair bit — about time too.

Revert to Type

"I want you to purge the thing and take it away."

"Nothing like a spot of purging," I agreed.

We were standing on the threshold of a small sunroom, into which late afternoon rays drifted through gently swaying curtains. The short man beside me, the one who'd suggested the purge, was dressed in a smart suit that whiffed of mildew, mothballs and a bottom-line fragrance of urine. He looked like the Hollywood actor David Niven before he died. Classy, British, a moustache, ancient. Over the other side of the space, on a solid oak desk, was a vintage Underwood 11 — 1940s and equally creaky.

"So what was it you wanted purged?"

"That typewriter. All the keys and the spacebar work, except the 'H'," the old guy said with some pride, his voice dusty. "They're the original glass-top tombstone keys."

"Neat," I said. I blew out my cheeks and made a loud sigh, didn't care if it were rude. "Honestly, though, looks like you gandered in the wrong parts of the Yellow Pages. We're not removalists or pawnbrokers."

"Didn't think you were, Mister—?"

"Scherer. Roy Scherer. We deal with stuff that's, well — crap." I was struggling to place my finger on precisely what it was we do, and 'crap' was a good word for it. Then I realized I had a better escape hatch. "Suzie, why don't you tell the gent?"

This was a perfect cue for my hyperactive 'assistant' to jump into the fray.

"Scherer and Miller, Investigators of the Paranormal and Supermundane," she announced, as our baby blue business card spun across the table like a stationery shuriken — Suzie was getting to be flamboyant with their dispersal. Sadly, the old fart misjudged the spin and dropped it on the floor. I didn't see him having the stamina to sweep up the card. He left it in the lint.

"Want a shot at another one?" Suzie asked.

"I think I'll give it a miss. So, about the typewriter?"

I passed fingers through my hair, doubtful. "What's the problem?"

"It's driving me to distraction — *clack, clack, clack, whiz-whirl, ka-ching!* at all hours — and then, when I storm in here to discover what the racket is all about, the bastard is docile and calm. Silent, even."

"As all good typewriters should be. What do you think the problem is?" I could be a persistent bugger, and I was guessing senility.

"I haven't a clue — you're the experts."

"Depends if the base issue is metaphysical or medicinal."

"I'm not mad."

"So you're saying it operates itself?"

"Precisely."

"Power surges?"

"This is a manual typewriter. There's no plug. Even so, the bugger starts up anytime it likes, typing away and then hitting return with that stupid bell. *Ding, ding, ding!* I feel like I have a tram in my apartment. It also leaves me messages."

"On the phone?"

"Of course not. It doesn't speak."

"Then it writes to you?"

"Yes, that *is* the inference." Our host was getting irritable. I'd been wondering how long that'd take, and this time there had been remarkably little contribution to the nonsense from the bespectacled blonde on my left. She was gazing over at the typewriter in analysis-mode as the old guy handed me some US Letter size papers.

On the first was a shopping list, typed in caps — PLEASE BUY: PAPER, RIBBON, CORRECTION FLUID, and something called MAC INE OIL.

"What's 'MAC INE OIL'?"

"Machine oil. I told you — the 'H' sticks."

"So you did. Hurrah," I muttered, putting the list to the back of the pile and examining the next note. "Okay: 'WOULD YOU RUB SOME OF THIS OIL ON MY KEYS?' Pfft. The typewriter has tactile tendencies. The 'H' is there here."

I didn't expect any response to a quip prime-time stupid before it left my lips.

"Can I look, can I look?" Suzie railed from nearby, the goddamn kindergartener.

I put up blinkers as I passed the papers back to our prospective client. I could still make money out of a ruse if I played my cards right. Definitely the man was bonkers, but a rich loon was always better than a mad pauper.

"I charge a hundred bucks a day, plus expenses."

"Sounds reasonable. This fee would cover the young lady as well?"

"She's a bonus. Now, is this your typewriter?"

"No. It was my father's. A writer."

"Classics?"

"Good Lord, hardly. Pulp — the usual kinds of horror, science fiction and detective stories. He made a pretty penny."

"I have to ask. Your old man's passed on?"

This old man cocked his head as he pursed his lips with a post-lemonish demeanour. "Well, now. What do *you* think?"

"Mm-hmm." He was too elderly to punch out and, anyway, I was too young for Marquess of Queensberry rules. I ignored the tone. "So — he died on the typewriter, or near it?"

"You believe it to be possessed?"

"Like you, mate, I haven't the faintest. But please answer the question."

"My father died in a hotel in Reno, on top of a two-dollar hooker."

"Thought you said he avoided the classics?"

"Oh, really now. You have the gumption to call this service?"

"I call it getting a job done."

"Roy. Shhh!" That was Suzie — who else?

I tried not getting annoyed and instead took out a pad to pretend to write. "Father nowhere near typewriter. Two-buck tramp." I rested my hand. "And how often would you say this machine...activates itself? Per day, I mean."

"Once, sometimes twice. Usually at night. The swine likes to keep me guessing."

"Have you tried feeding it?"

Yep, Suzie again, tossing in her all thumbs' two cents. The landlord and me combined forces to look over sharply, causing her to blush.

"Ribbon, I mean. *Ribbon.* Jeez, what were you two thinking?"

Time to ignore the girl — surprising, really, how often that occurred. "Why don't you just throw it out?" I suggested.

"What?" David Niven looked horrified.

"Open the window. Pick up the typewriter. Toss it."

"Do you know how irresponsible that is? I live on the fourth floor. What if it landed on someone's skull?"

"Well, all right, if you want to play socially behaved, why not carry the typewriter out of here, down the stairs or in the elevator, and stick it with the trash?"

"I'm eighty-two years old. You try lifting it."

"Sure."

I sauntered over to the bureau. There was an undusted bag of golf clubs leaned against the other side, so I moved this behind me, propped up on the wall. The sun outside was already hightailing. It'd be evening in a matter of minutes. I placed the writing pad in my pocket, eased hands beneath the rim of the machine, and hefted — well, tried my darnedest to do so. The monster weighed a ton and hardly budged. Stupid 1940s machinery. I took a step back to survey the situation and when I looked over I spotted a smirk on fossil-man's face.

"Sir, would you mind? We prefer to work in private."

"Certainly, certainly. My poor manners." He lifted his chinless jaw with that smirk and waltzed out in slow motion.

When the door closed, I had my moment. "Arsehole."

"Smooth," I heard Suzie respond over my shoulder.

Mocking? Oh, man. What kind of rubbishy situation had I stumbled into? My subconscious gnashing of chompers told me it was time to get serious. I again attempted to pick up the typewriter, when I accidentally hit the carriage-return button. Louder cursing from me swiftly pursued a loud *ka-ching!* — The carriage had hit dead centre of my crown jewels.

Worse still was Suzie's cackling giggle. I felt like pulling out my gun and blowing away either the typewriter or the girl — wasn't sure which would offer the most satisfaction. Probably neither, given the ongoing pain I experienced. "Shut up, will you? Gimme a moment. Crap."

"Double-crap."

That was precisely when Suzie stopped laughing and I ceased breathing, at least for a couple of seconds. I forgot all about the ache. Something wrong was happening to the typewriter, just as the last wink of direct sunlight disappeared.

Six long, shiny beetle legs — at least a metre apiece — slid out from the machine's casing, and it lifted itself upright, meaning the metal typewriter was vertical, with the keys positioned precisely where a beer belly'd sit pretty. As for the head that now emerged...fuckit, was that a head? Just above the Underwood logo was something looking like a rodent's muzzle, inverted, so there was a hole in the scaly face and two bulbous black peepers that stared straight at me, unblinking.

"Hey," I muttered — some sort of absurd, unintentional greeting — but the bugger was rude and stared without a word. "Ahh, the strong silent type." Very carefully I put my hands behind me, feeling for the dusty bag of golfing irons.

"*Clack, clack,*" the typewriter finally said. Not through the crazy mouth, but via its torso.

"Clack?" Suzie responded.

"*Clack, clack...*clickety-*click-clack!*"

"Talkative bugger, isn't he?" I muttered. "Suzie, what the fuck is that?"

"Oh, now you need me?"

"Sunshine, let it be said I always need you. I pretend otherwise — image and all." I doubt she believed a word, but needed speedy facts instead of infantile lip.

The ploy appeared to do the trick.

"Honestly? I'm not quite sure," Suzie said. In the corner of my eye I noticed she edged back, against the wall, but was impressed she held it together. I knew how much the girl detested insects and mice, and this was one very sorry merger of both. "Alien infiltration, akin to a hermit crab? Some kind of organic/mechanical hybrid? A rat trapped inside the contraption? Personally, I'm steering toward the first one."

"Remind me again."

"Alien infiltration — strikes me as similar to a report I read about a sentient typewriter in Tangier, though that came down to insecticide the people were inhaling. Could instead be a ghost in the machine?"

This last comment got the blighter typing: "*Click, clack* — ka-ching! *Clackety-clack-click!*"

"Careful with the clichés."

"No ghost? Okay, fair enough. You know — I think it might be attempting to communicate with us in Morse code," Suzie said, just as my fingers sized up a lob wedge.

"Open the window, will you?"

"Oh, sure — it's quite hot, right?" My pretty young assistant yanked up the glass. I noticed there was sweat on her temples. "A little fresh air will do us good while we decide what to do. First of all, is this little man using American Morse code, or Continental German? There is a difference. Hopefully it's the international standard version. Someone, somewhere, has to have a Morse code guidebook. Easier still to find online. Do you think our client has a PC? I know it's not exactly useful, but if we need to buy one we could put in a claim for the purchase with our next tax return, and—"

"Six!"

Yep, the choice of the lob wedge was better than the simple brutality of the driving iron. It conjured up a shot with a high arc that took the typewriter over a low bookshelf and the windowsill, clear into the evening air. I heard the *clack-clacking* diminish until an explosion of metal hit the ground far below. I'd never, ever, played such a rowdy game of golf.

Suzie jumped to the window and peered down.

"He communicating still?" I asked, as I merrily returned the club to its bag.

"I can't hear anything."

"Didn't take out any innocent bystanders in the process?"

"I don't know! Too dark down there to see. But it's probably in little pieces."

"You can thank me later."

The girl looked back at me with a perky, annoyed frown.

"You really should learn your correct sporting commentary. That was a golfing shot, yet you resorted to cricket — a 'six' is scored when the ball goes over the boundary rope without touching the ground. No one shouts it out except idle spectators. If it's golf you were mimicking, then you should've shouted out the warning 'fore' — and it's not spelt F-O-U-R but F-O-R-E. Okay?"

"Blah, blah, blah. Write it up in the visitor's book."

"You're completely — *completely* — shameless, Roy. You just destroyed a beautiful antique, and the sentient being that inhabited it. D'you know what we could have learned from this creature?"

"Meh, it prob'ly would've sounded all French to me, the way he kept dropping those H's." I gave her a big sham smile and headed for the door. Time to collect our pay.

The apartment was silent and most of the lights were off. David Niven had either done a runner or stepped out for a game of lawn bowls. Either way his wallet had gone with him.

After taking the old concertina elevator down to the ground floor we walked out and discovered our patron sunbaking on the pavement in the dark, his head sandwiched by a busted up, completely normal-looking 21.5 kg typewriter.

"Oh, Christ," said Suzie.

Me? I was transfixed by the spectacle. For the first time in a dog's age no snappy comeback veered my way. Some false teeth lay on a close-by nature strip. I stared in silence, barely able to breathe. A pool of black liquid ran into new cracks in the cement. I'd polished off a human being.

"Roy?"

"I'm screwed," was all I could say.

"Roy." Suzie placed herself between the corpse, the machine, and me. "Roy, you listening to me? Roy!" She slapped me hard, a stinger that struck the left cheek and the corner of my mouth.

"What?" I asked, still vague and slowly focusing on the girl's face. There was anger there, also a stubborn purpose I'd never seen Suzie display.

"Snap out of it. Now. We need to move."

"I killed the guy."

"You killed the typewriter. Whether the old man and the typewriter were some kind of bizarre kindred spirit, or if he had the bad sense of timing to be passing beneath when you knocked the monster out the window — well, we'll never know and it honestly doesn't matter. Pull yourself together."

"But — I —"

"But *nothing!*" Suzie glared up at me, holding my arms. "We are not going to jail for this, not for doing our job. We're simply going to walk away. To do so I need to tidy up things. What did you touch in the apartment? Roy, what did you touch?"

I tried to look past her but she dodged in the way again. A light rain had started to fall.

"Not there. Look at me. What did you touch?"

"I — the typewriter. The golf club."

"Which one?"

"The typewriter, the one just — a..."

"Which golf club?"

"The lob wedge."

"Right. Nothing else?"

"No." Water dripped down my face but I barely felt it.

Suzie turned on her heel, went to the dead body, and wiped over the fractured pieces of the typewriter with her sleeve. That done, she stood straight to peer up at the building we'd just left.

"I'll be back in a few minutes. Don't stray. But any fool stumbles across this mess, we'll meet a block down — thataway." The girl pointed towards the corner of Sholes and Glidden. "Understand?"

I glanced away. "Yeah."

"Roy." Suzie stepped back to me and placed her arms around my waist, her face coming close, hair wet. I never noticed before how dazzling she was, even with the glasses spattered with raindrops and the bloody sleeve. "We'll be fine." I heard thunder somewhere distant. Then she winked and headed for the entrance.

"Suze," I called.

She stopped to look at me, a resourceful smile on her lips. "What?"

"Don't forget the business card the old coot dropped."

"*Mmm*. More like it."

I started out writing East of Écarté *as a background piece for Floyd Maquina, my narrator from* Tobacco-Stained Mountain Goat, *intended to address a comment he made in the pages of* TSMG: *"Turns out they were Seeker Branch reps and were recruiting me because of my experience as a private investigator (I don't know why — I was a hack — but that's a long story for another day and another book)."*

But by August 2012, when I decided to steer the unfinished yarn into 'weird noir' territory to suit K.A. Laity's ace anthology (fittingly called Weird Noir, *for the fine people at Fox Spirit), it stood to reason I needed to ditch Floyd — who's rooted in a real if surreal, dystopic/dystrophic world — and induct my other detective character Roy Scherer, of Scherer and Miller, Investigators of the Paranormal and Supermundane.*

Aside from the fact he dabbles with the supernatural, Roy is most things Floyd is not. Floyd is more I: self-doubting, addicted to movies, a lush. Roy is the rumble-and-tumble type, cocky and cynical.

Here Roy is younger and fresher than in the other stories I've written about him and his partner Suzie. He hasn't reached the pinnacle of sarcasm and cynicism but he's started the trek.

Mocha Stockholm is a tiny wink at my daughter Cocoa, six years old when I put together this story (she's now seven). Cocoa's a similarly incredible force of nature, and while I write she often entertains herself practicing ballet beside me in our tiny Tokyo apartment that's 33 square metres.

She accompanies DVDs of performances by Aurélie Dupont, Gillian Murphy and Dorothée Gilbert. Like Mocha, Cocoa adores ballet and creates her own choreography on the fly, with touches of comedy, so of course I glance her way and it's had its influence.

The character of the male dancer here, Bruno Lermentov, is heavily based on Bruno the "Slobokian Acrobatic Bear" from Robert McKimson's Bugs Bunny cartoon Big Top Bunny *(1951) — a favourite for me and Cocoa — while the artistic director of the ballet company, Murray Helpman, is a loose nod to the great Sir Robert Helpmann, the Australian ballet dancer who choreographed* The Red

Shoes *(1948) and played the evil Child Catcher in* Chitty Chitty Bang Bang *(1968).*

In a review, Raven Crime Reads said "I particularly enjoyed... 'East of Ecarte' which made me feel that I'd wandered into the darkest recesses of Raymond Chandler's imagination." I mention this here 'cos the vaguest comparison with Chandler knocks off my socks.

Finally, there are some subverted quotes and character names buried in here from a wealth of ballet-oriented movies, everything from Dario Argento's Suspiria *to* Center Stage. *Why not?*

And do check out the original Weird Noir *anthology if you get the chance, "a brilliantly tough-talking, visceral and disturbing collection..."*

East of Écarté

I hugged the curve of the desk, partially playing sham detective but more honestly hungover and bored out of my brain, when the dame came to call — unannounced, as the choice ones usually do.

Which is an intentional play on words. This woman had no choice.

The fact was my employer not only underpaid me but also refused to invest in a receptionist, and this accounted for the fact our visitor wandered in with an addled expression stuck on her mush. I sat up straight to wave, before contemplating how stupid that looked.

If she noticed, the woman let me off the hook. She indicated the only chair on the other side of the bureau, her ironing-board posture putting mine to shame.

"May I?"

"Sure."

She was young, late teens sliding into early twenties, had long, golden-brown hair severely tied back in a way that framed a beautiful face with minimal makeup.

To balance this and likely buck any unwanted attention, the woman wore an abstract floral dress looking like Claude Monet and Jackson Pollock painted it in wild collusion.

"Are you Mister Miller?" she asked as my eyes adjusted to the glare.

"Sorry, he's out. I'm in."

"I see. I'm Mocha Stockholm."

"Course you are."

The woman frowned, though on that face the expression barely made a dent. I noticed her eyes mugged the colour of cinnamon.

"You know me?" she asked.

"Nah. Just sounded like a quip Humphrey Bogart would've rolled out — with far more flair."

"To which, Lauren Bacall would lob back her own face-slapping wisecrack?"

"The devil, you say...?" I grinned. "You know your classic cinema."

"A wee bit. My mum was a movie journalist, so I grew up force-fed on the stuff. She particularly loved her black-and-whites detective stories, Mister—?"

"Scherer."

"Mister Scherer."

"Call me Roy."

"Roy, then." She smiled. We looked at each other for several seconds. "Care to know why I've come today, Roy?"

"Oh, yeah, 'course — sorry."

I grabbed a notebook, and the first biro I scribbled with refused to work. I rifled through a desk drawer, searching for another.

"Would you mind if I smoke?" I heard the woman ask as I ransacked the bureau. What was her name? Mockba? Momo? Better to stick with Miss Stockholm.

"No worries, Miss Stockholm."

"Mocha."

"Mocha. Sure — so long as you don't mind sharing one of the cigarette's brothers. I'm out."

Mocha pulled her chair closer.

As she renounced good deportment and reclined back into it, the woman crossed a pair of obscenely long, narrow legs. I hadn't noticed before the minimal length of her overwrought dress.

She conjured up an ostrich-skin-covered cigarette case and slipped out two cigarettes.

"Help yourself."

Case in hand, Mocha leaned over and I prized one free. I tried my urbane best to snap up the fag with style, but my mitt shook. That would be the excessive amount of cognac, consumed the prior evening, revealing itself.

The woman lit our cigarettes with a Zippo that had the slogan *La Chauve-souris* inscribed in a flowing font across its surface.

Settling back to enjoy the moment I sensed the return of a wayward backbone, and granted my guest a grateful smile. She'd earned the truth.

"I have a confession," I said. "I'm not really a detective, just hired help."

"I suspected as much."

Mocha held the cigarette between her teeth as she placed the case and lighter into a small purse, and then she took it in her left hand.

"There's only one name on the business card — Mister Miller's. You're also a little young."

"No younger than you."

She pursed her lips, but there was a smirk there. "Too young to play the hardened, streetwise PI. You need to get out in the sun more often, weather-up the good-looks."

"You're a better detective than me."

"Something I've always aspired to. Let me guess: Part-time job?"

"Bingo. Pays the bills and saves me scabbing off my parents."

"They object?"

"I do."

The woman nodded, but I noticed she was looking over at the tattered venetian blind I had closed to fend off an offensive midday sun.

"The odd-jobs you do here. Surveillance, or that sort of thing?"

"Would be neat if true. Alas, no. Mostly paper shuffling and photocopy chores. I double-up as a cleaner and short order cook. I'm quite the whiz with an egg and a pot of boiling water. But I don't think Art trusts me enough at this point in the field, doing things like surveillance. Prob'ly never will."

"Art would be Mister Miller?"

"Yep."

With her free hand, Mocha pulled at the hem of her dress, which was riding too high on her thighs. I praised my lucky stars that Art had never invested in a wider desk.

"Speaking of whom," the woman murmured, "can I ask where he is? We had an appointment for twelve."

"That so?"

Mocha gifted me a laugh. "That *is* so."

This was a potential problem.

Art had been on the receiving end of most of the cognac the night before — two bottles of Château de Plassac, an undeserved gift from a grateful client. I'd drunk maybe half of one of them, Art the rest. Plus a couple of lines of speed. Given the current state of my brain, I assessed he'd be sleeping the cocktail off right into the next week.

I pretended to check a desk calendar my boss never used. "Stockholm," I mused, feigning diligence. "Named after the city?"

"No, silly — the city's named after me."

"Right." I looked up at the woman. "He's — um — indisposed

right now, out on a case, but give me all the details and I'll fill him in."

"Have you found a pen that works?"

"Right here."

I was holding aloft a gaudy pen with cute images of Minnie Mouse splashed all over the thing. Where the blazes had Art acquired that?

"Fine." The woman gave me a pleasant enough smile — difficult to read. "I think someone is trying to kill me."

I'd just crossed the t in 'think' — shorthand wasn't my forté — when she finished talking. The comment hung in the air like a predatory slap about to happen. I looked at her under my brow.

"You think...?"

Mocha glanced at the pad beneath my pen. "I think someone is trying to kill me."

"I know — you said."

"Well, you haven't finished writing."

"I'm not sure I need to — easy enough to remember."

I took a last drag on my cigarette, which was already burning at the filter. Damn.

"What I meant to ask is this: You think someone is trying to kill you, or you have actual proof of the matter?"

"I have these. See what you make of them."

Mocha had popped open her handbag — it was a Prada, no idea if counterfeit or real — and she took out a handful of twice-folded beige envelopes that she placed on the desk within easy reach. I picked them up and counted. Five in all, no address or postage stamp — just Mocha's name typed on the front.

"They were slipped under the door of my apartment," she said. "Well, four were put there. The fifth I discovered in my locker at the theatre."

"You're an actress?"

"Ballet dancer."

The perfect comportment of her legs crossed my mind. I

opened the flap of one of the envelopes and opened up an abnormally sized page.

Mocha leaned forward to place elbows on top of Art's ink-blotter map of the world, her chin in her palms. "It's U.S. Letter, eight-point-five by eleven inches."

"You measured it?"

"Well, like you, obviously, I thought this was a weird size. I checked into it. Whereas we use the international standard A4, U.S. Letter is the standard in—"

"The U.S.?" I hazarded.

"Spot on."

"Ta. Wasn't that difficult."

I turned my attention to the contents.

"Let's see: 'YOU WILL DIE!!' ... To the point, all caps, double exclamation marks for effect — making the threat childish. Not so sure of him or herself, since 'WILL' is employed instead of 'GOING TO'. Wow. You're right. This is a threat."

"Using a manual typewriter."

"Manual?" I stared closer at the print. "Old school. Scrub the childish quip. And looks like the 'L' drops down lower than the other keys."

Mocha narrowed her eyes as I showed the page. Straight after I had to shake my head to clear it of the vision. The woman's eyes were dazzling.

"I hadn't noticed that," she was saying.

I flicked through other envelopes in my hands. "All these letters are written with the same machine?"

"I'm fairly certain, yes."

"Similar commentary?"

"Pretty much. Things like 'Die, bitch', 'Prepare to meet your maker' — et cetera, et cetera. I haven't learned all of them by rote."

"Original content."

"Requiring writerly skill and excessive imagination."

"For sure. Any idea why some dipstick would want you bumped off?"

"I haven't the faintest." Straight after she lifted her head from her hands. "Actually, that's not exactly true. I was recently promoted to principal."

"Of which school?"

Mocha rolled those mesmerizing cinnamon peepers. "I'm nineteen. A little young to be a teacher, let alone running a school. I mean principal dancer at the company — what the French call étoile."

"Well, I'm glad we got that sorted out early," I laughed.

She charitably joined me. "That's true. Could have led to some disastrous misunderstandings."

"Oh, yeah. Now, back to the manual typewriter." Balancing the chair on its two back legs — which my boss hated me doing — I scratched my head. "Prob'ly it's easy enough to find in this day and age. What a giveaway."

"Then you'll take the case?"

"I'll have to run it by Art when he steps in. Guy's a busy man."

"Not your Mister Miller — you. Will you take the case?"

I stared at her. "Me?"

"I like the way you think, even while you're nursing what I can only imagine is the hangover from Hades."

"You noticed."

"Mmm. But I think we have something, a spark. I trust you, in spite of any — er — alcoholic tendencies."

"Well, I'm not qualified, anyway. I'm no detective. Art runs the show and he'd hit the roof."

"I don't care. Qualifications are often a ruse or no help at all. I'll pay you well — and I'll throw in a few front-row tickets."

"You have that kind of pull?" I guessed it must be a third-rate affair, probably some amateur collective doing rehearsals in a dilapidated warehouse on a forgotten back alley in Richmond or Clifton Hill.

"Right now, I seem to."

"Which company?"

"The national one."

"Ah." I seriously needed to reassess my detecting skills. "The big time."

"These days, with the world falling apart out there — I guess."

"Sorry to say, I'm not such a ballet fan, so the tickets would be a wasted perk."

"Any sisters?"

That made me twig. Art's kid Suzie.

I could imagine her killing for the tickets — or, better yet, strangling me if I passed up this kind of opportunity. A tough ten-year-old mad about ballet. I peered at my watch. God knows why. The old man wouldn't be back for days and, anyway, he wouldn't notice I was MIA.

"Okay," I decided. "You're on."

We entered the Arts Centre complex via a back door that reminded me of hidden panels used by ninja in old Japanese TV shows.

I didn't even see it there in the wall until Mocha stopped and swung it open. Just as I stepped forward, another skinny woman — coming from inside — whacked into my guide.

The glare this woman sent Mocha's way bookended the intentional nature of the bump. I would have guessed her age as early thirties, with crow's feet around the eyes and a boyish body she didn't hide. Pretty woman, but washed out and agitated.

"I see you're replacing me in the part," this woman said.

Mocha held her ground. "It's just temporary."

"Of course. Nobody here is a permanent fixture."

After that, the woman waltzed down the street. I'll give her this much — she waltzed well.

"Who's grumpy bum?" I asked.

"Neve Ryan."

"And the name is supposed to be meaningful to me, because...?"

"The darling of the company over the past decade — but she's being forced into retirement by our new director Murray Helpman."

"Bound to make someone grumpy. Any chance you reckon she could be the author of your fan mail?"

"Well, she doesn't like me."

"I don't like people, either — but that doesn't mean I send irate love letters or plan to knock them off."

"True. C'mon."

I followed the woman's lead along a narrow corridor wrapped in pale linoleum and very little else aside from intrusive fluorescent lighting above our heads.

"So this is ballet central?"

"The bowels of it."

Near an open door a wiry-looking middle-aged man in a baggy chocolate-brown suit, boasting a beige cravat around the neck and thinning hair up on top, intercepted us. He had a somewhat magnetic ski-jump nose undercut by a lopsided sneer.

"Darling," he purred, ignoring me as he washed bulging eyes over Mocha. "Where on earth have you been?"

"Having lunch with my friend Roy here. Roy, this is Murray Helpman — the artistic director of the company."

"Yes, yes, charmed," Helpman crooned, allowing his gaze to flick my way for all of one five hundredth of a second. "Now—" His attention had jumped back to Mocha "—I want to create, to make something big out of something little, to make a great dancer out of you. But first, I must ask you a question: What do you want from life? To eat?"

The man appeared genuinely disgusted at the thought.

"Don't worry, I threw down only a salad," Mocha assured him.

"With a liberal dashing of Thousand Island dressing," I added.

Helpman fairly swooned. Mincing with feeble, the man leaned against a wall, wiping his brow.

"Oh, my God! Insanity!"

"Roy's only kidding round," Mocha said, granting me a look that was thirty-three percent annoyed and the other two-thirds mischief. "No Thousand Island dressing, I swear."

Another man, handsome, taller and far more powerful-looking than Helpman, strode up to us in an overly tight pair of white tights and a loose black T-shirt with the word 'IF?' emblazoned across the chest.

"What is this I hear for Thousand Island dressing? I love the Thousand Island!"

"Oh, Bruno, shhh."

Mocha seemed disproportionately annoyed now. It was a sad thing to see the mischief scarper.

"Roy, this is my dance partner, Bruno Lermentov. He's from Slobokia."

"Is that a real country?"

"Ahh, of course, of course! Very nice to meet you, Mr. Roy," Bruno said, all odd eastern European twang, shaking my hand with a surprisingly strong grip that made my bones creak. Then he leaned in close, glittery eyes beneath a brunette fringe. "Am I not magnificent?"

"Sorry. It's a bit of a madhouse."

We were in a reasonably large dressing room that Mocha scored for herself. It even had her name on the door — my dream.

One wall was naked brickwork and opposite that a huge mirror sat above a dresser. Light bulbs surrounded the looking glass and a clothesline dangled across it just above head-height, holding an assortment of undergarments and jewellery.

Below, the dresser was jammed with powders, creams, rouge, lipsticks, brushes and other bric-à-brac I had no hope of recognizing.

"D'you mean it's a madhouse right here or the ballet company in general?"

"Both?" Mocha giggled.

I barely recognized the woman.

She'd changed into a sequined leotard with a wide, frilly tutu, while on her face she'd slapped a thick layer of white greasepaint, black eyeliner and ridiculously long false lashes. An ostrich-feather headpiece up top set it all off. Her midriff above the tutu was bare — a narrow, muscled thing that had absolutely no excess puppy fat. This was difficult to keep my hands off.

At that particular moment Mocha was grinding her feet in a small wooden box on the ground.

"Kitty litter?" I asked from my crap fold-up captain's chair by the door.

"Ha-Ha. No. This is ballet rosin, a powder resin we rub our toes and heels in to avoid slippage."

"Oh, I get it — a fancy version of the blue chalk we use on billiard cues for a game of pool."

"Mmm."

I wasn't sure what she meant by her tone there.

"Anyway, I have a performance. I've reserved a seat for you in the wings." She stepped out of the tray and pushed a ticket into my hands. "I'll see you after?"

"Sure. Might do a spot of snooping."

"If you're hungry — well, you'll have to pop out for something. There's a half-decent restaurant next door called The Archers, so try that. None of the other dancers have anything decent except rabbit food, and since he took over I'm certain Murray is trying to starve us all to death."

"How long's he been in charge?"

"Two months, ever since Pat Hingle's terrible accident."

"In what way terrible?"

"She was found in the loo — disembowelled, stabbed multiple times, and hung from a doorframe with her own tights."

"You call that an accident?"

"The police did. Anyway, I can't complain. Pat tended to ignore me, but once Murray took over he gave me the promotion."

The woman placed her arms in an 'L' position — the left one out straight beside her, the right pointed my way, and then she pirouetted on one leg several times, so swiftly her body became a blur. When she finished the rotation she struck a pose with her arms crossed low in front and one foot forward.

"*Bras Croisé*," she announced.

I couldn't help myself — I gave a healthy round of applause.

Mocha winked at me. "Warm up." Her gaze whipped over to a digital clock half hidden behind paraphernalia on that crowded dresser. "Gotta go, Roy — duty calls. Ciao!"

About three hours later, after countless curtain calls and once the orchestra had packed up and the audience piled out, Mocha came to find me in the right wing seats. She was still dolled-up, but had wrapped herself in a bland cream woolen cardigan and had her ostrich feathers at a jaunty angle. Surprisingly her makeup had held together okay. She also looked sweaty, and the complete package was sexy.

"So — what did you think of *Le Corsaire*?" she asked as she flopped next to me and stuck her pointe shoes on the chair in front. "I presumed you might enjoy it since there're pirates tucked away in the faintly ridiculous plot."

I glanced at her. "Honest answer?"

"Go on."

"I dozed through most of it."

"And I thought you were supposed to be keeping an eye on me."

"I had my leftie half-open."

"Does that count?"

"In my book, yep. Quite the struggle."

"Did you find any typewriters?"

"Forgot to bring my magnifying glass. Bring me up to speed on the yarn behind the ballet."

"There really isn't one. Remember I said it was faintly ridiculous?"

"You're kidding."

"It's the performance that matters. Kind of."

"Right." I rubbed my face and peered around the empty auditorium. "Big place. How many people does it hold?"

"A thousand at capacity."

"How many were here today."

"A thousand."

Mocha stood then and took my hand, which surprised me. I allowed her to lead me away from the comfy chair to a small set of stairs, and then up onto the stage.

Some of the spots high above still glowed, but the arena and its ramshackle sets created a dark forest effect that looked vaguely menacing — in a wire clothes hanger and papier-mâché way.

"Don't you get stage-fright in front of all those gawking plebs out there?"

"Sometimes my heart is in my stomach. Other times, I don't care. They're going to be building a larger theatre next door — it's going to hold five times as many people, apparently. Scary."

"Ballet is that popular?"

"I didn't think so, but I don't make these decisions. An audience of five thousand is too big — can you see the dancers at all from the back pews? Next up, they'll erect video screens in the rear for those people — which means they might as well save their money and enjoy the spectacle on a telly at home."

I decided on the spot the girl was cute when she soapboxed.

"How long've you been prancing partners with Bruno the Magnificent?"

"Ouch."

Mocha slid off the humdrum cardigan and watched it fall to the boards.

"You make us sound like some kind of glitzy ballroom dancing duo. We've been together a month, since I was elevated to principal. Bruno was Neve's partner before that."

"Bound to make waves."

"A drop in the ocean." Mocha smiled.

"So no death notes in your locker this afternoon?"

"Nothing. But we've only been here half a day. Rome wasn't built in twice that."

"Neither was my attention span. How long *did* it take to build Rome?"

"I don't remember them teaching us — we learned only the idiom."

"That figures."

I gazed up at the pulleys and ropes, lights and wire several dozen metres above, at the same time that I stretched the muscles in my back.

"Before you became a principal dancer you were one of those background people?"

"A member of the *corps de ballet*? Yep."

"What's the wire on them? Any grumpsters amongst that lot?"

"People annoyed by my promotion? I don't know. Haven't thought to take a survey." Perhaps feeling guilty, the girl picked up her cardigan and hung it on a small faux rock.

"When were you upped to prima?"

"Five weeks ago."

"When did the fan mail begin?"

"Five weeks ago."

I looked at her. "The same day you were promoted?"

"Yep — that was the night I received the one in the locker. After that they've been hand-delivered by the arsehole to my apartment."

"Before or after the announcement?"

"Which one?" Mocha was confused.

"The announcement about your upgrade — promotion."

"God, I don't know. It was ages ago."

"Try to remember."

Mocha frowned and her eyes darted about as she searched her memory. It seemed to be a losing battle, but then the girl parted her cherry-red lips and stared at me.

"Before? Crap — yes. You're right. It *was* before. We had a matinée performance of *The Sleeping Beauty*. Neve was Aurora, Bruno the Prince and I was the Lilac Fairy. Neve was so beautiful, Roy. I'd never, ever seen anyone dance Aurora so—"

I cleared my throat. "The letter, Mocha."

"Hmm?"

"The letter in the locker."

"Oh! Yes, sorry. After the performance ended I brushed out my hair, had a shower, got changed to go to the company fundraiser upstairs that evening — that was where the announcement about my promotion was to be made. I found the letter beforehand, squeezed into my locker through the grille."

"You weren't concerned?"

"I didn't take the thing seriously, wasn't sure if it was a joke or some silly stalker's handiwork. I didn't have the time to fret."

"Who knew you were being promoted?"

I was thinking of either Bruno the Magnificent or Neve, the forced retiree.

Incriminating ballet shoes best fit the two of them. Frankly, nothing would make me happier than to pin the wrong number tag on the guy who'd crushed my fingers — they still ached.

"Did Bruno or Neve know about the promotion?" I added.

"No. Well, I'm pretty sure no. Even I didn't know until the

announcement was made. I spotted Neve's face straight after —
she was horrified, but she also looked shocked. The woman
played a wonderful Aurora, but she's not that great an actress."

"Bruno?"

"Off chasing tutu. He'd slipped out straight after the encore to
catch a flight to Sydney. Some dancer up there he has his hands
all over."

I breathed out loudly and looked around us. We were alone. I
never realized a theatre would be so eerie when no one was in it.

"When is this place closed up for the night?"

"The theatre? They'll be switching off the lights in an hour or
two."

"Do they object to people hanging round like we are now?"

"Usually it's okay."

"So security is lax. People come, people go."

"I never gave it much thought. Yes."

After testing its stability I sat down on a prop representing an
anchor. "The key is the typewriter, but I doubt we'll find that
here. You'd hear a manual a mile off."

"We can't exactly ransack people's homes."

"Who says? Art does it all the time."

"And you?"

"The only ransacking I ever did was my older brother's room,
looking for his chocolate stash."

I performed the usual head scratch.

"Let's go back a way. Who would have known before the
announcement? Who decides these things? And had the time to
whiz home, type up the note on their fancy antique typewriter
that probably needed to be oiled down beforehand, and then get
back here — all this before the party — to make a letter drop?"

We glanced at each other.

"Helpman."

Straight after, I was seeing stars.

Something damnably hard had hammered me from behind

across the back of my skull, knocked me right off the anchor, and I lay on my face on the stage. The pain was excruciating and I thought I'd pass out — but didn't. I held on for dear life, since I knew life was probably something give or take in that moment.

It took a while to pull myself to my hands and knees, idiotic notions of protecting Mocha flying bat-crazy across my senses. I had to wait longer still to clearly see anything.

When I finally did, there was a sprinkling of blood on the floorboards around me — mine? Mocha's?

Velveteen stage curtains hung nearby and I used them to pull myself to my feet. I felt woozy and things threatened to bank sideways, but at least they'd stopped spinning.

Bruno the Magnificent stood a few metres away at the edge of the orchestra pit, a glassy look on his face as he watched me totter.

"You?" I said.

The dancer peered down at his right hand.

There was an iron weight there, something heavy enough to have been the object that whacked me — and, in fact, there was hair and a tuft of scalp attached to it, but the hair was the wrong colour.

It was black instead of my brown.

A thick trickle of blood from his hairline coursed down the Slobokian's face.

"It fell on my head, yet!" he declared of the metal weight, holding it aloft for conjecture, and then he collapsed sideways with a loud thud.

"A wonderful dancer, but in all other respects a cretin."

The theatre director, Helpman, came around the corner of a towering prop of the pirate ship the anchor belonged to. This newcomer kicked Bruno's body, which remained still, and he smiled.

"All that gutter English and poorly pronounced nonsense. Perhaps I should have bludgeoned him earlier?"

"Then you're the one that slugged me."

"Naturally."

"Where's Mocha?"

My skull puttered as I again fell to my knees. Yes, concern had come to bat, and I also decided I had to play for time — weak sister I might've been, but at the current moment I was in no state to put up half-decent resistance.

Time. I needed time. For a miracle to happen.

"And a fine question that is," Helpman nattered — like all good villains should, wasting precious seconds. "I thought she would be with you. Where *has* the girl got to?"

The man glanced about, displaying a relatively minor sense of unease.

If she'd taken a powder, good for her. Lot less to worry about. But I still needed the time I talked up, and clarity — p'raps I could even convince him to tip his mitt, for all the good that'd do me. Curiosity always was my weak point.

"Can I ask you something?"

"This depends, does it not?"

"On what exactly?"

"On the question, of course."

"Well, okay, whatever. Yeah." I shook my head. My vision was blurring again, but I kept to the chase like Art used to tell me about. "Anyway, d'you happen to have a manual typewriter?"

"Yes, I do."

"Does it get stuck on its 'L's?"

"Ahh. I see where you're taking this, Roger."

"Roy."

"I don't think your name is something you need to worry about ever again."

"Yeah, yeah, I get that. But one thing I don't get — you're the one who sent Mocha those crazy notes."

"Hands up, guilty parties!" Helpman raised five fingers into the air and he laughed in a mad, unnerving kind of way.

"Funny. Why? You promoted her to principal ballerina."

That killed the laughter.

"Dancer. Good Lord, nobody says 'ballerina' anymore."

"Dancer. Same question."

Helpman raised both arms now, outstretching them toward the empty seats of the theatre.

"Great agony of body and spirit can only be achieved by a great impression of simplicity!" he declared with a booming voice — either clearly insane or up for a bit of ham acting.

As I studied the palooka I also felt more than a little confused, and was pretty certain this wasn't concussion-related.

"I think you want to word that the other way round, mate," I decided.

"And who, pray tell, is the artistic director here?"

"I doubt you are. You strike me as more a professional nut-job."

"Oh, ho!" Helpman chuckled, without genuine mirth. "Do get these giddy expressions off your chest, before I crack your head wide open."

"No, I've got a better idea."

"You do?"

Time was working its little magic. I could see better and my head didn't feel like it had quite so many trolls tap-dancing about.

"Yeah, I do — let's bite the bullet here and now. You're going to kill me, so let's be upfront. I'm Roy Scherer and I work for a detective agency. The training wheels still haven't been detached, but there you go. I live in a mate's apartment, sleeping on his couch, and I have no money in the bank. My sad story in a nutshell. But Art Miller, my boss, knows I'm here and you don't want to mess with him."

I wiped the back of my head. It was wet. When I put my hand in front of my face, it was covered with sticky blood. I blinked a few times, feeling ill.

"Now you," I muttered. "What's your real name? I know Helpman is a sham."

"And why should I bother going into such detail?"

"Why not?"

He smiled. "Pathetic. My name is Ivan Boleslawsky."

"Okay. Never remember that. And your caper?"

"If you're asking me what this is about, you ought to direct the question to Mocha's mother. Mocha?"

The man turned full circle on the stage.

"Where the devil has she got to? She can't escape. I've locked all the doors, and the keys are right here." He tapped the breast pocket of his blazer.

I felt like I was going to pass out. Not yet. "Go on," I urged.

"Hmm?" The man stopped looking around. "Oh yes, of course, the story! Well, many years ago, Mocha's mother — a hack journalist, I must say — wrote a review of one of my father's movies. Do you know the famous Ruritanian director Rudolf Boleslawsky?"

"Nup."

"A great man. His cinema style was sublime, moving, and—"

"You talked up a review."

"Oh, yes. Thank you. This film 'review' was first published in *The Age* newspaper here in Melbourne. That would have been damaging enough, but the harpy syndicated the piece to *The Independent* in England and *The New York Times* in America. It even appeared in the esteemed *Ruritanian Gazette*. That five hundred-word critique destroyed my father's career and broke his heart — a year later he tried to drown my mother in the kitchen sink and was then committed to a mental institution. I was sixteen years old. It was a humiliating experience."

"For your dad, or for yourself?"

"Myself, of course."

I yawned. "Y'know, this yarn is about as interesting as the story behind *Le Corsaire*."

"How dare you!"

Bole-whatever-his-name-was strode straight over to Bruno's corpse and snatched up the weight from the dead man's hand.

"Now I'm going to return the favour by killing not just that evil reviewer's only child, but her rude, highly unprofessional prick of a bodyguard."

"My bad."

"Bad luck isn't brought by broken mirrors, but by broken shoes. Remember that."

"What's the point? You're going to crown me anyway."

"True."

The kook stepped slowly toward me. I still held tightly to the curtains and couldn't raise my hands to defend myself.

"Modern man is so confused, Roy. It's much better to work in the theatre — than in the horror of a world out there."

"Whatever."

That was when all hell broke loose.

Something fast darted out of shadows of a mocked-up grotto to my right, moving so quickly I couldn't hope to keep up.

I don't know when I realized the wildly whirling dervish was Mocha.

She hummed something familiar as she zipped, twisted, did a cartwheel — what was that damned tune? — and finally she somersaulted, catapulted herself into a handstand, scissor-kicked around Helpman's neck, and stopped right there.

"*Pas de deux?*" she said, her cheeks flushed even under all the makeup.

Helpman's eyes bulged, his head pinioned between Mocha's calf muscles. I could see he was stuck, and she wasn't about to let him go.

"Mocha," I warned, "watch out for the weight of iron he has in his mitt."

"Ta."

The woman knocked the metal away across the floor. Then she

leaned up close to her captive. The flexibility factor alone worried me — I had no hope of ever touching my toes.

"Ivan," she murmured softly, fluttering her enormous false eyelashes, "now I know your real name, let me tell the other part of the story, the bit you missed. I'm your harpy."

"What?"

"It was me. I wrote the bad review. The hack that destroyed your father."

"Preposterous! What nonsense is this? That would make you somewhere in the vicinity of sixty years of age! It was your mother!"

Mocha laughed.

"Oh, I've lived for a *very* long time. One reason my ballet is so good. Lots of practice. What you don't understand is that I've been doing this mother-daughter routine for centuries. Makes people less suspicious. By the way, I hate to be the bearer of bad tidings — but your father's movie really was awful."

A second later the woman spun abruptly, pushing off the floor with her hands, and I heard a loud crack.

Helpman, or Boleslawsky, or whoever the fuck he was, fell down across Bruno the Magnificent. His neck was bent at an obscene angle, and spread-eagled together on the stage like that the two men looked like an arty religious icon thrown together for some exasperating stage-play.

"Jeez. The horror of the world is right in here, pal," I muttered as I let go of the drapes and sagged.

Of course, Mocha caught me. This woman, I realized, was capable of anything.

"Roy, are you all right?" she asked quickly. "I heard every-thing. I'm so sorry I hid. I needed time to figure out my action."

"Guessed as much. I'm a good timewaster. Besides, in the end there you more than made up for the faux pas."

"I did?"

"Christ, did you ever."

I leaned back against her shoulder and could feel the woman's warm breath on my neck.

"I have a question, though — what'd you use on the bastard? Some kind of mixed martial arts?"

"Secret."

She eased us both down to the floor and I sat there on my backside, positioned between two sensational legs in white tights that I'd just seen kill a man.

Which was when I remembered.

"Stockholm really was named after you."

Mocha snuggled her face into my neck and granted me a kiss. "It was. Seven hundred years ago."

"Ominous. You may be an elderly lady — yet you still manage to rock and have a town to call your own. Now, let's get me to hospital."

"You're okay?"

"Never better."

I leaned over, dizzy, grabbed the keys from a dead man's pocket, and then gingerly stood up all by myself.

PART 3:

TOBACCO-STAINED OFFSHOOTS

I initially penned Tobacco-Stained Mountain Goat *as a four-page short story called 'Il Desinenza' when I was in my early 20s, and writing was still my single passion — this was before I got diverted, distracted and far too spread-out with music, the record label IF?, journalism, DJing, and generally having too much fun.*

In 1992, and again in 2001, I fleshed out the story to manuscript form, and then shelved it on both occasions to collect dust.

Somehow I dragged the thing back out in 2007, wiped it down, and began writing Tobacco-Stained Mountain Goat, *the novel, with great help from my editor Kristopher Young at Another Sky Press — who also decided to publish it...with a wunderbar cover by American artist Scott Campbell (a.k.a Scott C). I've included his original concept sketch for the back cover below.*

TSMG explores sci-fi/noir/dystopia and tells the story of Floyd Maquina, a seeker/detective of a near future in which Melbourne is the last remaining city on earth. Discrimination, environmental degradation and big business reign supreme, and Floyd, a lush, tries to save the day with help from his friends Laurel 'Nina' Canyon and Hank Jones.

After I published the novel (in April 2011) I wasn't keen to venture back into the same terrain, but I loved the characters — so ended up organizing an anthology with Another Sky: The Tobacco-Stained Sky. *This tome addresses the same post-apocalyptic/hardboiled world through the eyes of other writers and comic artists, as well as mine.*

Hence a few TSMG-related short stories and a batch of comic art that cropped up in 2012. Come Out Swinging *was one of the first, published online in July that year via the cool cats at* Shotgun Honey.

A one-page graphic version of this story, with lovely pictures by British artist Andrew Chiu, will appear in The Tobacco-Stained Sky. *I stuck a sneak-preview snippet in this book — just flip back to the frontispiece page at the beginning.*

Come Out Swinging

I stepped up to the plate and moved to king-hit the bastard from behind.

Sure it was cowardly, but also a pretty nifty manoeuvre, done without a moment to second-guess myself or opportunity to nut out a different course of action. His head was unprotected, an obvious target dressed up in messy, straw-coloured hair. A neck thicker than my waist propped up that head — quite some feat given the extra girth I'd put on in recent months of alcoholic mayhem and loafing about on the couch.

At least this wasn't going to kill him. No need to get blood on my hands, since the mitts were clean and I preferred them to stay that way.

Trouble was that the man apparently sensed me behind him, and second-guessed my intentions to boot. He ducked as I swung the gun, and I ended up glancing the handle off his scalp instead of getting in a heavy enough whack to knock him senseless.

Then, while I was off balance, he turned and grabbed me by the throat, huge fingers digging deep into my larynx, and a second later I'd been deprived of both the capacity to squeal and the ability to breathe. He lifted me up one handed, so my shoes no longer touched the ground, and I was ogling a human gorilla inches from my face, a dribble of saliva in the corner of his snarled mouth.

With his free hand he slapped me once, twice, a third time.

I was seeing stars, and other delusionary paraphernalia. It felt like this time, finally, the gig might truly be up. Thoughts shunted in between the sparkling stars, images of Laurel, and Veronica, and what would likely happen to both if I gave up the ghost, pulling up the personal tent-pegs here and now.

I still had the gun in my right fist. I could pop him in the jaw, put a slug in his eye, get it over with, but something held me back. I wouldn't call this a conscience — it was more like stubborn, idiotic madness.

Another slap knocked me silly. I could see specks of blood on the man's chunky, enraged face. Not his blood. Mine.

So I swung at my own blood, right at a big splash of it on his forehead, lined up like a bull's-eye. The gun barrel bounced off, but the man shook his head, like it hurt, so I tried again, and again. The fourth time rocked it — I fell flat on my bum, oxygen started pumping, and the gorilla stormed around me, like he was doing some kind of blind Indian rain dance, clutching his skull, screaming.

Then he barnstormed the wall, head first, and knocked himself out. He lay at my feet, unmoving. At least he'd stopped the over-dramatics.

My head was swimming enough as it was. I had to road test my voice, to see if it still worked. "Sleep tight," I muttered. Nothing more sparkling came to me. The weak quip would have to do — even if I did have an audience.

Laurel was bound and gagged over in a corner, next to a widescreen TV, like she'd been placed there as a second-thought decoration. I went straight over, leaned down, and touched her cheek. Her eyes were wide, even the one on the left that was swollen and ringed with blue-black.

Without waiting for applause, I undid her wrists and pulled off the material jammed into her mouth. Laurel could deal with the feet herself.

After breathing deeply a few times, apparently relishing the opportunity, Laurel looked straight at me.

"You look awful. Do you always make it so hard for yourself, babe? You could've just shot him. You had ample opportunity. Jeez."

I glowered at her. "D'you want me to put the gag back on?"

I wrote Dread Fellow Churls *specifically for the Crime Factory crew back in my hometown, Melbourne, since they were putting together a crime/noir anthology of Australian writers.*

This was a pretty superb collection called Hard Labour, *and was published in October 2012 with better pieces by Liam José, David Whish-Wilson, Leigh Redhead, Angela Savage, Adrian McKinty, Helen FitzGerald and other Aussies.*

However, I'd finalized this story earlier on in the year, at the same time that I was writing a particularly hard chapter of my novel One Hundred Years of Vicissitude.

This brushed up against the Nanjing Massacre by Japanese soldiers in China in 1937.

Since I wrote both pieces concurrently — and wasn't sure either story would eventually see the light of day — there were crossovers in style, dialogue and content. They're different yarns, yet the sampling (something I love to do in music as well) is clear.

Dread Fellow Churls *is a prequel story based on Floyd and Nina from* Tobacco-Stained Mountain Goat, *and while Floyd is the narrator, it's 'Laurel' who shines.*

OzNoir, reviewing the anthology at Fair Dinkum Crime, nicely wrote that "Rounding out my favourites is Dread Fellow Churls *by Andrez Bergen in which a drunk cop gets caught on a stake-out and has to rely on his partner to get him out; there is a distinct femme fatale feel to this.* Dread Fellow Churls *felt like a novel teaser rather than short story — left me wanting more."*

Dread Fellow Churls

You know, I have this theory that while oblivion is what you make of it, oftentimes it's a superior dram to reality.

Take the following situation.

After some strolling about in a kaleidoscopic neck of the woods in which all was sugar, spice and pretty darned nice, reality placed a stiletto heel to my throat, kicked sand in my eye, and asserted itself.

The first thing my cranky perception took in was a beige linoleum floor a few inches from my nose. As bland as that may have been, it was hardly disconcerting as I'd been in this position countless times before. What followed, however, threw me: tiny waves of spearmint that serenaded my way and made me flinch. I loathe spearmint. Give me peppermint anytime, but spearmint lays me low.

I was then yanked up with some object, hard and cold, poking about in my mouth. I assumed it was the stiletto. As the haziness cleared and the headache kicked in, I precariously balanced on two feet.

That deed accomplished, comprehension, or a distant cousin, sauntered up and slapped me about to clear the remaining fragments of oblivion. In instant retrospect I wish it hadn't.

I'm greedy. I adore my nirvana, lethe, insensibility, unconsciousness — however you prefer to dub it — but on this occasion snapping out of the bliss was a wee bit different.

I was propped up in a kitchenette with no clothes on, my hands tied behind me, and a gun barrel stuck in my kisser — none of these inconveniences, to my knowledge, volunteered. I could be wrong. After my screwy focus righted itself I stared along a metal muzzle, past the slide, over the rear sight, and straight into a single open eye in the middle distance.

While I was blinking rapidly that peeper over there walked the same beat at a lethargic pace. The iris was a faded variant of the bean-shooter between us. Grey. I couldn't check it against its partner as the other eye was closed — something to do with taking better aim. I don't understand why one needed to target at all in this situation. You could throw on a blindfold, yank back the trigger, and still spray half my noggin across a wall.

"Not a nice situation to be in. Not a nice way to be found. Eventually. In the nud. Embarrassin'," the man said. Turns out his mouth was as lazy as his eyeball.

"Speak up, son. You're mumbling."

Mark this down as a disposable line, intended to sound blasé but instead coming across desperate — more bluster than bravado. In any event, if anyone in this room had elucidation issues it was I, given the firearm's placement.

My triggerman was chewing on something I assumed to be gum. Spearmint gum. Yep, the smell made me queasy, but I put down the current nausea to the gun rather than the gum. Alternatively, p'raps, it was his presentation.

The bugger boasted a garish '70s body shirt, all Technicolor swirls, that hurt my head more. This shirt was open to the chest, revealing a bunch of twisty stray silver hairs. Despite the fact he was losing the other hair up on his head, this man was vain enough to apply a comb-over to bamboozle short-sighted folks. There were minor jowls spilling over the collar and all up he wasn't a handsome chappie. Still, there was something striking about him, a kind of magnetism. Probably it boiled down to his choice in kitchen utensils.

"Good work, Shitlock." A lip curl made best friends with a leer above disorganized teeth as he leaned forward, spearmint breath and all. "You found me."

"Better I hadn't," I decided around the gun barrel.

The man tossed back his head and was roaring a laugh or laughing a roar, I'm not sure which description best applies. Either way it wasn't pretty, and thankfully it was short. After shaking himself free of the fit, the goon stuck his free hand in his left pocket to snake out a blue polyester wallet, which was placed on the kitchen bench. This wallet had a name, "The Dude," embroidered in pink across one side. It flopped next to a coffee mug covered with pictures from the dated 1960s stop-motion Christmas movie *Rudolph the Red-Nosed Reindeer*. It's funny what pointless details you make out when you're staring death in the mush.

"Yo, you still with me?"

The pistol did a bit of tea-bagging around my palate and almost knocked out one of my molars. I think oblivion had been creeping back in. This guy was having none of that.

"So, I'm going to show you something. Something I keep, for special occasions."

"Like this one?"

"Like this one."

"Let me guess," I grumbled as best I could, "pictures of the grandkids."

My gunsel spittooned a comic "Tsk, tsk," tilted his head to one side, and sighed thereafter. "Goes to show. There I was, beginning to have great faith in you as a detective. Goes to show, right?"

I tried to say something but it came out slurred, so the man kindly removed the impediment to my speech.

"That's the thing about faith — it tends to leaves you disappointed," I said. I'm not sure this rated highly in the speech stakes.

"Mm-hmm."

The man obviously concurred. He stared at his gun, and gave it a quick wipe-down with the gaudy shirt.

"For fuck's sake. You know that's disgusting? You're drooling all over the thing. You'll get it rusty. I'll have to grease it down after all this with machine oil and a clean rag. Give it the kind of love and attention I'd never waste on any woman. So, where was I? Oh, yeah. Showing you something. Right?"

"Apparently."

"Apparently. Keep the comedy coming, Alcho-Boy."

Don't ask me what he assumed I thought was funny. "Apparently" didn't ring amusing to me. Nothing made particular sense as my head pounded in tandem with my hammering heart. Comedy was sitting on a backburner some place very far from here.

Keeping his weapon pointed my way, the man grabbed The Dude and unfastened its catch to open the wallet up with a show of great ceremony. He removed a strip of photographs, perhaps half a dozen in all. Just when I thought my grandkids deduction had reclaimed for me Holmes' deerstalker, I looked at the pictures. Instead of showing cute children with baby teeth missing and a little league trophy or two, the happy-snaps displayed women without hands, without feet, screaming in pain and misery or just plain dead — trophies of the arsehole that grinned at their corpses.

The arsehole now bee-lining a similar grin my way.

I tried not to stare at the pictures but I must have done so for a few seconds as I took it all in, and then I looked away. I looked at the wall to the right, the one on the left, over at a greasy, oil-spattered stovetop just beyond the man, and up to twin fluorescent globes attached to the ceiling. Anywhere but at the photographs or at the smiling lunatic who held them aloft. I felt benumbed. Some fool had surely shot me with a stray anaesthetic, but the same bastard pulled it out before oblivion could weasel my way.

Things had started out so much simpler.

It'd started out with a medicated kip some twelve hours before and an uncomplicated tussle with a Cossack. On that occasion I'd had clothes on and laid out the blighter with a cricket bat. God knows what the willow was doing there on a set of wild Russian steppes, but I wasn't one to complain — playing Whac-A-Mole in my dreams was a downright hoot. The sad thing was waking up — the reality check, as I've already mentioned.

After toast with Vegemite and a strong coffee with a slug of payless whisky, the call came through. I wish I'd skipped it. I could've stayed home and watched old pirate movies. Instead I answered, and as reward was summoned to Branch HQ.

In a gesture of hare-brained personal protest, I wasted my time going in on public transport, taking a surreptitious swig from a hipflask every few minutes. At a public loo near the office I chugged down a quickie cigarette and washed my face. A gargle with Listerine was just the kind of eau de cologne I needed to mask the juice on my breath, and I was as good as new.

Kind of.

After arrival and the usual security check they parked me in a waiting room — so I twiddled my thumbs and did what it recommended on the door. I waited.

Half an hour later they moved me into the Briefing Room.

Once the lecture started I barely listened to the patter. I had my mind instead busy conjuring up the image of a giant tumbler, about three metres in height, filled with brandy served at room temperature — ice be damned. The glass was big enough to go in for a dip.

But right then, as I lingered over a choice of appropriate swimwear, my area supervisor, Ophelia, stepped up to me. The middle-aged woman was all scowl. She shoved her index finger into the middle of my ribcage, as if making some kind of physical exclamation mark to round off a sentence I hadn't bothered hearing. Poking me was her expertise — it hurt like hell — and the big, fat glass in my mind was spilled.

"Damn," I muttered.

"This Dev is dangerous, Maquina. You paying attention at all?"

"Sure, boss. Front and centre, etcetera, etcetera."

"Good to hear."

She picked up one of the mug shots from the table. It was a black-and-white number, so I never suspected the perp's dress-sense would hurt my eyes. It also must have been taken a few years before, as the man's jowls were in training mode and he had all his hair.

"Take a good peek. Make sure you take it all in. Remember this face. Because Dain's killed at least four women that we know of, one of them a Seeker like you."

"Then why aren't there two of me to deal with the loser?"

"We don't have the resources right now." Ophelia blew out her cheeks and exhaled. "Look, if someone else is freed up, I'll put them on the case. Till then you're flying solo."

"So I can rack up a few more hours in this blissful little job. Amen."

"Be careful with the quips, Floyd. And be careful in general. This individual is dangerous — this isn't your usual round of Activities."

The hell it wasn't.

Straight after I skipped out the door I followed the usual routine: first stop, Seeker Branch. Check. Next stop, watering hole — Ziggy's gin mill.

I sidled down there through a rash of pedestrians and heavy rain, pushed the entrance door aside, took the stairs three at a time, and grabbed a stool in the far corner by the bar. Ziggy winked at me, grabbed my usual starter, and then I got loaded up on a triple-shot and at least half a dozen chasers. I admit I lost count.

Somewhere in the middle of this parade Laurel Canyon put in an appearance.

She shooed away the person occupying the stool next to mine, removed her sunglasses, and ordered us another round. Then she side-glanced my way and looked amused.

We'd gone drinking together on a number of occasions but I barely knew the woman. She played a deck of marked cards close to her chest. For my part I'd rambled too much about a lifetime of sordid issues, while she'd barely disclosed a morsel.

Still, there was something about her that appealed to me. It went beyond the rough-around-the-edges beauty, a Lauren Bacall mouth, and a propensity for ample amounts of alcohol that matched my own. All of these tidbits helped, of course, but as I say — there was something more.

"Floyd. Can I ask a stupid question?"

Laurel tossed this query my way right before she did a quick run of lipstick across her kisser. She didn't bother using a mirror. To be honest, right then I was almost as taken with the woman as I was by my current drink.

"Sure."

"D'you always get this tanked before you go stake out someone?"

"Occasionally." I pretended to think the matter through, and then gave up the ghost. "The alcohol helps me maintain a stiff upper lip."

"I hate to be the one to tell you, but the upper lip looks like it's sagging."

"A fine art. A few more rounds and it won't know which way

gravity is — and voila."

"Ah." Laurel smiled, and then finished her glass. "So that's how it works. 'Nother drink?"

"You're an angel."

I'm sure I don't need to spell this out, but needless to say I was smashed when I got around to doing the Activities thing.

The rain didn't help. It just stung and made me more miserable. So I lurked about under cover in alleyways and door alcoves for a bit, fidgety and bored, pining for a cigarette and another slug. At one stage I did slip under a threadbare veranda in front of a shuttered-up store and lit a ciggie. I left myself dangling. I'm not surprised my quarry nutted me out first, tiptoed up behind me, and conked me on the skull. God knows what he used as a blunt instrument. It felt like the same cricket bat I'd used on the Cossack in my dream. Yeah, yeah — so much for paying attention.

Which brought me to the here and now, dressed down with a gun in the gob and about to be rubbed out.

This serial killer was planning to play courteous. He'd alter his modus operandi just for me, and I'd blundered into the mess thanks to my alcoholic prowess. Salut, Floyd.

"It's a little chilly here," I said as I carefully pulled my face away from the gun barrel. "Can I pin my diapers back on?"

"Nah, l feel safer with you wearing only a smile." The man snickered. "A Seeker. I'm thinking about collecting you people. The other one squealed like a pig when I cut off her fingers. I started with her thumbs. After the fingers I went with the toes. Then I started on some private bits and pieces. What will you do when I poke round down there?"

His single open eye whipped to my divested crotch.

"Yodel like a castrato?" he suggested.

Crap. I could feel perspiration breaking out on my face. I'm not sure if it related to the alcoholic excesses earlier on in the evening or the fear marinating my senses right now. I doubt he'll get any opera from me, just the pleas I barely keep in check and a whole lot of screams. I'm not one to gush but they're hovering there on the cusp, threatening to break loose.

"My partner will notice that I'm not at my post," I said. It's a pretty weak attempt, uttered in barely more than a whisper, but I'll go with anything right now.

"Sure. But if he's as drunk as you were, it'll be easy to deal with him too. Drunk — as a skunk. Hilarious. Who pays you for this kind of professional behaviour?"

I didn't answer. There was nothing to say, and my voice failed me regardless.

"Yeah, I think I'll start down there," the bastard continued in that goddamned lazy drawl, the eye fixed on an area I'd have much preferred him to forget. "Now, where's me knife?"

That got me bucking. A gun is one thing, but a shiv?

"For fuck's sake," I began as I strained against the ropes at my back, "why don't you—?"

"The knife, the knife, my kingdom for the knife. Where's the knife? Tra-la-la, oh the knife, glorious knife, hot sausage and mustard!"

The man was singing a shambolic collusion of *Oliver!* and *Richard III* in such a grating falsetto it drowned out my squeals — meaning I gave up trying to be heard.

So it came as a complete surprise when, right about then, he cut the crooning.

The single grey eye bulged, joined a second or two later by its companion—which was, it turns out, the same colour. He'd lost his aim and the gun clattered to the floor, just as the second button of his tawdry shirtfront popped free and something created a pointy bulge there beneath the material.

"I do believe I found your knife, mister."

The voice making this declaration was said in such a sweet, singsong tone that I barely recognized it. It came from just behind him. The arsehole fiddled with the buttons of his shirt, turned a fraction, and shuddered. He nodded his head in a bouncy kind of way, his face sagged like a sack of old potatoes, and he slid down to join the shooter on the lino. Looked like gravity did get the better of the stiff upper lip on this occasion.

Laurel was standing in his place, shorter in height but immeasurably superior eye-candy. She had indeed found the shiv. It was in her gloved right hand, a long hunting number, and the knife had just been used to skewer the man and his offensive wardrobe — thank God I wasn't the only one up for poking on the carte du jour.

Laurel kicked the corpse once, and then arched an eyebrow at me.

I had something tinkering with my vision — I'll swear it was sweat — and I couldn't clear it away since my arms were still bound behind me.

"Jesus wept, Laurel. Timing."

"Not bad, right?"

"I'd give you a round of applause but my hands are otherwise occupied."

"Then I'll try to picture it." She gave me a once-over and laughed. "Say, don't you have any sense of shame? Where on earth are your clothes?"

Neck-Tied *was also written for* Shotgun Honey, *and thus abides by their specific guidelines: "Crime. Hardboiled. Noir. Something like that. 700 words maximum. Make it tight. Make it hum." It was published in November 2012.*

Let it be known I love Shotgun Honey — *it's filled to the brim with excellent writers like Matthew C. Funk, K.A. Laity, Mike Monson, Paul D. Brazill, Christopher L. Irvin, R. Thomas Brown, Katherine Tomlinson, Benoit Lelièvre, Court Merrigan, Fiona Johnson, Allan Guthrie, Matthew J. McBride, and about a million others I dig — so I'm really happy I slipped in there.*

Check out shotgunhoney.net.

In this particular offering the narrator isn't Floyd, but it's definitely another Seeker — someone a tad more direct, perhaps.

"Finding an adversary's weakness makes sense in this solid little story," responded fellow scribe (par excellence) Patti Abbott after she read it online.

Ta, mate.

Neck-Tied

There's blood on my hands yet I'm well-nigh choking to death.

The weight behind me, somewhere I think near to my own, has that fishing line wrapped around my neck and is yanking hard. I've cut my fingers up trying to stop the wire slicing further into my throat—I can see bone sticking out from my left thumb.

How long has it been since I gobbled down a last breath of oxygen?

Feels like hours, probably only seconds. Passing out, I know — edges of everything blurring, head pounding, neck silently screaming on its sweet lonesome.

Desperation dictates my next manoeuvre, a frantic shove backwards that sandwiches my attacker between me and a mantelpiece stuck over the fireplace. I hear the wind come out of him, the wire loosens up the smallest fraction, and that's enough for me to stick my left hand through the garrotte and take the pressure of the wire on my wrist — instead of further mutilating my fingers or my collar.

The blurring folds in on itself and there's a moment of clarity.

This is my moment, I realize, one final lucky chance prior to giving up the ghost.

So I lift my right arm high and quickly hammer back with the elbow, praying to some empty mead hall of Norse gods that I get this right and nail the bastard holding me, rather than smashing up my funny bone on the concrete wall.

I'm lucky.

I hit something soft, and it's not a pillow.

The wire unravels from my neck, I swing round, and I lob a haymaker right where the head should be. Only it isn't. This time I really do hammer the wall — I feel a few knuckles crack.

"Goddammit!" I hiss a croak, snapping my left arm free of the wire, and then cradling my busted-up mitt in the fingers of the left hand while I hop up and down, trying not to bawl. I can still barely swallow and I gulp at air like a deranged guppy. Can't quite recall when I remember about my assailant.

I try to pull myself together and look to the floor.

There, spread-eagled by my shoes, is a small man probably half my weight. I'd been amiss. Looked also half my height. From the state of his right eye, which had ruptured, I could more accurately say my elbow had struck him there, instead of in the chest or stomach like I presumed. Messy. Currently out for the count, the bastard will need medical assistance and an eye-patch post haste.

I take my fine time as I try to clear my throat, making unpleasant sounds.

In addition, there's the fishing line at my feet to inspect. I hold the weapon aloft, looking past the bits of skin and droplets of blood. Superior piece of workmanship — a strong, braided monofilament core wrapped up in thick, waterproof PVC sheathing. The perfect weight and mass necessary to cast an artificial fly with a fly rod, and not a bad choice for doing a Gurkha on someone.

I measure the length and make some quick calculations.

Wondering about strength versus weight contradictions, I flex the wire and pull hard. It cuts again into my fingers. Actually, there's blood everywhere, all over my clothes, mine, and I suppose I'll also need medicating soon enough.

But in this day and age it's difficult to find decent fishing line, so I carefully roll up the line and stick it in my coat pocket, and then squat beside the dwarf. He's waking up. Hasn't yet realized he now has two-dimensional vision. There's one question to ask before I call in to Branch and rat out the silly prick.

I grab him by his shirt and yank him up into a sitting position. He swoons but anyway manages to focus the leftie my way.

"Any idea, mate," I ask, "where I can find some decent live fish?"

In the earlier manuscripts of Tobacco-Stained Mountain Goat, *Floyd's wife Veronica played a bigger part, though she wasn't always called Veronica.*

Laurel took on a large chunk of her persona in the final version, but I had still implied Veronica was alive and kicking in the final version I sent Another Sky Press. I didn't say so out loud — it was only an inference, one within the confines of a virtual reality 'Test' — but to my mind she survived.

We ended up editing this out — a particular scene in which Floyd hunts down a group of Deviants in the apocalypse that is Richmond, and targets that final one on the street, but lets her go.

She, to my mind, was V, not dead after all — and I decided to expand upon the revelation with this story for The Tobacco-Stained Sky. *Whether or not you agree this really is Veronica is up to, well, you.*

Again, a Peter Lorre reference.

This was written at the same time as One Hundred Years of Vicissitude *and* Lazarus Slept, *in early 2012. The thread was there.*

And I changed the narrative from first person to third just prior to inclusion in this collection.

In-Dreamed

There's a soft breeze, a whisper that's supremely gentle. She drifts on its current, floating above ground, sight unseen. There is some kind of movement nearby, impenetrable in the blackness. Can't see anything at all. She must be dozing, and this surprises. Since when did she lucid dream? Oh, yes. Always.

"Guv." A distant, entirely unwelcome call to arms. "Guv — wakey, wakey."

Shit, she knows that voice. Taylor. Forces open her eyes.

'Taylor' is such a solid name — the kind of family handle you'd picture being pinned to a chisel-jawed leading man in old Hollywood, like Charlton Heston or Burt Lancaster, rather than weighing on the shoulders of this scrawny, chinless wonder. Instead of deep-set, strong blue eyes, his are bulbous and brown — the only movie star he resembles is a poor man's Peter Lorre, and the surname comes across as the punch line from some sly genetic joke. This Taylor would be better off as a Bernbaum.

"I was dreaming," she says, holding his bulldog gaze. No more to be said, no need to get into vindictive pet theories now.

"You sure it was a dream?"

She attempts to smile at that — the man can tickle her funny bone sometimes — but the cheek muscles feel stiff, awkward. Figures they need a workout. "There's a valid point. Debatable, right?"

"Right. Sleep aside — you want an update of the here and now?"

She'd prefer not. "Do I have a choice?"

"Course you do. You could angle at more shut-eye and maybe get your throat cut while you kip."

"Charming. And I thought the verdict was out as to whether or not I'm really sleeping."

"All the same. Gotta hurt." Taylor slips a knife down into plain sight from where he hid it up his sleeve. He'd like the others to believe he has the disappearing/reappearing skills of a magician, but this kind of trick is a basic stretch of street-hooligan know-how — nothing enchanting.

She plays it blasé. "Mmm."

"Mmm to you, too. We got company." The small man studies the blade in his hand. Polished to perfection, this was something to treasure, but it has a chip broken out of the edge, making it twice as dangerous. A thing like that could hook onto an internal organ and tear the blighter out in the follow through.

"Police?" she asks.

"Dunno. Zero in the uniform department, and they haven't got all that batty armour the new blokes get about in. I'm thinking Seekers — plus a couple'a tourists."

"Then you do know." Placing hands on the filthy parquetry floor — they're just as filthy, anyway — she uses them to push her numb bum into action. The legs do the rest of the work, but when she lurches sideways, Taylor sticks out a steadying hand — the same one holding the knife.

"Careful with that," she mutters.

"Sorted."

"I'm not certain you know what 'sorted' means."

"Hush. The window."

Annoyed, she wades through rubbish, broken furniture and torn-up linoleum. The window is huge, twice my height, with the glass chiselled out; fly wire ripped and flapping, and the rain beating through. She doesn't need all that space, requires only a couple of centimetres to check the devastated world two storeys below.

Four people, armed with umbrellas, two hundred metres away.

The first she picks out — also boasting salt-and-pepper hair and a beastly moustache visible from this distance — is a middle-aged man who sensibly elected to wear a suit in the rain, carnage and pools of rancid water down there. Bright boy.

The second intruder is a fairly large bounder with a round, friar's face — hardly intimidating. Number three, however, is someone she can't see properly, bundled in a long coat and Fedora hat. A worry.

Last one coming, spinning circles around the others with a big camera, is a skinny individual dressed in an equally oversized white coat, the letters 'ITC' on his back — wasn't that a TV company? Not willing to trust her memories, the woman unpeels from the windowsill.

Straight away, Taylor is in the ear. "Verdict?"

The tattered thing she dares still to call a heart is racing, but covering the fear proves easy. "Hard to say."

"That's a cop-out answer, if ever I heard one. And I've heard a few."

"From me?"

"You? Often."

"That so? Live with the disappointment." She lets him see the roll of the eyes. It'll be a quarter of an hour before those people reach this place, if they come up at all.

Both Archer and Tux had silently entered the space and they

stand on either side of Taylor, looking at the woman, waiting for something. Barked orders? She frowns, feels like kicking them. It was bloody annoying that they'd made her their ad hoc leader without dreaming to ask. Why? Because she'd been the one to leave the Hospital first, when the three of these arses were malingering, too afraid to set foot in the rain? That didn't take leadership, it was blind panic on her part. Taylor at least hedged. Even though he threw about the word 'guv', she suspected he used the moniker precisely because it annoyed.

She decides she needs space, distance from their hangdog eyes, so peers out the window and up at the forbidding sky. Meanwhile, behind her, Tux croons "Rain, rain, go away, come again another day." The only dirge he remembers.

Wasn't wise to go near the windows. How long'd they been here? Hours? Days? Impossible to tell. There was minimal difference between day and night, thanks to the perennial downpour that blotted out the sun. Surprise was they'd made it this far since the breakout.

Breakout — what a misappropriated expression. The only breaking-out they'd perfected was the sweat in escaping from Hospital.

Before that, the sum total of her memories revolved around needles. Needles and machines and rack-mounted gear, of small white rooms and a slab where they deposited people and placed bags over their heads. Time after time after time. They had the gall to name the procedure 'social conditioning', but it was just a variation on idInteract gaming madness in which people died — mostly her. In these scenarios they took away the ability to speak, made her dance in zany roles, and injected some kind of irrational streak into the brain — so that she was continuously unable to sense it was fake-and-bake.

On each and every occasion this led to seizing upon a handy weapon in a stupid attempt to escape, which then led to her dispatch — by gun, knife, fist, foot, and once via a frozen leg of lamb. The pain of death remained after she awoke, every time, or p'raps each demise took with it another part of the remaining shreds of life.

This time, however, was different.

When she came to and ripped off the bag, the room was empty, the door ajar. She disconnected from the leads and plugs and cables and a catheter stuck in her arm, then staggered over and peered into the hallway. It was also devoid of life. No one there. Nobody to ask the time or bar one from leaving.

So she fled through a small door at the edge of a tunnel, all the time petrified of discovery — and what that'd entail — but this never came. Having taken a service elevator to the upper level, she discovered a flooded bluestone laneway swept with rain — and three others, like her discursively covered in white patient gowns, huddling under an twisted awning. Bewildered, lost.

The permanent drizzle was never going to stop her.

She pushed straight past them and out into the rain, letting it wash over, cleansing, even as it stung the eyes and began eating away at clothing and skin. She had no idea why the others followed, of how she'd collected three stray dogs named Taylor, Archer and Tux.

Taylor, you know.

Tux got his name since he'd been a tailor — surprise. Word in the wards said he'd been delivered up to Hospital gift-wrapped in a morning suit and waistcoat — nailed on his wedding day. However long later, Tux remains that good-looking, medium-heighted groom, but he's also rake-thin and health services had sucked the vigour out of him — he lost a bout with sanity ages ago. Tux acted like a shadow and wore the expression of a lost child. You'd think, for a tailor, he'd have some pride in his wardrobe, but out of the lot of them his clothes were in the worse repair.

And Archer?

Well — while his name may conjure up notions of some Grecian warrior-king like Odysseus, with a swanky helmet and a longbow — you'd be well wide of the mark, though let's hang onto 'wide' for later use.

He was diabolically strong, built like a brick shithouse, about six-and-a-half feet, almost as wide, none of this girth cellulite. Archer had a boxer's swollen and deformed ears — what did they call them? Cauliflowers? — and his shaved head and broad jaw line were already sprouting a shade of red, peppered with grey. There was nothing to read on his face, simplicity its blessing. He also didn't speak.

The woman wasn't aware if this was a conscious decision or they'd stolen from him the ability to talk. Archer hadn't said a solitary word since they'd fled the Hospital complex, and she'd heard nary a peep from him in the times they met in the holding cells beforehand.

So there was very little subtlety or elegance to the man — you'd never be able to squeeze a Corinthian helm over his thick skull — and this was one of the reasons they'd made it so far. The man was a godsend, no matter that he wasn't godlike.

Which left the woman.

Who is she? A peachy question.

She thinks, once upon a time, she was a nice person — caring, respectful, in love. Rather pathetic. But after so long locked away, she can't say for sure. She gets the sensation that she's been leeched of anything that ever mattered, of losing hold of the past. The memories are so elusive she's discarded a fair few of those as well.

Doesn't know how long she was Hospitalized, and doesn't give it too much thought. None of them do. There were no calendars in there, no generous souls predisposed to dish out timetables. It felt like years, probably was. Time enough for most of the people she met to vanish or die. A treadmill of 'treatment' and needles and examinations, of being herded into tiny communal rooms where twenty-five odd people slept, shat, fought, copulated and ate in a space measuring fifteen square metres.

She was married once, long ago. No children, thankfully, though she was four months' pregnant when admitted to Hospital. The medicos threw in an abortion, gratis, the very same day. Was sick, some disease she don't know the name of, would no doubt have died as well, but they cured her — though choice never entered into the equation.

She had no notion of why they did that, not initially, yet gradually put two-and-two together, in between medicine hits supposed to keep her zapped out. Leverage, that's what she was, nothing more to it. Being kept alive meant she could be flaunted as a bartering tool, just like the other 'lucky' patients she met, the survivors, the ones who stayed round. The others who disappeared or died — they had no such use.

At first she submitted to all the pain and humiliation, the abuse, the medication. Hid in the recesses of the mind, far back as possible, but eventually they hacked through. Was a time, a black spot, when she lost any sense of self, of awareness. Didn't know how or why she started swimming against the current. Once she did, though, she made it duty-bound to wipe clean every remaining morsel of who she was and what she'd been. The few memories clung to — being a wife, almost having a child — she kept to torment herself at the lowest depths.

The past. That's all it was. A dead currency. She runs fingers over the stubble of the buzz cut on her scalp, feeling the occasional scar, counts five different ones, each with their own story.

She notices Taylor's hand straying near, and then brushing her hip.

He's getting predictable. If she doesn't act now, he'll move up and get still more adventurous, so she slaps away the hand. Nothing more necessary. He understands she won't let him go further, but she wonders how long he'll play ball, now he has a knife. For the time being he's still one of her strays.

The woman frets about Taylor, and not just because of his ill-fitting name. He's a Recent, hadn't been in Hospital all that much time before they escaped.

Tux was in there longest and Archer predated herself. Taylor, no. She didn't trust him. You never could put faith in a Recent. A sizeable part of her hated him as well — he hadn't experienced what they had, never would appreciate the wonderful depth of Hospitalization. He still had life hanging on his shoulders, draped at a jaunty angle like a misappropriated fox stole.

Now she's rubbing her face as she stares at the three men seated helter-skelter on the muddy floor, between them bits and pieces of a dead man's weaponry: a large rifle, a double-barrelled pistol, a shotgun, a long narrow tube (a silencer?) and grenades of various sizes. The dead man had been carrying all of that, armed to his teeth, but none of the munitions stopped Archer snapping his neck.

The woman had used herself as bait — tossed off the rags to stand straight-backed, some kind of nonsensical pride in her posture, in the middle of the showroom floor downstairs. Surrounded by mannequins equally naked, littered like the slain troops of an Amazonian army — limbs missing and body parts without obvious owner. She'd shivered in the humidity as the soon-to-be-dead man approached, couldn't see his eyes beyond the opaque black visor under a metallic helmet, but knew well enough that they'd be washing over her, ogling, just as Archer crept up from behind, wordlessly grabbed the man's helmet, and twisted it to the right.

Snap-o.

That left Taylor to do additional handicraft with his knife — "A warning to any other arseholes," he said, in between slicing and dicing — and then Archer had hung the dead man on a wall between cracked, weary colonnades, high above those fallen, equally mangled dummies.

What on earth were they on about? What could they do there-after? And why the hell did she remain with these sorry excuses for humanity?

Better to go it alone. Better. But where? Why bother? She had nothing. Even the rags around her were beginning to disintegrate. She feels itchy — probably this has less to do with the old hessian sack she'd appropriated as a camisole than the fact she hadn't showered in an age. The last time was a dousing under a water canon alongside a dozen other people. Freezing water that knocked her back into a wall and dislocated the left shoulder.

She tugs the sack round and rips it at the front, in order to be able to move the neck more freely (as well as scratch a bit), but realizes she tore it too far and now you could see her sternum bulging through thin skin above a shrunken breast. Without looking to check, she senses Taylor's eyes on her chest and therefore manoeuvres the sack again so it's more discreet.

"What do we do, guv? Ambush those people and kill 'em?" Taylor asks. "They look dead-easy, making a racket — it's like a goddamned carnival." His knife again pops out from the sleeve. "Maybe we could make them perform a jig for us. I could do with some light entertainment."

The woman decides she's had enough.

"For fuck's sake, I'm not your governor, not your boss, not whatever. How many times do I have to tell you this? Don't dump the responsibility on me — I don't care what any of you do. Any of you. Get it? I can't stand this role."

"Even so — what are you planning?" This time it's Tux speaking, in that pale, well-nigh inaudible voice.

"I don't know."

"Neither do we. We can do that together...can't we?"

Tux and Archer are looking like little lost souls, heavier than they seem, pulling her down again. Taylor has an easier expression, nice and lecherous.

"Agree. Safety in numbers, and all that," he says.

Safety? She almost laughs out loud, but decides to save such merriment for another day. It'd been years since she'd waltzed with the concept of safety and wasn't expecting an invitation to dance anytime soon. Safety was beyond them. They were Deviants, Devs on the run, and they'd murdered someone. The law would be out in force and they'd be lucky to survive twenty-four hours. Safety? Quite the joke.

Their combined hangdog expressions, however, do pay dividends. The woman relents before she understands what is happening.

"We've got three choices," she decides. "We split up, go our separate ways. We stick together and do a runner. Or we stay here, to make a dumb stand."

After a second's silence, Taylor speaks. "I vote for number three, the dumb stand thingy," he announces. Of course — the man continually confuses stupidity with bravery, and only because he seems to have his rancid heart set on impressing the woman in his field of vision. "Right on, Blondie?"

She sighs in return. "Stick with the 'guv'. A tad more endearing."

Archer and Tux aren't capable of deciding for themselves and, like the woman, they don't trust Taylor as far as they can toss the bugger — so they wait for her decision. If this matches Taylor's, all the better; if it doesn't, they'll have a hell of a time making a choice. This causes her to sigh and settle on easy.

"Why not?" she mutters. "There's nowhere to go, anyway. Right?"

Which is when they hear noises outside, in the alley leading to the back entrance of the ancient department store. Soft voices first, and then there arises such a clatter.

The woman glances at her companions, a finger to the lips.

Taylor has picked up the dead man's bulky pistol, which he tucks into his Hospital tunic. He then offers the assault rifle her way, like some kind of off-season Christmas gift. She shakes her head. Wouldn't know what to do with the thing. Archer also refuses — doesn't need it, what with the strength of his bare hands — and so Taylor hands it over to Tux. The shotgun he hides in a dry spot beneath some rubble. "Back-up," he says.

The quartet below is trying to find a way in.

They're talking a lot now — which strikes her as odd — until someone yells at the others. Then they hear a door being jimmied, followed by its creak and grind upon opening.

"Shhhh!" one of the newcomers hisses.

These intruders are like a comedy act. How are they supposed to take them seriously? Even Tux has a lukewarm smile.

More whispering ensues a floor beneath. They'd soon enough find the cadaver down there, the one she led astray, Archer killed, and Taylor disembowelled. That should cut the comedy.

Ten more minutes passed.

She'd motioned everybody to their places. They heeded without dispute, fanning out quietly, far enough away from one another to lay the trap, but still able to see each other in the darkness, amid falling water geysers that shower down from the smashed ceiling, courtesy of the torrential rain.

Above the sounds of gurgling water and the pound of that rain, there's footfall on the back staircase, the one leading up to this level. Floorboards groan. Down the corridor, closer to the stairs, Taylor lifts his pistol. He gives the woman an awkward wink, and then aims at some place she can't see.

They all hear the crunching sound, so loud you could hardly hope to miss it, despite the interference of the leaky roof — a fool had put his shoe through the floor. Taylor has a ringside seat and he's silently laughing.

Someone promptly yells "Christ!", and this seems all the cue Taylor needs to fire off a round. Only, he doesn't. This shot comes from her left, closer by, and almost takes out the woman's eardrum. Tux — it was Tux, with the assault rifle in the opposite doorway, his face dark, unreadable.

There's more clattering around the corner, some kind of thrashing in water, and then an eerie yodel. Another person — a man? — screams.

In the darkness, she can only just make out the lanky individual with the movie camera, as he staggers into view, spinning in circles, apparently filming. Someone else grabs him and they melt away into shadows near Taylor's position. Did Taylor see that? She's unsure, frets, and panic rises. There's a wealth of noise, chatter and shrieking going down — chaos has kicked its way into the quartet's little home.

"Hey, you fucking arsehole!" she hears a voice rant nearby. Not one of her boys. "Help him! Get him the hell outta here — now!"

Get whom? The person Tux'd shot?

Still can't see anything from her position, and to be honest the panic has abated and she's mulling on surprised. She'd expected trigger-happy action from Taylor, not Tux. Looking across the corridor at Tux, she realizes she didn't think he had murder in him.

Another shot rings out, this time sourced from Taylor, and half the yells end.

Seconds pass, nobody moves. Silence, aside from the gush of the improvised, raging waterworks — an abstract fountain complex thrown together by a madman on acid.

"Floyd! Are you all right? Floyd!"

The woman freezes, pinned up against a sagging, buckled wall with floral wallpaper and a sea of mildew.

Tux frowns when he sees her face, but before either can further react, there are scattered footsteps and a spotlight suddenly swings round the huge space. Taylor is caught right in the middle of this, shielding his eyes, and then something happens to his waist — it bucks to one side — followed quickly by an echoing explosion, and he falls in silence.

A man in a hat, cast only in silhouette by the roving spotlight, grabs Taylor's gun, tosses it away — and then sprints in the direction of the woman and Tux.

"Crap!" she hisses, throwing herself across the corridor and diving into the room behind Tux, the one where Archer lurked. That spotlight framed the doorway she'd come through, followed by the thunder of three explosions. Tux reels past, staggering, and he ends up crashing through a wood-covered window and falls out.

"Go!"

For the first time since she met him, Archer has spoken, but she has no time to cherish the moment.

The big man pushes at her as he thumbs the open window, and then he turns away and vanishes into twisted shadows beside the entrance. She doesn't need any more counsel, jumps for the windowsill as someone barges through the doorway behind her, and takes a leap as a bullet whistles past her ear.

Two storeys aren't as easy as they might sound.

The height had broken Tux's back, but judging from the bullet wounds in his chest and stomach, grapefruit sizes torn out, he would've been dead anyway.

She hadn't busted her spine but crunched some bone in the right ankle at the end of the drop — heard it snap when she landed — and the pain now is blinding. Even so, she makes out two more shots high above. Archer. Assumed he would never say another word. So there remained only her, just as there had been when she first started.

The woman hobbles along, unable to put any decent weight on the busted foot, but having decided to refuse to stand about — anyway just as painful —to be recaptured and Hospitalized, or more simply gunned down like the others.

"Stop where you are!"

That's a man's voice somewhere behind her, same one she'd heard in the short fight upstairs. The warning serves only to make her move quicker, despite the torture.

"Shoot, man!" someone else is bleating back there, all whiney. "I've got a brill long-shot, but you've gotta do it now! Shoot! Blow her away! Do it!"

She refuses to look back, focuses ahead, and then the first man's voice speaks again. She barely hears it, but the message carries: "Fuck you."

It's said right before she hits a corner, one where she can scramble to safety away from a bullet, but the woman can't resist — she has to turn and look.

The killer with the Fedora is there, his gun hand lowered, and the skinny camera kid is gesticulating wildly, shouting in his ear.

He ignores the boy. His and the woman's eyes meet, for the shortest moment. It's enough. She has to smile — though she doubts he sees this — and then she's rounded a brick wall into the next street and ducks down a secondary alleyway. Needs to open up as much distance as possible, no matter the agony the leg delivers up. Time enough to scream, mope, wail and bawl her eyes out later.

But the lane has no end, the straight lines of the brickwork around abruptly swing to diagonal, and she's swimming in inky darkness. A white pinpoint appears. Wonders if she should head there, or retreat in the opposite direction, but the light's getting bigger and the current is headed that way. Treading water, she's indecisive, shooting pains speaking nonsense from her ankle.

And suddenly she's awake.

Sitting up on the side of a plasti-steel cot, cords and wires hanging from places all over a half-naked body.

An extremely elderly nurse is unstitching the devices, pulling them out, rolling them up. The woman has a pert mouth with thin lips and zero expression on her face. It's like looking at another wall.

On three other cots nearby lie the shapes of people. They're hidden beneath plastic sheets, so she cannot see their faces. They seem to be breathing, but there is no other movement.

"These gentlemen failed."

The announcement comes from a slightly built, middle-aged man standing near the door. He has a grey beard, a drab plastic folder tucked under his arm and a starched white outfit, but his voice is rich. There's a nametag that reads 'Dr. Kern', pinned above a biro in his shirt pocket.

"Failed what?" she asks.

"The Test."

"What test?"

"The one you undertook just now."

"Oh. So that's what it was. Right."

"Don't overly worry yourself. Far more eminent is the fact that you passed, Patient... *er*—" He consults cheat-notes in the folder "—14111922. Congratulations."

As the nurse leaves the room, the doctor steps forward and hands his patient a beige business card, made of some kind of plastic hybrid. It had the name from his tag, plus the words 'Management Control Division'.

"I can imagine you're rather tired of Hospitals by now," he waffles on. "How about a nice change? We have a job opportunity for you at MCD, out in the real world."

She glances at him. "How real?"

"Terra firma, I assure you."

"No more games?"

"I can't guarantee that."

"But a job."

"That's right."

"As one of the good guys."

"Precisely. With Controller Branch. Hunting down and rounding up the bad sort."

As she sits there on the side of the bed, the woman chews her lower lip. All this has unravelled quickly — is it any more real than the warzone she just escaped? Still, she is at a loss for options and realizes it doesn't matter. The man might've been channelling Mephistopheles, but virtuous alternatives failed to present themselves. They always had been missing. Besides, what had the world ever given her? At least now she'd be the one with the stick.

"All right," she says.

"Bravo. Welcome to the team." He hands over an A5-size clipboard. It has several sheets of paper on it. A contract. The pen is already in her hand.

The good doctor is rattling out a stream of kooky caveats, something about how he needn't remind one that, as a Controller, she'd be in a position of authority and therefore bear a certain amount of responsibility, plus there'd be a brand new identity — Constance Ockelman — and some secrecy provisions. Blah, blah, blah. She tuned out the moment the flow began.

"What happens to them?" Having interrupted his speech, she nods at the three people on the beds in their shrouds, could only guess they were her companions. One of them was certainly as mountainous as Archer.

"If they're lucky, they recover."

"And who are you? Really?"

The man rubs his hands together in a childlike manner, but his chuckle comes across wizened and fractionally sinister. "The future, my dear."

Slowly, she raises her leg. The ankle is stiff, but it isn't broken. She rotates her foot and smiles. "Whatever. Are you paid to sprout that kind of nonsense?"

"Actually, I do like to indulge in a spot of theatre sports on the side."

"Mmm. Do me a favour?"

He looks mildly irritated. "You will find we are already doing that — by giving you a second chance."

"Still."

Dr. Kern's expression assumes a dubious glint. "Name it."

"Revive them." She sweeps here renovated foot in the air with a wave that takes in the motionless trio under their plasti-sheets.

"Why?"

"We make a good team."

"Difficult. The procedure can be...tricky."

"Oh, I don't know about that. I'm sure you'll succeed, since you've revived me after I 'died' — several times over."

The good doctor is impressed. "You remember."

"How could I forget?"

"Most people do. The trauma is too much for them. Very well, I'll see what I can arrange regarding these gentlemen. All three?"

"Mmm. Even the little guy. By the way, is his name really Taylor?"

Kern again scans his notes. "Yes, it says so here. I believe that is the case."

"Well. There you go."

Linoleum Actress *was the first short-story I'd written in years, put together straight after publishing* Tobacco-Stained Mountain Goat *in 2011 — for a new website,* Dirty Noir, *which was co-run by a fellow Aussie writer named Doc O'Donnell.*

It's something that spins out of the hardboiled scenario in TSMG, *and to my mind the narrator could easily be Floyd Maquina...but not necessarily.*

I decided to reboot it for the anthology The Tobacco-Stained Sky, *this time as a graphic story with artwork by Canadian Michael Grills* (Runnin' With a Gun), *and a couple of months later inserted the written version into* One Hundred Years of Vicissitude *— as Wolram Deaps' surly yarn about the fate he wished for Floyd.*

Incidentally, Linoleum Actress *is also the name of one of my Little Nobody EPs, released through IF? around the same period with remixes by Justin Robertson, Paul Birken and Sebastian Bayne.*

Linoleum Actress

The first thing she does is she powders her nose.

She unzips her tobacco-coloured Louis Vuitton purse in the same manner a lioness, basking in the sun on an African savannah, tends to flick her tail — in a deceptive, lazy kind of way, but in reality it's a quick and precise gesture.

She drops her hand in the bag and fiddles about a few moments before her long, slender fingers emerge with a compact. Leaning toward the half-length mirror attached to the wardrobe, as I said, she powders her nose.

I've never seen anybody do it with such style.

Straight after her eyes in the mirror shift to mine, she smiles a fraction, then changes her mind and blows a kiss.

I'm pretty certain it misses, and that was the point. Attention returned to herself in the mirror, she adjusts the bra strap on her left shoulder, straightens out the dress strap next to that, rotates both shoulders to make the ensemble sit better, and pushes her hair back.

"What're you looking at, babe?" she says in a distracted kind of way.

I don't answer. I just stare at the beauty in that reflection and find it remarkable that such a serpent could sit so pretty.

"Snake got your tongue?" She seems to know my every thought, and I find that spooky. Not that it matters now, I guess. Her laughter is husky and it drifts around me. I loved that sound. I loved her. I thought the feeling was mutual, but I'm beginning to suspect I was wrong.

She's on top of me now, the aroma of lilacs intense, pressing her face as close as possible to mine, so that our eyes meet and her two hazel peepers become one in my struggling vision.

"Cyclops," she whispers — it's our age-old game of affection, yet right now her tone sounds more vicious than vivacious.

Straight off the bat she breaks away, sits up, and stares down at me. "Well, you are rather boring today, my love. You could put in a little more effort."

She eases herself off my lap, heads into the kitchenette, and pushes two slices of bread into the pop-up. The cap's off the tequila and she's swigging straight out of the bottle. She's wandering that savannah again, eyes pushing wild, before a return to civilization and pouring a shot into a glass.

She paces the kitchen waiting for the toast. The way she walks takes her out of my sight every now and then, but I can hear her breathing and can still smell the perfume.

"You got any Vegemite?" she asks. "Oh wait, found it!" Her next pace takes her to the fridge, where she peers inside. "Oh crap. Margarine? I hate margarine, you know that. Why couldn't you get Western Star butter instead? A girl might get the feeling that you don't care about what she wants." The toast pops, and then she's laughing to herself as she spreads condiments. In her next breath she's singing Foghorn Leghorn. "Oh, doggy, you're gonna get your lumps. Oh, doggy, you're gonna get some bumps…"

The way she stands there on the linoleum floor, I'm watching her from behind. She definitely knows how to move that body of hers in that tight satin dress — truth is she always did, especially in my field of vision. Her hips sway as she spreads and serenades, and it's a mesmerizing sight.

Finally breakfast is over, followed by a sizable slug of tequila, and she comes back into the bedsit — with the bottle — to stand before me.

"I'd offer you some brekky," she says, "but I have a feeling you'd just play mum. You know?" After she swirls the tequila around a bit, she glances at it and back to me. "So, what's your poison? ...Oh, wait, you've already had it." She leans over me on the couch and pries away the empty tumbler that's been stuck in my mitt for the past half hour. "How's that paralysis coming along, babe?"

She puts a playful finger to my mouth, though I can't feel it. At all. I also can't catch the lilac anymore.

"No need to answer. Shouldn't be long now. Probably your vision will start botching up next."

I can still see her clear enough, but the edges of my eyesight are starting to get haggard, and that haggardness is creeping in from all sides. She sniffs the glass that she took from me and frowns.

"Say, you can smell the extra bonus stuff a mile off. You really have only yourself to blame. Someone who was a bit more cautious would've whiffed this before the first sip. But you just love your booze, don't you? Down the hatch before you even stop to breathe." She sighs. "Well, I was nice, anyway — at least this concoction isn't as painful as others. It's also not very quick. Sorry about that."

She's right. At the moment I'm feeling nothing, my senses numb, but as I say it's been over thirty minutes according to the big, kitsch, 3D crucifixion-scene clock on the wall.

There is a query nagging away at the back of my noggin. I just wish I could enunciate it through dead lips, or express it to her with my fading eyes; some kind of mental Morse code. Hell, sign language would be fine, if my fingers still worked.

The question was a simple, one-word no-brainer: Why?

She picks up the phone and makes a call, and right about then the lights go out.

A slap brings me back to consciousness.

I can barely see but I do make out a small white saucer held up a few inches from my face, with a lump of distorted yellow gunk sitting on it.

She's showcasing the thing like a '50s Tupperware party hostess.

"It's incredible," she says, "what these days a girl will do for thirty grams of butter."

Before you browse the following artwork, I'm going to get all finicky.

As Floyd Maquina would say, it'd put you in solid with me if you'd already read my two previous novels Tobacco-Stained Mountain Goat *(2011) and* One Hundred Years of Vicissitude, *which are stand-alone tomes but connected by about 5% of content.*

Some of that percentage turns up in the following short 4-page comic strip, which I did in collaboration last year with wunderbar Argentinian artist Marcos Vergara.

It's kind of like the missing link — a story intended to stand alone, but also the absent jigsaw piece between one scene in One Hundred Years... *(Chapter 35, pages 226-229) and another in* TSMG *(the chapter 'The Salt of the Turf', pages 167-168).*

Hence we have characters that could be Floyd and barkeeper Ziggy, along with Wolram Deaps and Kohana.

To cut further to the chase, it kind of explains away the presence of the Webley revolver in both novels...if you want to see it that way.

I wrote the story in a bit of a hurry as I had a tight window of oppor-tunity to work with Marcos, and this was one of my first attempts to write comicbook-style for an artist.

I love what he sent back.

Get Busy
Andrez Bergen
Marcos Vergara

IT'S BUSIER
THAN THE
AUSTRALIAN
GRAND PRIX IN
THERE

TRIPLE-VODKA SHOT, ZIGGY

WITH A SQUIRT OF LIME JUICE.

ON THE TAB, BUB?

TAP

DARN TOOTIN'. TIME TO DRINK MYSELF STUPID

THERE'S A TIME FOR THAT?

BLUB BLUB BLUB

I'M WONDERING IF THERE'S A TIME THERE ISN'T

③

149

This next romp is actually an ending — the one I toyed with for the 1992 manuscript of Tobacco-Stained Mountain Goat, *back when I called the book* We Are Not Afraid, We Serve.

Hence the title here.

I abandoned this finale when I did the final version of TSMG, *the one published through Another Sky Press in 2011, but not because I disliked the tangent. I just felt* TSMG *was already so oppressive, it needed uplift in the final chapter.*

So, when I decided to do a self-indulgent compendium of short stories and other odds and ends, naturally I grabbed this off the rear-end of the old manuscript, rewrote the thing so it now stars Floyd's Seeker Branch buddy Hank Jones, and gave it a wayward wax and polish.

We Are Not Afraid, We Serve

Annoyingly floodlit and humid it might've been, but I continued to walk the underpass burrowing deep beneath City Centre.

In the plus column, there was zero traffic at this time, so I could proceed down the middle of the road with carefree abandon, at least till catching sight of a security post.

I had no idea of my plan of action once I reached the Senator's abode — if I reached the place, given the excess of sentries and surveillance doohickeys I expected to encounter between here and there.

The tunnel, only four lanes wide, stretched on indefinitely and time was precious. I could probably find a more convenient entrance from within the Dome, above me, but this route offered a discreet alternative. Working off a few excess kilos would never hurt.

Having rounded a gradual turn, I spotted my first guard-house directly ahead. I fled the road to press up against a wall, and straight after recoiled — chocolate-brown seepage, hopefully from the Yarra, oozed down the concrete.

In an attempt to steady ransacked nerves, I scrutinized the small, two- or three-man building. How many people were there? What was my excuse for passing through? Hi, saw your lights on, thought I'd drop in? Why should the bozos begin to believe such a rort?

Turns out, however, that fabrications weren't required.

The lights were off, and I couldn't see anybody from this distance. As I carefully stepped over toward the bungalow, I made out no life at all. While this hung as odd, I couldn't deny confirmation when I leaned against the cracked plasti-glass, looked inside, and saw dark shadows in which nothing moved.

The crack puzzled me. This stuff was supposed to be harder than steel, so what could have caused that? And why wasn't it replaced? Poor-man's maintenance didn't ring credible here.

From the wide open door, coming out of hidden speakers in low volume, I caught the sounds of an old big band number about a girl from Kalamazoo. Floyd would probably know the name of the tune, but he wasn't here to quiz. There was a camera suspended above the doorway that refused to swivel even when I waved up at it. Surely I was a target large enough for even a malfunctioning device.

I edged forward to the entrance, still puzzling over why there weren't any guards. It might've been a lower-rung concern, but anyway this underpass would slip into the high-security umbrella, being in such close proximity to politicos like Kenbright. It was inconceivable that they'd leave a post unguarded for even a few seconds.

I glanced around, jumpy re: the lack of personnel, riding notions that it had to be a trap. Without taking the time to procrastinate further, I stepped into the building — and tumbled back out again. I stopped myself from landing on my bum by hanging onto the doorframe.

"Shit," I muttered, at the same time as I dragged my eyes away from the vivid tableau on the floor of the security booth.

I'd glimpsed enough — two methodically gagged and bound guards, with their throats cut ear-to-ear as an apparent after-thought. The men were as dead as discarded doornails. This had to have happened recently. The gashes looked too fresh and blood wept from them, easing around the edges of vinyl gaffer tape.

I looked outside in the tunnel proper for some sign of the pricks who'd done this butcher's job, without success — and straight after plucked up enough wayward courage to go through the guards' pockets. Their holsters may've been empty, but one of the guys had a small pistol tucked up under his left armpit. Bingo. Flimsy as it was, this would do fine.

I extended the gun, a nine millimetre Glock 26, before me as I left the death-trap, turned full circle, and decided upon the bizarre: nobody was here. Who would do this much carnage, only to scarper? Why weren't alarm bells a-klanging? It didn't make for good sense.

My thoughts turned back to Kenbright, and then Léna.

This had to have something to do with the Senator, though what was another matter. Perhaps it was an attempt on his life? Could Léna have done—? No. I shook my head, my own attempt to lob out idiotic notions.

Whatever the case, if she were with him, I had no time to lose.

I started to jog along the remainder of the tunnel, panting the further I went. I was nowhere near the best condition for this kind of exercise, and I'd forgotten my shorts. Though I kept an eye on the terrain ahead, there was no peep from a single soul. Within minutes I entered a cavernous underground parking garage where priceless vehicles sparkled in uniform rows.

I bent over, hands on my knees, heart pounding, gasping for air. God, I felt like I was going to die. Finally, I dragged in suffi-cient oxygen to raise my head.

The Senator's limo was parked over by the elevator shaft.

Even amidst all the other expensive crates it was impossible to miss the car's hot pink exterior. Kenbright was known for his kinks. The rumour mill said the jerk ironed-out those kinks with a steady succession of young women that people tended to never see again. The thought of Léna as the full stop to this chain jolted me.

With the tiny Glock clasped in both hands but arched down a fraction, I weaved from car to car. The limo had its engine off and I couldn't see its driver.

The other titbit I'd gleaned was that this chauffeur had a black belt in karate — meaning she could double-dip as personal bodyguard. The only martial art I'd mastered was bathing other people's cats, so I figured the miniature gun would have to fill in for five digits of death.

I reached the limo and peeked through the tinted window.

Oh yeah, the chauffeur was there, all right, but hardly playing coy. All those after-hours karate lessons had been given the finger.

Her eyes were slitted and stared at some attractive space over my left shoulder. I was tempted to take a gander, though it was pretty obvious she was dead. I couldn't see a mark on her, and there was nothing behind me.

I turned anyway and leaned against the pink vehicle for a while. I had my arms crossed in front of me as I focused on a nearby exit sign. My tummy growled. Damn.

I'd like to think I was capable enough to mull over the odds and ends and thereby make a decision, but it was pointless trying to slot the pieces into a reasonable whole — none of this clicked, neither disjointed nor lassoed together. The only thing making an impression, the thing that had brought me this far, was Léna's life being in danger. Mine hanging on the line, too, was beside the point.

Since today's bill of fare appeared to be the act of stealing things from dead bodies, I took the driver's ID, headed over to the elevators, and then pushed the button. Nothing happened for several seconds. I wondered if the lifts had been locked-down, but I heard a comical 'ding' and a pair of doors slid open.

I stepped inside. It was too bright in there. I found myself squinting.

"Level Forty-two," I announced, swiping the appropriated ID card across the panel.

After the doors closed I felt a soft upward motion. Toward — what? An awaiting Senator Kenbright surrounded by body-guards? A squad of trigger-happy cops? Christ knew, and Christ bloody well cared. For my part, I had no idea and decided to give up imagining. What a waste. All of that was beyond me now. It always had been. I was screwed the moment they hammered through the Bill of Deviations, but was too much of an overweight blockhead to know it at the time.

As I mentioned, the only worthwhile pursuit was helping out Léna.

She deserved that much — I owed her. She'd given me the time of day when most people look at the fat man as nothing more than light relief. So I raised the handgun before me, level with my gaze, and waited for the elevator to open.

We stopped at forty-two according to the red-light display, and the metal doors slid apart on cue — to an empty, ill-lit hallway. I hopped out and aimed in both directions along the corridor, playing pistolero, but again there were no moving targets. All I saw were a couple of other doors, an antique chest with some purple flowers on top, and a large Renaissance-style painting showcasing a chubby, naked lady on a settee, enjoying a bunch of grapes.

The painting looked like the real deal. Old, faded, apparently oil on canvas, though it could've been acrylic or recycled poop for all I knew. Something small caught my eye. When I leaned closer to the picture, I saw a black, oval sticker with white writing — it read 'if?' — stuck to the woman's buttocks. Right. That would've devalued the thing a significant percentage.

I pulled myself back to the here and now. One of the wooden doors was slightly ajar, so I headed over to that. The closer I got, the more I was able to distinguish the sound of some kind of slow piano riff. I carefully pushed the door open to a gloomy, average-sized room. The lack of illumination was a worry, though it was the middle of the night, and I supposed it would help mask my movement. This appeared to be a den, with an orderly secretaire and desk, and a bookcase concealing an entire wall. There was another door, closed, that I slowly eased forward.

The master bedroom, I deduced. Who needed Sherlock?

These quarters were huge, with a canopied four-poster bed in the centre, and next to the bed a candelabrum with dozens of burning candles in it, all of them a different shade of pink wax.

They threw enough light for me to see a naked female form lying face-down on the bed, hands tied together with a fuchsia stocking, and large red welts crisscrossing her back. She wasn't moving. I crossed the floor, leaned over, and pushed back blonde hair that obscured the face.

Léna.

I'd already guessed as much. I recognized her backside and the glorious flow of her shoulder muscles, cherished the colour of the hair.

The woman's eyes were closed. They would never reopen.

From the look of the bruising around the neck I assumed she'd been throttled. I worked the gun across my forehead, feeling the pain of its sharp sight cutting into the skin. I believe I was attempting to blot out the other pain, the one inside me. She was dead — in the same boat as my wife Courtney. The same vessel I'd be hitching a ride on in a short while from now.

What a bloody waste. Not me. Her.

I sat on the bed beside Léna, memories hammering my head from within as I bludgeoned that same head, with the gun, from without. This had to stop. The pistol was too flyweight to induce decent physical damage without pulling the trigger, and I needed it to inflict retribution on the arsehole who'd done this.

So, I looked at the murder scene afresh. At the woman in particular. I touched her cheek. Vaguely warm. There were wires leading from the bed that weaved across space, on into an idInteract console propped on a nearby table. Further checking it out was unnecessary — you didn't need flights of fancy to conjure up the idIotic programs Kenbright would get off on.

Anyway, I could still hear that damnable piano concerto.

It was louder here, music I recognized, a cheesy piece used in some recent TV advertising. What'd they been hawking? Cars? Plastic, more likely.

I tore my gaze from what I told myself was no more than a corpse, lurched up, and rounded the corner of two further doorways in a blundering hurry.

The source of the music was a flyweight, elderly man wrapped in a towel, toga-fashion, seated before a grand piano. Above the keys he tinkered with was the brand name 'Truffaut', written in flowing gold leaf.

When he saw me in the doorway to his right, the piano player sat up straight.

"Deaps sent you for me, didn't he?"

I glared at the man, spots in my vision. "Deaps? Wolram Deaps?"

"I know he wants to silence me. I've become a liability."

"Dunno what the hell you're talking about. I came for Léna."

"Oh." Both his mouth and then the man's eyes widened themselves into ridiculously formed 'O's, as if to emphasize the statement. Then they sagged. "You're far too late. She's dead."

"I know that."

"Yes, how silly of me — of course you do."

"Why?" My voice had taken on a croak that sounded pathetic. "Why what?"

"Why murder her?"

"Well, now. I haven't an inkling. I think it was accidental —

the other times it was definitely an accident. These things happen."

"Right."

The man scratched at his black, rakish, RAF-style moustache. This was obviously dyed, since the thinning hair on top of his head was close to white. I noticed that in doing the scratch he'd stopped playing the piano, yet the music continued unabated. This bloke was all sham.

"Senator Kenbright," I said.

"Yes, yes, that is my name." The man sighed, like he was irritated with my incompetence. "Well, what are you waiting for? Do your thing."

"What thing?"

"The thing you people are paid for. Putting others out of their misery. Why are you waiting?"

"Beats me. Maybe you got me confused with somebody else? And, to be honest, I just changed my mind — I'm here to arrest you. I'm thinking that way you'll have a whole lot more misery ahead."

I took out my Mitt-Mate and made the call. "Jones, H. Seeker Two-Five-Two-Six," I began. "Ophelia—? Hank. I have a doozie."

It felt right. Shooting this bogus piano player would be far too kind.

Besides, it stood to reason that someone had set up all of this. The bundled guards and gift-wrapped chauffeur weren't mere wallpaper. The Senator mentioned Deaps, which meant it could go all the way to the top. Possibly? Probably.

Better to do this by the book, win a few Tinkertoy medals in the process, and then cry into my drinks later. God — Léna.

"So, I'm to be Relocated," the Senator mused. "Might I at least put on something decent? There are bound to be reporters."

"Nah. I like the look of you just as you are. You're lucky I'm letting you stick with the towel."

"May I smoke?"

He lifted a silver case from the top of the piano, but I knocked it across the room.

"Put a lid on it, wanker. Jeez."

Kenbright looked like I'd hurt his feelings. "I am not afraid. I simply served my country," he complained.

"Sure you did, laddie. Me, too. Choice career move."

"You know, aren't you a little fat to be a Seeker?"

"Fat and happy, mate." I could hear the sirens already. "Fat and happy."

The next experiment was something I toyed with last year, reviving a kind of collage-based story-telling technique I worked with in the early 1990s — when I did a weekly superhero comic about fellow staff members at TAC Insurance in Melbourne, using (mis)appropriated ID tags — but grew out of when I quit my stab at a corporate job.

I wanted to tell a simple tale, minimalist, possibly even the story of the Hospitalization of Floyd's wife Veronica (never actually seen in Tobacco-Stained Mountain Goat, *except through the narrator's blinkered memories).*

Then again, it could be the arrest and Relocation of anybody in this suffocating near-future dystopia.

The story also gave me an excuse to dabble with some silly art, utilizing some of the new software that's available, and 'twas fun.

Since the story before last was how things (kind of) originally finished, I'm going to now serve up the prologue to Tobacco-Stained Mountain Goat *that went out with the novel when it was published in 2011.*

There is a reason for this, aside from the fact that I feel it sits pleasantly by itself — I'm going to follow this up with the original prologue (here titled Prologue Thingy*) that went with the final manuscript in my submission to Another Sky Press in the U.S. in October 2007.*

At the time I was suffering from dire lack of sleep — I'd rewritten the novel in three months, while working full-time and coming to grips with being the dad of a child not yet two years of age.

I got this surprising, mind-blowing email back from Another Sky on October 22 that year: "Submission received! In fact, a couple of us here have already looked it over. This is unusual — we get a lot of submissions and there's usually a delay before we actually have a chance to review something. But somehow you skipped to the front. Anyway, getting to the point — we totally dug the sample you sent and we'd love to read more of Tobacco-Stained Mountain Goat. *I guess you jumped to the top of the pile for a reason."*

A year or so later, as we plodded on the early editing pleasantries, Kristopher Young — the guy who runs Another Sky — said this amazing thing in an interview. I kept the byte because it knocked my socks off and helped inspire me to follow through on some particularly grim editing moments with TSMG... *and to continue pursuit of this writing thing (thanks, Kris!). The quote goes thus:*

"We're working on a project right now by a guy who has an extremely unique voice. I've never read anyone with such a unique voice. An Australian that lives in Tokyo. He's extremely well-versed in film noir. It's this noirish-Australian-Japanese conglomeration of ideas. The thing is it's a beautiful labour, but it needs a ton of editing. I am probably going to be spending another year of my life, minimum, finishing this epic novel."

Little did he suspect it'd take more time than that.

Funnily enough the rambling, somewhat pretentious Prologue Thingy *you'll wade through (after the final version,* Fear of that

Misplaced Black Bat*) was attached at the beginning of my original submission to Another Sky. It was one of the first things to go.*

We ended up throwing it out the window, although you may recognize some of the text since this was threaded into other parts of TSMG, *most notably the new intro...which you'll get to read first now.*

Anyway, if you're still vaguely interested, you can then go grab the pdf and epub versions of the whole novel — gratis — from Another Sky Press at anothersky.org.

Fear of that Misplaced Black Cat

I never really knew the old Melbourne before the Wall, with its sundry pub music, its boutique-club glamour, and vaguely dissident art, a not-so-contaminated Yarra River, all-night warehouse rave parties, superlative eateries, and its easy multi-cultural charm — I was still only a kid then.

What I really got to know was the xenophobic, rotting hulk of a city it became in the epoch after the shuttering of the place to an outside world on its last legs. Now, the city is divided into a dozen culturally cut-up and socioeconomically distinct districts, you know, each occupied by swarms of police and trigger-thrilled security types, and separated from one another with blockades and fences, along with a shocking case of paranoia. The centre of the city — that's the Dome — is a play area reserved for the rich. Then there's the subterranean Hospital zone, but let's not get into that here.

Melbourne may look a little worse for wear, a little bombed out even, but it's nothing compared to the ghastly ruins of the other cities out there. Our city suffers from a chronic case of overpopulation, it's true, but the rest of the lot is devoid of us riffraff altogether.

Oh, I was going to tell you, wait, I was going to tell you about this guy, goes by the name of Floyd Maquina. Now, Floyd was broke and had medical bills to pay to support his ailing spouse, so the government offered him some sort — I don't know — some sort of a job.

Anyway, there he was, poor chap, unhappy as a lark, without a cent, and soaked through to the bone.

This is how the dream unravels in my plagiaristic mind — a preemptive attempt at a spot of streetwise narration plundered from the opening monologue for the 1949 classic, *The Third Man*, read with either the cynical edge of Carol Reed's racketeer, or the more inanely optimistic offering from Joseph Cotten's protagonist in the Americanized version.

Your choice.

The words are smeared just a bit into a ramshackle riot that attempts (badly, I must say) to correlate with the mood, the alternative locale, and the entirely crap circumstances of the here and now.

Hell, I don't know if you've ever copped a screening of *The Third Man*, but if you have it'd put you in solid with me — and would certainly help out with all that descriptive nonsense we otherwise have to indulge in to set the scene hereabouts. Whether or not you've seen the flick, or even if you just need a few friendly slaps to remind you, there's a pivotal scene over an hour into it that perfectly captures my predicament: cue a transient form, a man maybe, skulking in a darkened alcove off the side of a nighttime Viennese plaza.

There's a cat seated at the figure's feet, preening itself. A light claps on in an overhead window and you get a glimpse of the man's face, replete with a flirtatious, mocking expression — it's Orson Welles as the iconic Harry Lime, a character we've previously assumed to have been measured up for a concrete kimono. He's resurrected himself, shades of Lazarus, and — ah, forget it. Who am I kidding?

I've nowhere near the smug self-assurance, let alone panache, of Orson Welles when he takes that first visual splash in *The Third Man*. I've more the personality of his co-star Joseph Cotten's Holly Martins in my B-movie attempt at an opening reel.

Besides, the contemporary location shoot — in Melbourne, Australia — isn't quite as safe, orderly, or classy as Reed's post-World War II bombed-out Vienna, Austria.

I apologize for all the confusion — chalk it up to a delusion that should be excised and dumped on the floor of the editing suite to be swept out with the rest of the trash.

So, quickly pull back to a wide shot of the street in an attempt to resuscitate this narrative. Keep it simple — no out-of-focus fade-ins like they employed in the old black-and-whites, or the Salvador Dalí bender in Hitchcock's *Spellbound*. Simply diffuse the colour and crinkle-cut the edges of the frame as heavy rain begins to fall.

Someone — that's me — is leaning against a wall on some second-rate street. Cut to my aged, scuffed, and soaked-through shoe, then pan to where our absent film-noir cat is supposed to be. Damn.

There's not, it seems, an available tabby or tortoiseshell to be found anywhere within this dream.

Mind you, this all backed by the crackle of a single-channel soundtrack: maybe some guy twanging away on a zither, or a shamisen.

Or wait, perhaps Irving Berlin could rise from the grave to conduct a bunch of dusted-down tuxedos and cocktail-dressed dames. I could go still more self-consciously future schlock here like Cabaret Voltaire and Throbbing Gristle did back in the 1970s, say something into a mic, splice 'n' loop the tape, sprinkle in some of my dad's tortured guitar strumming from when I was little, and then have the sheer audacity to call it this dream's musical score.

Now that we have that sorted, jump cut, in godawfully hopeful Jean-Luc Godard style, to my own perspective. This is where it all starts, really, with this recurring dream — and I wish to blazes the truth had more pizzazz.

Prologue Thingy

Where to start, where to start... I'm muttering these words; it's just one of those anxiety-ridden moments, so pay no heed.

Intros.

I mean who really needs 'em...?

Apart from all those tweed-clad, armchair, fireplace-hovering critics — and their bloody book-toting hounds — who say that prologues're the most important part of the narrative; that they set the scene, that without an intro the reader has no idea what's happening; that you've gotta reel in the characters, and by extension the reader, *blah, blah, blah*...oh yeah, and I should use way less semicolons in the process.

Definitely don't create your own peculiar lexicon.

But after a hundred and one spotted attempts (including sweaty revisions, frantic erasures, crazed scribbling and rancid Dalmatians) to embark upon this unwieldy beast of a story, I'm well and truly washed-up on the fucking introduction front.

Maybe I could skimp from the Tristan Tzara bag of tricks, go all Dadaist here, cut up these paragraphs, stick the words in a knapsack, then take 'em out again to be reassembled in verbatim hotchpotch style?

Or make it more postmodern, do a Brion Gysin/*The Third Mind* party-trick twist, and pitchfork deconstruction in the process?

Shake my booty on the same trail that Cabaret Voltaire and Throbbing Gristle did back in the '70s, say something into a mic, splice 'n' loop the tape, sprinkle in some of my dad's terrible guitar strumming, and call it intro muzak...

Am I rambling yet?

The sooner it's over and done with, the better; invariably intros are just a waste of space anyway — unless it's something quirky like Richard Basehart uttering "My name is Ishmael" at the beginning of John Huston's celluloid 1950s latex whale rejig of Melville's *Moby-Dick*.

How about a classic-yet-desultory opening line stealer like Bernardo's "Who's there?" in *Hamlet*, or something pompous and gay like the chorus in *Henry V* that inanely cogitates, "O for a Muse of fire, that would ascend the brightest heaven of invention," ad infinitum, etc, etc. I checked those out on the Internet, just to pretend I'm all literate.

Or even — yeah, sod it all, even something irrepressibly cheesy, like the schlock-scroll spiels at the beginning of all the *Star Wars* movies.

Man, at least they have something to say, however silly. Shakespeare and Melville waffled on too much. They were like old-school Freud.

And I feel like I'm going in similar psychosomatic circles here.

If I were original enough to be the lame-arse trendsetter who declared, "It was a dark and stormy night", I'd be halfway towards vaguely chuffed.

Me?

I've got *Dune* on my mind, goddammit.

Just a smidgeon, but that's enough; it junked up the works in my headspace a moment ago. And I'm talking about the dud moving picture, not the dime-store novel.

Ever copped a dose?

Yeah, yeah — I know. It's not exactly a knockout and nothing to brag about if you *have* seen it. But the point here is that if you had, it'd make things a whole lot easier here — putting you in solid with me as a result.

And don't crack upright and foxy about the book being superior; I wouldn't have the faintest idea. I've never read it. In fact I don't think I've ever even seen a copy anywhere. It's as rare as hen's teeth these days, like most other dusted-up paperbacks and hard covers.

Anyway, don't ask me if this part's in the book, but in the flick Virginia Madsen's prologue narration kick-starts with the words, "A beginning is a very delicate time."

…and you know what?

I'd bet a dollar against a dime that more honest, rattle-brained sentiments have rarely been uttered, muttered, elucidated or thrown up for conjecture.

That's how it figures, because I'm completely aware of it right now: the beginning bit and the delicacy issue chucked together in a hell-for-leather free-for-all. Then maybe gently stirred, definitely not shaken, in a philosophical cocktail replete with stuffed olive — or better yet stuffed with my own waffling verbal horse manure — and run through with one of those wooden toothpicks you find in ramshackle Chinese diners.

Bloody hell.

Now I'm getting all noir and Raymond Chandleresque — even though I have nowhere near the amount of talent possibly found in the mole on the instep of his little left toe.

This wasn't my intention. Where was I? Oh, yeah.

An introduction. The point of everything, that'll steer you clear into the story itself. Amen to that.

Oh shit, I'm out of space and over the word limit now, aren't I? *Bollocks.*

Ahem.

At least Headhunter *has an interesting history — well, so far as I'm concerned.*

It's actually a chapter of Tobacco-Stained Mountain Goat *that was excised from the novel. I very much wanted to keep it in there but my editor, Kristopher Young, convinced me it diluted the story.*

I decided to dig the blighter back up, change the perspective so it's Floyd's former mentor Colman at the centre of things, and we get to find out what happened to Ant Hope after the CPs picked him up in TSMG (on page 106, if you have a copy).

In case you're wondering (or not), the character of Colman — first name undisclosed — is partially modelled on a great Sydney-based chum of mine, a fellow hack journalist, dad and lover of fine spirits...or any alcohol for that matter. And the gold Krugerrand gossip from TSMG was based on a genuine experience we went through together in Newcastle (Australia) at a crazy arts festival.

This story has a longer history than that, however. It's part of a novel I'd been pottering over for years, but never came close to finishing, called The Cricketers *— set in a dystopic, futuristic society in which cricket is used as the ultimate spectator sport.*

Yes, it was very much influenced by Rollerball *(1975) as well as the surreal moments of* Catch-22 *and the sports' evangelism of* The Natural *and* Field of Dreams. *There's also a nod toward Australian mini-series* Bodyline, *which starred Hugo Weaving* (The Matrix, Captain America, Lord of the Rings) *in one of his earliest villainous roles — as English cricket captain Douglas Jardine.*

There are probably many reasons I never finished getting beyond the draft stage, including the above-mentioned superior romps — so I slipped my favourite part into TSMG, but then that was removed when my editor (correctly) noticed it didn't sit well with the rest of the story.

So here it is, anyway, as a bit of a lazy stand-alone.

First up, some unhealthy sporting stats: (1) Whereas in baseball players wear mitts to field, cricketers field barehanded; (2) A cricket ball is of similar construction to a baseball, but slightly harder and denser;

(3) The fastest ball bowled by any bowler in cricket is 161.3 km/h or 100.23 mph, and the fastest baseball pitch clocked-in at 162.3km/h or 100.9mph; (4) Batters' helmets became mandatory in baseball in 1959, but were not in common use in Test cricket until the early 1980s; (5) Cricket fields take up an area the size of about 175,000 square feet or 16,300 m^2, whereas in baseball the fair territory area is about 110,000 square feet or 10,000 m^2; (6) While a baseball match is usually in the vicinity of three hours, a Test cricket match can go on for up to five days.

Headhunter

Truth to tell, he was more aggrieved than bored.

There had been some bacterial problem with the latest crop — rendering it useless, even after he did some repair work, hacked away the disturbing black growth, cut the plants at the bottom, trimmed off remaining fan leaves, clipped the trim leaves as well, and stuck those in a paper grocery bag for drying and to keep as hash. All of it was spoiled. He could blame the goddamned weather but everyone did that already.

Not that any of this accounted in meaningful way toward the grief.

Instead of wallowing in self-pity he scraped together the remnants of his last stash, rolled these up, sealed them with a kiss and a flick of a match, and got stuck into two bottles of reconstituted rum — a combination that bent his head enough to produce a weird nostalgia for the carefully hidden muses of childhood.

Something to steer away from the news. Of her death. Of the requirement to tell his sister.

The last time Colman paid any sort of heed to the cricket was decades before — when Allan Border was still playing — and in the pickled recesses of his memory he couldn't revive a bare ten percent of the rules of the game. Who the bollocks really knew them all, anyway? Cricket was such an anachronistic sport.

Aside from escapism, probably it was Ant who subversively motivated his arse to switch on the telly and tune in to the grand final, though he would never let this on to the bugger.

Colman raided the fridge, and then sat back on the couch with about twelve ring-in Coopers Ale beside him, lifted a deep ceramic bowl off the coffee table, poured into it some dried vegetation, and started mulching the remnants of the remnants.

Thoughts of Floyd wafted by. Dog-eaten memories, mostly, a majority fond. He felt his eyes begin to water, pushed the balls of his hands into either temple, pushed hard, forced himself to stop the waterworks and banish the kid from mind. For good.

The ploy was a success.

As he carefully ground away, Colman decided not to care. Josephine could wait. Madeleine was out for an evening's canasta and here he was, home alone, steadily getting rather off his tree. While doing so he tuned out to the sporting shenanigans on the TV.

It took just a few seconds' bleary vision to twig that this game had changed significantly.

In fact, calling it a game — or a sport for that matter — was a sham, one surely punishable by a stint in Purgatory. Instead, picture a gladiatorial outing more on par with one of Richard Wagner's Arthurian operas, *Parsifal* in particular, the one with a long-winded death scene for Amfortas — the Grail Honcho, or Fishing King, or whoever the hell he was.

A long time ago Maddy had forced him to sit through this '80s Kraut film version of *Parsifal* by some terror called Hans-Jürgen Syberberg. It went on and on in excess of four hours. Towards the end, he'd gone stir-crazy, railing for the guy to sod off and kick the bucket, and swore aloud he'd well-nigh learned the

German language.

In return his wife cold-shouldered him, picked up her purse, and left the cinema without a backward glance.

Here — by 'here' Colman meant slap-bang on the telly screen — the lead-up pomp and ceremony for this grand final at Hylax Stadium Mk. III in the Dome were bothersome bummer enough. Think 'rousing' music and grating performances by awful local rock wannabes. He felt like he might go deaf and blind — or set off on his very own quest in search of a chalice of half-decent entertainment.

Not that there weren't bonus extras: lazy fireworks and terrible performers, semi-naked cheerleaders in poor-taste, erotically tight threads. A mass exodus of thousands of kids pouring out across the ground carrying different coloured cards that, once coordinated, resembled the Australian flag and, on the reverse side of the placards, a boxing kangaroo.

Then came a scratchy, orchestral dirge of 'Waltzing Matilda', distorted over the stadium's PA — or was it his single functional TV speaker causing that? — hotly pursued by the latest pop starlet sensation warbling the national anthem. She sounded like she might have been deaf as a post, but likely he was getting old and cranky.

The commentators blathered on with disposable inanities throughout, then reported that while 185,000 people were right there in the stadium, the match was being broadcast to an audience of approximately ten million homes in Melbourne. Were there really that many places to suffer in this skip of a city?

They were talking up the stats of both teams and players involved — centred upon the Australians, of course — and it became obvious where bias resided. Bias. Colman's thoughts wandered. A child. Corinne. The hospital.

No. Desist, he told himself and forced his attention back to the telly.

After an interminable amount of verbal guff, at last some

action rolled into view. The World XI was the first team to emerge from the dressing rooms.

They wandered onto the field in a straggling line led by Ant Hope, and the resounding silence surrounding them was, seconds later, followed by boos, hisses and jibes from the crowd, along with a tempest of empty bottles, cans, cups, plates, diapers, shoes, and the proverbial kitchen sink.

When the cameras zoomed up close on the team members rather than the tossed paraphernalia, Colman saw a multicultural collection of faces that looked jaded, bitter, morose. Ant's mug held onto the impassive. Full marks — he covered well.

Meanwhile, the commentators rambled on, forcing Colman to kill the impulse to crank down the volume and escape their monotone excess. He knew this hellish fiasco needed to be 'enjoyed' with the vicarious add-ons.

After about five minutes more of the rubbish, the stadium lights dimmed, spectators hushed, and the TV pundits stopped blabbering. Bliss. Then a ring of a dozen huge spotlights lit up the pitch in the centre of the stadium, as well as the ceiling of the Dome far above.

The poignant moment scared the hell out of Colman, mid-puff on his joint.

An inordinate amount of dry ice smoke washed across everything, including a parade of scantily-clad girls marching in Akubra hats and green and gold sequined bikinis, when four noir hover-choppers appeared out of nowhere and descended into the arena to the blaring soundtrack of AC/DC's Brian Johnson growling out 'Back in Black'. God, he hated that song — preferred the band's former lead singer Bon Scott, since the man had died with style, choking on his own vomit.

As soon as the vehicles landed, the Australian players jumped down, clad in tawdry gold and green lamé jumpsuits. They were triumphant smiles, self-confident grins, arms held aloft to soak up the standing ovation and adulation from a mammoth crowd.

The announcers, barely audible above that roar, wet themselves with glee. Relighting his spliff, Colman examined the face of Ray Massey when he was introduced, to thunderous approval, on the stadium PA.

Ant's arch-nemesis and his ex-girlfriend's current snog, Massey looked the part of a cocky arsehole — but, then again, most postmodern cricketers did.

The cameras swooped onto every one of the Australian team's eleven players, predictably via their best angle, and Colman sussed they'd caroused with their fair share of cosmetic enhancements. Each one of them would've looked right at home as part of a Mattel action-figure range in some diabolical toyshop.

Statistics, records, favourite food, the size of their stamp collections, shoe measurements, star signs, blood types and marital status flashed up for each. He'd never seen a bigger group of people who thought that 'driving' qualified as a worthwhile hobby.

All, without exception, cited Vegemite as their favorite topping on toast for brekky, and Melbourne Bitter as their favourite beer. Colman couldn't abide that. While Vegemite admittedly remained the nectar of the gods, he was a Coopers man himself — but guessed that the company logos on their shirtfronts meant these people could never infer otherwise.

The man threw an empty Coopers plasti-can over into the corner with a resounding clatter, and then opened one of its brothers as he concurrently rolled and lit another gasper.

Thought he'd pass out with the mind-numbing absurdity of things on the telly, but maybe that was more due to the effects of mixing grass with wine and beer, even if the latter liquid refreshments were synthetic chicanery.

Did that ancient adage — the one about beer after wine being fine — still apply when the substances themselves were fake?

It seemed like hours had swung by at a snail's pace before the match began, and Colman sensed he didn't need to be The

Amazing Criswell to predict what would happen next.

The World XI, batting first, started disastrously.

They played like kindergarteners reluctantly inducted into the Under-18s, tossing away their first three wickets for just twenty-two runs before a fourth player retired injured, his foot broken in three places by "a Miles Mander trademark sand-shoe crusher" — as one studio armchair critic described the devilish delivery.

Colman's head was beginning to freewheel, but a surprising level of clarity in there surprised him. He puffed out and leaned on the table. The announcers adored this Mander character in every possible which way: "Bowler of the century," they went on, "Greatest cricketer of all time" and "Best pecs on the field," along with "Coolest haircut in cricket" — meaningful observations, the lot of them.

They also asided that his fastest recorded delivery clocked in at 176 km/h.

Ant had ratted out the fellow to Colman a few weeks before, thankfully over drinks to dull the pain. Seems that in the past year he'd not only split helmets, caused concussion, and broken bones on a regular basis, but two World XI players had been killed by his deliveries, another was in a coma, and a lucky fourth had permanent brain trauma and would never walk again.

Genetic enhancement had been legalized (under the cuff) in sports a decade ago, and Miles Mander was the natural conclusion to this kind of GM manipulation of the human physique. He swayed in the breeze at well over two metres in height, his shoulders somewhere near that wide.

It was obvious he deserved his nickname — the 'Verminator' — but, given the blocky facial lines and heavy brow, Colman felt that Ivan Drago would be a better handle. You could hang bamboo blinds from the man's forehead.

Ant had said that Mander perfected a deviation on the old

Bodyline tactic used by the English early in Don Bradman's career in the 1930s, except Mander didn't just bowl straight at the batsman's body — he aimed purposefully at their heads.

Headline? the man pondered. *Nah, that'd cause too many newspaper copywriters headaches.* Boom-boom! Colman shook his skull, laid down the spliff and stared at it. Perhaps it would be better, he decided, to stick with the beers.

And the telly. Ahhh, the telly.

Most of the World XI batsmen pictured there seemed to be equal parts shell-shocked and terrified, though he doubted this had much to do with homegrown cannabis. Even a cheap, relatively spaced-out amateur punter like him could see that these cricketers wore far too much protection to be able to fluidly move, and put excessive effort into evading Miles Mander's deliveries instead of trying to hit them.

Hell, if he were stuck in their place he'd do exactly the same thing, or even better duck and run for cover in a convenient bunker some place.

So he wondered what kept these fellows going out there to face permanent injury or possible death; what vice-hold grip or sordid means of coercion the Cricketing Authority used to keep them popping up their heads as human cannon fodder.

A fourth wicket tumbled with the score on thirty-one, and the crowd's jubilation reached fever-pitch as the ousted batsman began his slow, pathetic walk across the oval to the dressing rooms, dragging his bat as he went.

What a sad-sack individual.

Empty bottles and loaded jeers came flying out towards him, making Colman consider if the helmet and body-armour were more intended more for this situation than the playing of the game.

The commentators were beside themselves and he caught Ant's name being touted. Sure enough, there was the man and his goatee, emerging from the dressing room.

Ant patted his despondent teammate on the shoulder, and then walked briskly across the grass, using his bat to swat away a bottle that flew too close. There was a determination about his face that Colman hadn't seen lately — if ever — and the announcers drew attention to the fact Ant wasn't carrying a helmet.

"Ludicrous," one of them declared; "Complete stupidity on Hope's part," spat out another; "What kind of role model for kids does he think he is?" grilled a third.

Ad nausea. *Fucking hell. Whatever.*

Ant lined himself up at the crease then wandered out to the middle of the pitch to chinwag for a few seconds with the other batsman. The Australian players hovered round them like a bunch of ravenous, genetically knocked-together seagulls.

Then Ant smiled a fraction, returned to his end, and batted up.

Miles Mander was bowling.

The crowd chanted, in out-of-kilter manner, his nickname (the Verminator) before resorting to the simpler "Kill, kill, kill — thrill, thrill, thrill."

This chant surged to a resounding roar as Mander loped in with the ball and let it fly in an absolute flash. With far more graceful a flourish, Ant hooked the ball over his shoulder and it went flying into the sky and right over the fence — into the crowd.

The umpire took his time before he lifted his arms into the air to indicate six runs.

Colman's friend — yes, he would admit it, he was suddenly willing to impart the honour in this proud, gung-ho moment when he was considerably off his head — well, Colman's friend stood his ground and stared down the bowler, a man who looked now less in league with Dolph and a lot more like a stunned Lou Ferrigno reflecting on glory days as the Incredible Hulk — not the prettiest sight.

The bowler's brow dropped an inch further down and he fumed.

The crowd was, tip to toe, silent. Even the TV commentators had shut up. This required the services of a celebratory toke. Colman lit up again and chased the smoke with half a can of beer.

The Hulk returned to the end of his run up, glowered a bit, chewed gum, spat on the ground, rubbed his crotch with the ball, shook his head like a frenzied bull, and then charged in. The crowd rediscovered their collective voice and screamed away in a grubby frenzy of expectation, albeit decibels lower this time round.

Ant leaned back and easily smacked the ball away through mid-wicket, to the boundary, for another four runs. Quietude prevailed.

"Oh, you bloody beauty!" Colman tossed another deprived can into the corner, heard the empty plastic thunk as it smacked into its predecessor, and opened a fourth Coopers.

The third ball ended up being smashed away for four runs through mid-off, earning scattered applause that picked up around the stadium.

Interesting.

The next delivery? A great big hit back over the bowler's head for six, followed by rowdy, more sustained hand clapping and cheers. Twenty runs in about six minutes.

Drinks were taken, the Australian players gathered in a hyper-active huddle. Officials clad in astoundingly ugly lime-green suits joined them.

Advertisements took over the screen, so Colman drained the can, practiced his slips-cordon throwing technique, and opened yet another. By this time he was hypothesizing that something was amiss. Some action, completely unscripted, was about to go down.

Time for the emergency stash.

He mulched, gathered, rolled, licked, twisted, and sought out the lighter — then sat back to ponder. As much as he'd baited, pissed off, harangued and ridden Ant Hope over the years, there was no one he was more proud of in that drunken and philosophical moment.

The World XI weren't intended to play like this. Win occasionally, certainly, but by supposed chance, poor umpiring decisions, and only ever by uninspired minimal margins. Colman figured that was intended to keep people from guessing the obvious ruse at play.

The Australian team was the star here. Its members were the celebrities, the demigods. They weren't supposed to be upstaged. Ant had mentioned this on countless occasions. It was part of the contract he'd signed — but was also pretty much apparent to anyone with half a cerebral cortex.

When the ad break was over — he'd suffered through about a dozen inane commercials for Melbourne Bitter, Vegemite, Hylax plastic projects, PCs, cars, DevWatch, even a new-fangled MCD public announcement — Ant and the other batsman had returned to their creases and a different bowler was on.

That bowler, a pretty innocuous individual, delivered his six balls — without score — to Ant's batting partner. This made Ant go crazy. He was yelling at the other batsman after each delivery, but the guy acted nonchalant and simply padded away each ball without trying, like he wanted to stay down his end of the pitch.

Probably that was the case.

Because then the over changed and it was again David versus Goliath — or rather, in this case, Ant taking on the rampaging Hulk.

Miles Mander's first ball was a wide, so far from Ant's outstretched bat that the wicket keeper barely got a hand to it, and Colman was surprised the delivery didn't take off the man's fingers.

The next ball reared up at Ant's unprotected throat.

Somehow, he got down under it and hooked again, a much

bigger shot this time, one that flew right up into the air, toward the overhead stadium lights, and there was an insanely huge explosion as one of the two-metre bulbs was trashed by the ball.

The crowd erupted then, as one.

They loved it. Colman loved it. Hell, everyone and his dog would love it. "You funny card thrower," he muttered, smiling in silly fashion. The communal roar on the telly distorted the sound coming through his crap speaker.

On-screen, Ant remained poker-faced while receiving a standing ovation. The Australian players again huddled together, talking, yelling, and gesticulating wildly.

In that moment, to be completely honest, Colman started traveling a wild flight of fantasy, one that mixed together James Caan in *Rollerball*, Russell Crowe in *Gladiator*, even Ralph Macchio in *The Karate Kid*. He skulled the rest of his existing can of amber fluid, lobbed it in indiscriminate fashion, and popped open the last of its ilk. For fuck's sake, even the dimwit commentators were flighty and carried away.

The next ball crash-landed further delusions.

Mander stomped in like a raging rhinoceros on heat to let loose a ball later clocked at 182 km/h. His fastest ever, they said.

Ant was skilled enough to give himself a chance to swing at it, but he didn't have time to connect with his bat.

The ball, instead, connected with his head.

PART 4:

RANSACKING THE ARCHIVE
(i) 1989

When, in 1989, I returned to Melbourne after some time carousing in London, an unsettled and listless post-punk/faux goth without a heart in either scene, I pottered away over the next three years on an early, somewhat primitive version of the manuscript that would eventually turn into Tobacco-Stained Mountain Goat.

I was at uni, doing a thesis on industrial music in Britain in the 1970s, and had some minor pretentions to whittle away at. I obsessed over the music of Front 242, Cabaret Voltaire and Ary Barroso, loved directors Terry Gilliam and David Lynch, and pretended to read Umberto Eco and Brion Gysin.

I still had vague dreams of publication of my fiction but drifted toward film-making and music, and it was precisely at this juncture that my friend's father, Tomek Sikora — a Polish artistic photographer of some note — asked me on board to write short prose pieces for his more experimental visuals.

These were subsequently placed together in a limited edition, glossy coffee-table book called Behind the Light, and it won some photography award or other...in spite of the writing. But this was my first publication and funnily enough was the last outlet for my fiction (aside from journalism) until TSMG was published in 2011.

Though I'm not into the style/content now and find it a wee bit embarrassing, I decided to stick in four of these 23-year-old pieces.

Seems I also used to like flaunting adjectives and semicolons.

I did consider removing 'em and tidying up, but that wouldn't be exactly fair to the spirit of history. I've pulled enough 1984-isms already.

Mirror, Cracked

The mirror, cracked,
Reflects two diverging faces
Where one once was.
A partition that reflects the state of my soul —
Reflects something split, torn, slit, rendered;
The discord, disruption, dissension there.
Pain where once joy was nurtured;
Affliction overcoming vitality.
Love gone, hate gone.
Just two empty eyes from diverging faces
That stare back into my empty heart.
Eyes cold, emotions cold, life cold.
The mirror, cracked,
Bears an image of what could have been,
What would have been,
But for my own failure.
One shard of glass, from
The mirror, cracked,
And one swift movement.
That's all.

Destroy! Destroy!

Violence and destruction;
A lust to destroy, render, crush!
Equality and reason as a weakness
To be dispelled;
Morality cauterized!
The only right is their right,
The right of power and dominance
Over others too feeble to fight.
They find strength in their own belief
Of their own superiority;
Smash all else —
Pathetic! Pathetic!
Destroy! Destroy!
Steadfast love of themselves!
What a wonderful ego trip,
Orgasming all over themselves
And their presupposed superiority!
Ignorance as wonderful!
Blind belief as catechism!
Racism and bigotry their icons!
...stuff that.

Bliss

She tries to ignore him.
He is so far from her spiritually,
But he is too ignorant to understand that.
She tries to invert her thoughts,
To that comforting inner sanctuary where she can
Escape his insipid advances:
Those dreams of escape from the cruel restraints of this place;
Her dreams of freedom to live something more than this,
Where others could respect her for herself and —
His rough hand slides clumsily along her wrist,
And then to her thigh.
The pause in her thoughts is brief, and resentful,
Before returning to her dreams of escaping this appalling
    existence;
This town of pointless indifference and stale lives.
He's pressing close to her now.
She can smell his breath of tobacco and alcohol and wheat;
He's mumbling drab nothings in her ear
As his hand creeps towards its predetermined destination.
He's just like all the others; wants exactly the same from her,
And nothing beyond that.
She clings to her dreams with furious strength.
Dreams of eluding the passive fate of her sisters and her
Mother and her grandmother in this stifling place
Arriving, working, fucking, marrying and eventually dying
In utter apathetic ignorance.
She hates this place and these people.
Hates it all.
His calloused fingers pry at her dress and he laughs inanely;
She pushes herself further into her dreams.
Dreams of escaping.

Two Remaining Trees

Two remaining trees
Upon a ruptured grey plain, scarred and desolate;
Dawn mist or smoke and the stench of filth.
They file past the trees in sombre silence
Or melancholic oblivion,
Their grey faces empty and bare;
Their heads bowed, thoughts absent.
Barely registering a sniper shot a mile away
And a distant, short cry.
They file onwards in their ragged grey line,
Stepping wearily over rotting carcasses and
Meandering along familiar water-logged planks
Past smashed wagons and a fallen airplane
Across the strangled, infertile earth.
A languid sun struggles on the horizon,
Its stagnant presence a mockery of the past;
Its pale glow outlining the two remaining trees
Where once a forest and life grew.

Andrez Bergen

Memories

There are faces around — his family.
He can no longer hear her voices, or feel their presence.
Memories drift past, diminishing one by one;
But he clutches at a single memory.
It's her.
She smiles that smile. She's there, by the window, and
She is just as he remembers her.
No one else notices her presence, strangely.
He lies there, watching her yet not seeing her.
She is waiting for him — he can see it in her warm,
Welcoming eyes.
And he is happy.

Coma Home Now

He sees a picture of home.
It shouldn't be here, so far from home,
But in the half-light it could easily be home.
Almost forgotten —
A silo in the middle of a sun-drenched field;
The deserted tin mine
From a long-lost boom,
And the crumbling chimneystack.
Forgotten, cauterized memories struggling now
To resurface. Of home, of family, of friends,
Of childhood and living and breathing.
Things that are so alien now; foreign and
Tormenting to revive.
He huddles there on the rotted floorboards,
His head propped up on an empty wine cask,
His eyes transfixed by the image splashed upon the
Fallen drape, where no image but emptiness should be.
It could easily be home. The home he'd deserted in
His blind rush to live and experience.
Home created by the neon of the street outside;
Cold, austere and colourless, just like the city.
The image is the past, and just as irretrievable.
This is his reality, around him: the squat, the poverty,
The meaningless existence, the broken furniture and
The ruin of human frailty;
Valeska curled up beside him in a ball,
Unconscious and oblivious in a blur that will soon be his.
The needle, in his shaking hands, promises that —
An escape from the awful memories that rear before him,
Of vitality and warmth, love and sheer joy of living —
Unbearable thoughts now! —
It could so easily be home.

He couldn't stand that; not knowing what he now lived.
With one short manoeuvre, home vanished and reality
Passed out in a welcome coma.

PART 4:

RANSACKING THE ARCHIVE
(ii) Japan

So that was 1989. Done. Honestly? I feel like gluing those pages together.

Much later on, for a few lucky years in the early to late 2000s, I worked as a freelance journalist at the Yomiuri Shimbun *newspaper and as the Tokyo Correspondent for a swag of overseas magazines, doing commentary on things Japanese.*

Easy.

This was before Internet killed the biz, but I love the 'net so the murder was okay.

The upcoming articles were originally put together for Geek *magazine in the U.S. in 2008-09, and reprinted in British magazine* Impact.

If you have a keen eye — and have read One Hundred Years of Vicissitude *— you might notice that some of this hoo-har filtered across into that novel.*

Chanko-nabe: Food of the Sumo

Sumo is one of Japan's more internationally famous sports, probably because the spectacle of two exceptionally fat men — in a nation of exceptionally skinny people — wrestling one another, clad only in loincloths shaped like sexy G-strings is, well, hilarious.

What most accidental spectators don't realize is that there's so much more to the sport than its remarkably hefty *rikishi* (wrestlers).

Behind the bulldog bravura of cataclysmic grappling that goes on in the ring are centuries-old traditions like the Shinto-related throwing of salt (that one's for purification).

And sumo competitors' hair, which is precision-slicked into top-knots, is coiffed using a waxy substance called *bintsuke abura*, the main ingredient of which comes from the berries of the Japanese wax tree, *Toxicodendron succedaneum* — a member of the same family as poison ivy. It's been used cosmetically and in hairdressing in Japan for around a thousand years, and is also used by geisha as a waxy base for their makeup.

Incidentally, this July [2008] the Japanese newspaper, *Nikkan Sports*, reported that a 15g container of the oil rose from ¥685 to ¥735, prompting sumo stars to demand a pay-rise.

Even that remarkably revealing loincloth, known as the *mawashi*, has a story: it's made of silk, approximately 30 feet long, weighs up to 11 pounds, and sometimes bears the name of a sponsor.

Ryogoku, located here in Tokyo near the historic centre of this monolithic metropolis, is the home of the sumo. Right outside the west exit of Ryogoku JR station stands the mammoth Kokugikan, the Sumo Hall, with a capacity of 13,000 people. Three of the six national Grand Sumo tournaments happen here.

Unlike ogling geisha in Kyoto, trainspotting sumo sorts in the streets around Ryogoku is relatively easy, especially since the practitioners of the sport aren't exactly the waif-like types that geisha or maiko typically are.

But sumo wrestlers would be nothing without their diet, and — yes — we dangle the word "diet" here in its most strictly ironic sense. You want find these people anywhere near a Diet Coke or low-fat mayonnaise.

Chanko-nabe is the food of the sumo — a huge, simmering hot-pot that's chock-full of meat, fish and vegetables, best mixed with soy sauce, but sometimes also blended with *mirin*, *miso*, saké, and *dashi* stock (shavings of dried skipjack tuna mixed with edible kelp).

Leftover broth is often then consumed with a hefty plate of noodles.

It's as highly nutritious (think protein-city) as it is gut-busting, and is the principle dish gorged by sumo wrestlers to extend their hefty waistlines and add to already-impressive girths.

Some wrestlers enjoy the concoction so much that they quit the ring and instead become the *chanko-cho*, or chief chanko chef, for their wrestling stables, and eventually open their own restaurants — often with sumo memorabilia from their workhorse days adorning the walls.

And, to my blinkered eyes at least, there's no finer chanko-nabe to be had in Ryogoku, than at a fine establishment called *Yoshiba*.

The building that houses Yoshiba was erected in 1948 as a prominent sumo wrestling club and practice stadium for the famous, 200-year-old Miyagino stable, and nine years later the premises were handed down to the stable's coach, former distinguished *yokuzuna* (sumo grand champion), Yoshibayama, who passed away in 1977.

After that, the building was recast as a restaurant (in 1983), maintaining the sumo ring and the practice rooms in their original state.

Yoshiba, named after the aforementioned yokuzuna, is hardly a small place itself. The restaurant can seat up to 250 people, it boasts a sushi bar and a voluminous fish-tank, and while the place is invariably busy, the service from the staff is brilliant — so much so, it leaves you despondent that the custom of tipping is a foreign one in Japan.

There's also daily entertainment in the sumo ring in the centre of the restaurant, which veers from guys in *yukata* (summer robes) singing traditional sumo songs, to a group of rowdy musicians strumming away on a *shamisen* in a more quirky, contemporary style.

But the focus here, of course, is the chanko-nabe, and the seriously skewed attempts to finish this herculean dish. Give yourself a day or two to recover — and try not to remember that sumo champions and their lesser ilk guzzle gallons of the chunky nectar on a daily basis.

Ouch.

Genji: The Millennium Man

This month, I'll avoid the slacker excesses of recounting my trips abroad, and get instead all scholarly. Think chalk and Harris Tweed jackets (harristweedscotland.com), then I want you to reflect back on dusty high-school history tomes, or literature classes, that dealt with the older-school inanimate; kick those frazzled Yuletide season brain cells back into gear, and try to recollect the few times you've surfed through Wikipedia with practical purpose.

Then imagine me scrawling across a patchy-coloured blackboard, in pink chalk 'cos I can't seem to locate the cooler green one, this simple question: What is the oldest novel in the world?

If you're automatically toeing the Anglo-Saxon belletristic line (a lot of us here are native English speakers, so you'll be forgiven), you may end up clutching at a name like Shakespeare. Hopefully you suspect his is the possible name of an author, not a novel or a fictitious romantic lead, but you'd be backing the wrong horse, anyway. He's too new — by almost by half a millennium.

Know the original, anonymous source material for Robert Zemeckis's motion-capture action movie, *Beowulf*, which hit screens in 2007? Think that's a contender? Well, it's timely enough — put down on parchment at some stage between the 8th and 11th centuries — but it's a poem, hardly a novel, and if the original inscription does fall into the 11th century, then it's too late anyway.

And while the earliest contestants for "prenatal novel" bounce between *Satyricon*, possibly written by Gaius Petronius in the 1st century AD, *Daphnis and Chloe*, written by Longus in the 2nd century, and a couple of other novels hacked together in archaic Greek and Latin tongues around the same period, these in no way relate to the modern "classic" novel, with more emphasis on character psychology — which is where *Genji Monogatari* (*The Tale of Genji*) slinks in.

Composed by a noblewoman at the Japanese imperial court — Shikibu Murasaki — in the early 11th century, the vast opus has been anointed the first psychological novel, as well as the first full-length novel still to be considered a classic — although some cranky people decry the honorary status, and whether or not Murasaki wrote all 54 chapters.

It's something most of us can relate to on some level.

Armchair critics continue to insist that the real writer of 16th-century Britain's best-known plays may not in fact have been John and Mary Shakespeare's wee tacker, Howard Hawks never owned up to his directorial work on *The Thing from Another World*, and only recently was the mystery surrounding the "real" version of Ridley Scott's *Blade Runner* explained away.

Last year [2008], November 1 was proclaimed Classics Day in Japan, at a ceremony in Kyoto — attended by the Emperor, his wife, and 2,400 other, lesser VIPs — that was held to mark the millennium of the *Tale of Genji*. At least, they were celebrating 1,000 years since Murasaki first mentioned the story in her diary, on an otherwise dull day's activities, on Nov. 1, 1008.

We have to wait another 12 years before we can celebrate the millennial end of the story, which is supposed to have been finished in 1021. Like the great Gothic cathedrals of Europe, this yarn took over a decade to complete, but the ink was dry 45 years before the Normans invaded England, "Harold Rex interfectus est", arrow through the eye, and all.

Yuki Shibamoto, the 25-year-old daughter of regular NHK actress Kyoko Maya, and herself a star of the new Toho movie, *Watashi wa Kani ni Naritai* (*I Want to Be a Shellfish*), was selected as the Genji millennium's poster girl, and made a big speech at the Kyoto bash, garbed in contemporary wear snatched straight out of the Heian period — the era in which Murasaki cosied up to court.

Picking Shibamoto was a canny decision, with respect to Murakami's title character, Hikaru Genji.

While he might be the devilishly handsome son of an emperor, for political reasons — namely that his mom was a low-ranking concubine — Genji has no hereditary title, and he instead ekes out life as an imperial officer. As the tale unfolds, we quickly come to realize just how much of a womanizing character this guy actually is, tempered with a debonair edge that leaves the womanized swooning.

Unfortunately, the impact isn't always mutual — Genji often finds the dalliances dull — and sometimes said romps are fatal affairs for his partners.

In an iddish twist worthy of Oedipus and Freud, our hero also has a penchant for his dad's new wife (the beautiful, responsive, Lady Fujitsubo), while having to deal with his own cold, haughty spouse, Aoi no Ue.

The *Tale of Genji* is partially a mix of James Bond's bedtime antics, with the costume dramatics of Richard Chamberlain and Yoko Shimada in the mini-series, *Shogun* (1980); a dash of Don Juan histrionics distilled into a Romeo and Juliet potboiler.

There's also kidnap, court intrigue, danger, sexual decline, chronic infidelity, more deaths, and other plot contrivances recently found in dramas on this side of the Pacific, like *The O.C.*

Which makes Genji, even a thousand years later, more than just required reading at grade school. It's prescient, psychological, seat-gripping stuff for people of all ages, instead of just teens.

Take that, Josh Schwartz.

What you'll read next is pretty much self-explanatory in the title.

I put this together while winding up my novel One Hundred Years of Vicissitude, *and dove into the specifics of the March 1945 firebombing.*

I'd done a spot of research in the early days of the novel, in around 2008 — when it was nothing more than a notion — but this was a little too much and I needed to vent.

My very supportive editor Stefan Blitz at Forces Of Geek provided the outlet valve, and this article went online there last year just before the novel was published. Which may explain why it starts out like a promotional leaflet before getting to the point.

I skipped using the pictures here. I don't think they're necessary.

If you've read One Hundred Years of Vicissitude, *you may recognize some of the language and details, since the novel and the article cross-pollinated one another.*

Funnily enough, I copped a little flak after the publication of the novel, along the lines that I went too 'soft' on the Japanese, focused too much on their pain, and didn't pay adequate heed to the Japanese army's heinous crimes in China and elsewhere during World War II.

'Scuse me if I'm wrong, but an atrocity's an atrocity — doesn't matter who the perpetrator might be.

Apocalypse Then: How 300 B-29 Bombers Burned Tokyo

Over the past year or so I've been immersed in the writing of my second novel, this time with the focus on Japan from 1929 on.

One Hundred Years of Vicissitude is a blend of historical novel, surrealism, a mystery and noir; there's fantasy and a wee bit of romance in there as well, and I'm always ready for a hardboiled moment or two.

Included in this mix is an homage to classic Japanese cinema by the likes of Akira Kurosawa, Seijun Suzuki, and Satoshi Kon, along with actors Toshiro Mifune and Meiko Kaji.

There are nods to manga and comicbooks, medieval potboilers, Melbourne, Lewis Carroll, and Osamu Tezuka — along with the only visit to Tokyo by the *Graf Zeppelin*, saké, an eight-headed dragon, the sumo, geisha, James Bond, the Japanese Red Army, and a lot of other wayward stuff people might expect of me.

Also included is a pivotal dramatic tipping point, one that relates to the firebombing of Tokyo in March 1945.

Not long after I first arrived in Japan in 2001, I remember an elderly student, a child in that firebombing of the evening of March 9 and the morning of March 10, 1945. He recounted a story that the Kanda River ran red.

Whether from blood or the reflection of the fires all around, I was too timid to ask.

For the novel I ended up doing a lot of research into that fateful night. After doing so, I abridged several pages to put together a three-page summation. I toyed with this as the prologue for *One Hundred Years of Vicissitude* — but ditched the notion and instead integrated most of the facts and figures into survivor Kohana's diatribes about the event, early on in the story.

Coincidentally, I was writing up the fictional account here in Tokyo this past March, around the same time as the sixty-seventh anniversary of the aerial strike — though I was too immersed in the yarn to notice.

If you're squeamish, you may want to bounce out now, in light of one of the final pictures here, which shows the aftermath of the March 9/10 bombardment.

Disclaimers out of the way, let's start with the B-29.

You might recall the one from the opening credits of the *Watchmen* film, emblazoned with "Miss Jupiter".

The American B-29 bomber had every right to call itself a 'Superfortress', since the contraption was a flying stronghold.

This was the largest aircraft inducted during World War II, a four-engine beauty flaunting a dozen 50-calibre M2 heavy machine guns mounted in five turrets, and one 20-millimetre cannon in its backside. All that was missing was a catapult.

While the plane's length doesn't ring so impressive — 99 feet, or just over 30 metres — the wingspan was 141 feet (43 metres) and it had an area of 1,736 square feet.

The bugger weighed in at 33,600 kilograms, prior to cramming in its particularly lethal payload.

The B-29 pushed the throttle to 357 miles per hour and it had a flight ceiling of 12 kilometres, making it practically immune to ground-based anti-aircraft fire and enemy fighter planes such as the Mitsubishi A6M Zero — which flew slower and lower.

I don't know how you feel, but all these facts and figures bamboozle me. In a nutshell, this was a huge thing that was well-armed, flew higher and faster than anyone else, and carried a lot of bombs.

"The success of the development of the B-29 is an outstanding example of the technical leadership and resourcefulness which is the American way of doing things," U.S. Major General Curtis LeMay wrote in the foreword to the airplane's Combat Crew Manual, which also includes Disney-like cartoons and useful tidbits like what to do in case of snakebite.

What the Combat Crew Manual did not discuss were the recurring engine problems and the crash in 1943 of the plane's second prototype, killing its 11-man crew and 20 civilians as it narrowly avoided Seattle skyscrapers, finally hitting a meat-packing plant on the ground.

The B-29 also acted as a high-flying postman, dropping propaganda leaflets that said things like "America is not fighting the Japanese people but is fighting the military clique which has enslaved the Japanese people," alongside images of Japanese soldiers shoving civilians over a cliff.

There were also happy-snaps of Japanese cities with the shadow of a B-29 looming across.

Each Superfortress was crewed by eleven men, who typically tagged the forward fuselage with a kitsch painting of a half-naked pin-up girl, along with monikers like 'Dauntless Dotty', 'Fertile Myrtle' and 'Jughound Jalopy'.

However, unlike its successor the B-52, the B-29 never inspired a hairdo.

Perhaps barbers remembered this was the same aircraft that did a fly-by in Hiroshima and Nagasaki, gifting each city respectively with atomic bombs named 'Little Boy' and 'Fat Man'.

After hostilities ceased, the B-29 was reverse-engineered by the Soviets (from crash-landed aircraft that had been interned during the war) to create the Tupolev Tu-4, and the first aircraft to break the sound barrier, the rocket-powered Bell X-1 piloted by the legendary Chuck Yeager, was launched from the bomb bay of a modified B-29.

The 334 B-29s that flew over Tokyo from the evening of March 9th through to the early hours of March 10th, 1945, were also a break from the mould.

For this lower-altitude raid, dubbed Operation Meetinghouse, they had much of their defensive armament removed so as to be able to carry more fuel and greater bomb loads.

"You're going to deliver the biggest firecracker the Japanese have ever seen," U.S. Major General Curtis LeMay reportedly told his crews beforehand.

He was spot on. They didn't come together, like the Valkyrie swooping to select the dead on some Norse battlefield. The bombers came in waves of three planes every minute, 334 Superfortresses powered by 1,336 twin-row turbocharged radial pistol R-3350 Duplex-Cyclone engines (manufactured by a company originally founded by aviation pioneers Orville and Wilbur Wright).

They flew in staggered formation from as low as five thousand feet.

Tokyo's residents, who had become accustomed to nightly visitations by the B-29s, paid little attention to the warning sirens.

The aircraft had 2,000 tons of incendiary explosive — a hotchpotch of white phosphorus and napalm, the new jellied gasoline mixture concocted from a Harvard University recipe of oleic acid, naphthenic acid derived from crude oil, palmitic acid derived from coconut oil, and aviation fuel — neatly tucked away in their bellies.

This luggage they dropped on a city with a wartime population of about five million.

The M-69 cluster bombs, nicknamed 'Tokyo Calling Cards', sprayed napalm over a 100-foot area before or after landing, and then exploded; sending flames rampaging through densely packed wooden homes. Asphalt boiled in the 1,800-degree heat; super-heated flames air sucked people into the flames. U.S. aircraft returned to their bases with blistered paint underneath. The fires could be viewed 150 miles away.

Operation Meetinghouse was the most devastating air raid in history.

Two percent of Tokyo's residents, between 80,000 and 130,000 people, most of them civilians, perished. The lucky ones died quickly in the initial explosions of TNT charges; others would be burned or boiled alive. 25 percent of the city — 267,000 mostly wood-and-paper buildings in the downtown Shitamachi quarter — was destroyed.

Tsukiji Fish Market (these days one of Tokyo's most popular tourist attractions) and Kanda Market were swallowed up in the conflagration.

One million people were made instantly homeless.

"We scorched and boiled and baked to death more people in Tokyo on that night, 9-10 March, than went up in vapour at Hiroshima and Nagasaki combined," LeMay later boasted.

More people died in one night than the combined military fatalities in the Vietnam War for the U.S., Australia, New Zealand and South Korea.

There were casualties amidst the raiders.

About 42 of the bombers were damaged, 14 B-29s crashed, and two hundred and forty-three U.S. airmen were lost.

While some planes were shredded by flak, several had non-combat related technical problems and one aircraft was struck by lightning. A significant number of B-29 losses were due to vortex updrafts from the fires that tore the wings off one bomber.

A B-29 nicknamed 'Tall In The Saddle' crashed in Ibaraki, killing nine crewmembers. One of the three survivors was executed by the military police and the other two, interned to Tokyo's military prison, burned to death in an air raid by another 464 B-29s on May 25.

After seeing action in the Korean War, the B-29 was retired off in 1960 and replaced by the Boeing B-52 Stratofortress — a plane perhaps better known because of the hairstyle, a cocktail (combining Kahlúa, Baileys Irish Cream, and Grand Marnier), and the band.

On December 7, 1964, the Japanese government conferred the First Order of Merit with the Grand Cordon of the Rising Sun upon General Curtis LeMay — who had by then turned his bombing attention on Vietnam, suggesting the use of nuclear weapons and declaring, "We're going to bomb them back into the Stone Age."

It was no accident that the gung-ho character of General Buck Turgidson, played by actor George C. Scott in Stanley Kubrick's biting satire *Dr. Strangelove* (1964), was based on LeMay.

Time to leap back from the abyss, or at least the heavy-handed content of the last article, and go somewhat lightweight here.

I'm not often a fan of my own articles — sometimes I dig particular parts, and I'm always proud to see them in print, depending on layout — but I start nitpicking straight after they weasel off the press.

This one, however, still reads okay to me five years after it was published in Geek *magazine in the U.S. I ended up nicking a chunk of it to include in* Tobacco-Stained Mountain Goat, *though* F Troop *was left on the cutting-room floor.*

Obon a Go Go

Compulsorily celebrated in mid-August in most regions of Japan, Obon week is one of the country's three major holiday seasons — which plays havoc with domestic and international travel, and raises the prospect of completely booked-out accommodation or outrageously stiff hotel rates.

On top of these, business itself comes to a virtual standstill — as much as this is possible in an über-metropolis like Tokyo. Most shops, banks, ATMs and stores are closed for the duration of the week, during which employees, and obviously the artificially-intelligent types that run the ATMs, are coerced by their bosses to take mandatory vacation (or leave-without-pay), all in observance of this thing called Obon.

So what's all the big fuss about, anyway?

While Obon is *the* annual Buddhist event in which to commemorate and memorialize one's ancestors, it's also believed that the freewheeling spirits of these dearly departed return to this world in order to visit their relatives. And — you guessed right — it all happens round Obon week.

So the festival has shaped-up as an significant traditional custom in Japan, as well as a bit of a late-summer cleaning fiesta: people from the big cities return to their home towns to visit and clean their old folks' graves, then scrub their own places too.

Colourful paper lanterns are propped up in front of houses to guide the ancestors' spirits home (just in case they've forgotten), there's a swag of ceremonial food and saké on offer, and Japanese rediscover of modicum of religiosity.

But the big deal and the biggest fun at Obon time are the oh-so-special evening dance-offs, dubbed *bon odori*.

Kids and their grandparents don summer kimonos (*yukata*), and as the bon odori music plays, they perform a dance routine that is, in some respects, choreographed the same way throughout Japan.

There are specific moves that I like to call "The Shoveler" and "Vogue", but these get lost in the (written) translation here.

The typical bon odori dance involves people lining up around a high wooden building made especially for the festival, called a *yagura*, which doubles as a bandstand for the musicians, taiko drummers, and guest crooners. It also bears an unnerving resemblance to the ever-collapsing watchtower in '60s U.S. sitcom, *F Troop*.

Some dancers proceed clockwise, and some dancers sidle counter-clockwise around the yagura, depending upon the particular festival, but never the twain shall meet.

Amidst the traditional soundtrack is inserted a bunch of *enka* classics and famous anime TV tunes, like those for *Doraemon* and *Pokémon*—and grandmas are just as likely to bop away at these, with adept panache, as their whippersnapper descendants.

Somewhat creepily, it's also a widely held belief that those spirits of deceased loved ones are jigging in step at the same time.

There are even more traditions and customs to round out this one-week extravaganza — kids who've caught goldfish at carnival booths are often subsequently heard shrieking as ghost stories are told, Buddhist shrines are decorated in outrageous new ways, processions of people march in the streets, and fireworks fill the sky. You'd swear you can even smell brimstone — but it's probably just gunpowder.

At the tail-end of Obon, floating lanterns are lobbed into rivers, lakes and seas in order to guide the spirits back into their world, perhaps so they can choreograph new heavenly dance moves for next year's event.

This piece was published via Australian cinema-oriented magazine Filmink *in 2010 as put of a twin-article effort to correspond with the centennial of the birth of famed Japanese writer/director Akira Kurosawa.*

You know Kurosawa, right?

If not, you should. In Tokyo 103 years ago — on March 23, 1910, to be pedantic about it — Akira Kurosawa was born the youngest of eight kids to middle-aged, middle-class former samurai stock. He lived to see his 88th birthday, made 30 films over 50 years, most of those productions are essential viewing for even the most half-hearted of movie buffs, and when you talk Kurosawa you really need to flaunt a thesaurus.

Close this book and go grab one or two of the following: Yojimbo, Drunken Angel, Seven Samurai, The Hidden Fortress, Stray Dog, Kagemusha, Ran, The Bad Sleep Well, Rashomon, Sanjuro, High and Low, The Quiet Duel.

Rashomon *(1950) scored the Venice Film Festival Grand Prize and an Academy Award for Honorary Foreign Language Film in 1951, while* Seven Samurai *won the Silver Lion at the Venice Film Festival in 1954; he was nominated for Best Director at the Oscars for* Ran *31 years later, and then treated to the lifetime achievement Academy Award in 1990.*

Given I'm a huge fan of Kurosawa and his favourite actor (Toshiro Mifune) the slant here is obvious.

But I haven't put in the larger piece I did on Kurosawa, as this included quotes and opinions from various film-makers and Japanese creative types, and I haven't been able to get permission to reprint the story in this tome — so let's stick with the Mifune rap.

These men have had an incredible working bond and both heavily influenced my fiction. But if you still haven't checked out any of the movies mentioned, I recommend doing so.

Pronto, like.

Toshiro Mifune: Sexy Beast

1984 might've been the year that the Macintosh was introduced, *Terms of Endearment* won the Oscar for Best Picture, and Australia swapped national anthems (finally ditching 'God Save the Queen'), but it was also the year that a major Japanese magazine conducted a national poll; when the results were in the actor Toshiro Mifune, at age 64, was declared the winner of the 'Most-Japanese Man' competition — singled out from all Japanese males, past and present, over the nation's known history.

This is no minor feat when you fathom that the Japanese trace their recorded history back two millennia.

Mifune was prolific in the acting industry long before attempting English language roles in Steven Spielberg's *1941* or the TV miniseries *Shogun*.

His filmography at imdb.com tips the 180 mark, over a hundred of which were produced prior to his turn as Lee Marvin's violent Man Friday in *Hell in the Pacific* (1968); the list stretches from his first film in 1947 through to the his death at age 77, fifty years later.

It's no accident that Akira Kurosawa, the writer/director with whom Mifune did his superior work, orchestrated most of these Japanese films. By the time the rest of the world cottoned on to the actor, he and Kurosawa were estranged, having made their last film together in 1965 after a partnership that lasted almost two decades.

There's his well-meaning rookie cop, eerily akin to a young Gregory Peck, who loses his gun on public transport in *Stray Dog* (1949); the ailing yakuza gangster in *Drunken Angel* the year before; a brash samurai charlatan in *Seven Samurai* (1954); his hyperactive, paranoid dynamo in the *Macbeth*-as-*jidaigeki*-drama, *Throne of Blood* (1957); the bespectacled salaryman with the slow-burning vendetta in *The Bad Sleep Well* (1960).

Perhaps the most memorable and famous of Toshiro's roles is the blasé, mysterious stranger in *Yojimbo* (1961) and its sequel *Sanjuro* the following year — himself the role model for both Clint Eastwood's and Bruce Willis's Man with No Name characters in *A Fistful of Dollars* and *Last Man Standing*.

The stand-out collaboration is debatable, but if you want to angle things in Mifune's corner, toward the movie in which he rattles bones most as the sexy beast/enfant terrible of old-school Japanese cinema, you're going to have to settle on 1958, when the actor was 38 and at the height of his stagecraft.

Star Wars aficionados interested in finding out the source material for Episode IV are duty-bound to investigate a B&W movie made that year by Kurosawa in the widescreen Tohoscope format, starring Mifune, and originally released in Japan in December — because *The Hidden Fortress* has most of the key elements of a plot used 19 years later when the first *Star Wars* movie was released.

But in truth it's Toshiro Mifune, above and beyond the superior script and direction, who shines.

Cast in the principle role of General Rokurota Makabe, the actor's turn here sparked the whole 'sexy thing' reference in the somewhat dubious headline for this article — and without doubt contributed to his man's man award in 1984.

As a samurai, General Makabe is perhaps the scariest, most fearless and honourable man alive — as well as one of the more charismatic and inspiring. He's got that rousing leader quality, the sort Russell Crowe delivered in *Gladiator*, Edward James Olmos brandishes on *Battlestar Galactica*, and King Hal throws about in the pages of Shakespeare's *Henry V*.

It's also the kind you just didn't get at all from Orlando Bloom in *Kingdom Of Heaven*.

Think effortlessly debonair, man-of-action panache, and gravelly speeches that'd embolden even an inert, pen-pushing sloth like myself to pull myself to my knees, yell a bit, shake a blunt spear about in the air, and cheerfully follow both his magnetic persona and/or twinkling eyes into battle — at least some of the way, before diving for cover.

You just know that Makabe is like Lieutenant Colonel Kilgore in *Apocalypse Now*, and he'll never actually cop an injury at all. The guy wears serious bravery on his sleeve, and acts like it's a regular wristwatch.

Most of all, though, while the steely scowl and the gruff baritone are the hallmarks of any encounter with Mifune in the reels of *The Hidden Fortress*, there's also a barely repressed machismo that hovers there as he strokes his chin in thought, seemingly not amused or divorced from the events that transpire around him — then throws back his head with riotous laughter, more than a little bit mad.

Each facet is a thrilling moment that keeps your eyes glued on this fascinating, sexy beast of a man and his scene-chewing performance.

The next article was written at the end of 2011 for recently revived Geek *mag over in the 'States, and I plagiarized some of it to shoe-in to* One Hundred Years of Vicissitude.

Not just the Bond references and the saké, but the Toyota 2000GT convertible (Kohana's car), piranha, sumo, and the 48th printing of Instant Japanese: A Pocketful of Useful Phrases.

I also nicked the Siamese vodka earlier on for inclusion in Tobacco-Stained Mountain Goat.

The article for Geek *was introduced with the following disclaimer/fill-in paragraph at the beginning:*

"The Bond movie *You Only Live Twice* turns forty-five this year [2012], and to celebrate JapaneseCultureGoNow!'s Tokyo-based correspondent Andrez Bergen has turned its sights on the arguable classic to answer a slew of innocuous questions. For starters, is it one of the best 007 movies, or in bed with the worst? Does it stand up to contemporary senses as well as it did in 1967? And what exactly is the correct temperature for saké?"

007 Dies Twice

Let me confess to you here and now that the 1966-67 production of *You Only Live Twice* is my favorite James Bond film, and it wasn't just the title-sequence that snagged me.

I'm subjective about it, of course.

I first saw the movie on the telly back in Melbourne (Australia) when I was in primary school, and I'm fairly certain it was my first James Bond film — although quite possibly *Dr. No* or *The Man With the Golden Gun* preceded it. This was definitely one of my first doses of 'Japan', alongside the TV series *The Samurai* — which was oddly successful in Australia from the 1960s on.

You Only Live Twice and *The Samurai* provided me with a rather skewed idea of Japan and are one of the subliminal reasons I moved to this country ten years ago.

While *You Only Live Twice* tends to be mauled by disgruntled critics trying to build on their largesse, I love so much about this film. It slightly pips *Goldfinger*, another classic, and rides roughshod over all the Roger Moore outings.

Even though he later said that the original novel was "Ian Fleming's worst book, with no plot in it which would even make a movie," Roald Dahl (*Charlie and the Chocolate Factory*) worked on the screenplay and Lewis Gilbert (*Sink the Bismarck!*) directed. There's a thoroughly rousing score (by the late, great John Barry of course, with Nancy Sinatra — Frank's daughter — doing the vocal work-out in one of the series' most memorable songs), and Little Nellie remains one of Bond's most quaintly unprepossessing technological contraptions.

Here we had spy intrigue at the height of the Cold War (ahhh, nostalgia), with the evil organization that is SPECTRE fuelling fiction between the United States and the Soviet Union, while Her Majesty's Government tries to run interference to stop matters blowing out into World War III. There are space capsules aplenty, a gaping-jawed UFO, a rousing helicopter battle, and James Bond is 'murdered' (in bed with a femme fatale, of course) at the beginning of the flick.

On top of this, much of the movie was set and filmed in 1960s Japan, so we get often hilarious doses of sumo, women, *nihonshu* (saké), a Shinto wedding, exotic pearl divers, devious salarymen, Bond's counterfeit Oriental makeover, and the clumsy ninja at a training school located slap-bang next to the spectacular World Heritage-classified Himeji Castle.

Siamese vodka and piranha are also shoe-ins.

It's a treat to see Connery wander through 1960s Shibuya, visit a sumo bout at the real Kuramae Kokugikan, since closed and replaced by a bigger sumo stadium in Ryugoku. We also get to indulge in one of the series' best, and more amusing, one-on-one fisticuffs inside the offices of Osato Chemicals — a cover organization for SPECTRE.

Osato Chemicals was set inside the real life Hotel New Otani, a ten-acre oasis in Chiyoda, here in Tokyo, that used to be the private garden of a 17th-century lord but was reinvented as a hotel in 1964 to coincide with the Tokyo Olympics.

Straight after visiting Mr. Osato's office, Bond exits via the main entrance and is almost murdered by a carload of hired gunsels before being rescued by the cool Japanese agent Aki (Akiko Wakabayashi, from *King Kong vs. Godzilla*) and they dash off together in her sleek Toyota 2000GT convertible.

The hotel's extensive, gorgeous gardens were also used in some of the ninja training scenes in the film.

Other parts of *You Only Live Twice* were filmed outside Tokyo — in or near places like Kyushu and Miyazaki — as well as Spain, the Bahamas, and back in England.

But here in Tokyo Bond took an *onsen* (hot spring), a massage by scantily-clad young women, chased skirt, then was escorted down to Tiger Tanaka's private transportation hub — cue personal train — at Nakano-Shimbashi Station, not far from Shinjuku on the Marunouchi Line.

Ernst Blofeld's hideaway volcano set (erected not in Japan, but at Pinewood Studios back in the UK) and the Tinkertoy rockets are downright superb, especially for someone who grew up on *Godzilla* and *Thunderbirds* — which also happened to be a hit in Japan.

The set was also obviously a huge influence on Mike Myers for both Doctor Evil's appearance and that of his base of operations in the Austin Powers romps.

So what if I later learned that James fired blanks in his declaration that the correct temperature for saké is 98.4 degrees Fahrenheit (it's only one of many appropriate temperatures) or that his casual afternoon drive to Kobe, with ill-fated flame Aki, is actually a five-hour ride?

I had a minor crush on the other Bond girl in the picture Mie Hama, as Kissy Suzuki — Bond's sham ring-in bride later on in the yarn — and to this day remain mesmerized by the vocal cords of Tetsuro Tamba (Tiger Tanaka), though I've since learned that most of Tiger's lines in English were dubbed in by another actor, Robert Rietty.

Oh yeah, and this nifty flick has the "Welcome to Japan, Mr. Bond" line itself that I've appropriated and delivered to mates at Narita Airport on countless occasions... with far less panache than Charles Gray or Tamba/Rietty.

You Only Live Twice is also the reason that the month I arrived in Japan I promptly purchased the 48th printing of *Instant Japanese: A Pocketful of Useful Phrases*, first published in 1964, by Masahiro Watanabe and Kei Nagashima.

It's collected dust since but looks cool on the shelf, even if I'm the only one who makes the connection to that silly Moneypenny moment early on in the film.

Along with Akira Kurosawa, Mamoru Oshii, Kinji Fukusaku and Satoshi Kon, Seijun Suzuki would rate in my top five of Japanese movie directors. I love the guy, and use present tense since — as I write these words — Suzuki's still alive at age 90.

Yep, he's another one who's had significant impact not only on how I perceive cinema, but how I write fiction and the scene transitions in same.

In fact the reappearance of the gangster Katsudo Shashin, in Chapter 30 of One Hundred Years of Vicissitude, *is a direct reference to Suzuki's* A Tattooed Life.

This long-winded homage was written for Impact *magazine in 2011.*

Seijun Suzuki, Branded to Thrill

If there were a dictionary of Japanese filmmakers, the entry for Seijun Suzuki would read something like this:

Suzuki, Seijun *(Japanese filmmaker, born Seitaro Suzuki, 1923). Has a penchant for the surreal, the bizarre, odd lighting and set designs, and an irreverent sense of humour. Directed* Tattooed Life, Tokyo Drifter, Branded to Kill, *and the musical* Princess Raccoon. *Better known in Japan as an actor; just celebrated his 88th birthday.*

Tragically, a hefty percentage of the Japanese population — even part-time film buffs I know — aren't aware of the guy's directing chops. When I mention Suzuki's name and his originative movies from the '60s, the most people offer up is usually just a blank expression.

Possibly this has to do with just how alien his concepts were to an emerging Japan twenty years after World War II, and the fact that he was blacklisted by the studio system in this country for 10 years.

In the 1960s Suzuki's studio Nikkatsu, a purveyor of youth-oriented flicks and film noir, tried to defang the director's flights of fancy. While he focused on the subject-matter of yakuza gangsters — a turn-off for most women — Suzuki's offbeat, somewhat bizarre eccentricities even now seem to sit well only with leftfield Japanese audiences who enjoy the latter likes of Shinya Tsukamoto (*Tetsuo, the Iron Man*).

Which means it appears that a grand total of very few people in this country know and appreciate the man's directorial efforts. And actually it's pretty much the same outside Japan — throw about monikers like Akira Kurosawa and Yasujiro Ozu at posh dinner parties and you'll win friends. Mention Seijun Suzuki and you'll likely get a shrug and a follow-through cold shoulder.

To be honest, I find this unawareness just plain sad — not that I found it easy to discover him myself. It's been only five years since I first viewed one of Suzuki's movies. I knew of the man's most famous flick, *Tokyo Drifter*, but hadn't had the chance (or, honestly, incentive) to see it; when I received a promo copy of *A Tattooed Life*, I had a couple of hours to kill so copped a viewing of that instead.

And was smitten — so much that Suzuki rates an homage in my novel *Tobacco-Stained Mountain Goat* (on page 12, in case anyone has a spare copy lying about. Ahem).

What snagged my senses wasn't so much the underlying premise of on-the-lam yakuza gangster 'Silver Fox' Tetsu who hides out with his artist brother in a small town, doing labour work. It wasn't even the tale of intrigue, revenge and love.

What I loved about *A Tattooed Life* (*Irezumi Ichidai*, 1965) was its twist two thirds of the way through, when it went from Dorothy in dull, monochrome Kansas to vibrant, Technicolor Oz; the lighting, colour composition and set designs change from the straight-and-narrow to those bordering on madness — and, instead of ruby slippers, our hero Tetsu whips out a katana sword and hacks his way home.

It's like two completely different movies compressed into one, both fighting for control, but the madcap surrealist venture wins the debate hands down.

By contrast *Tokyo Drifter* (*Tokyo Nagaremono*, 1966) is all about style.

The title reeks the tone, 1960s Tokyo drips the stuff, and the central protagonist exudes it in spades.

Ostensibly the story of Tetsu, aka the Phoenix — a yakuza hit man trying to go straight — we together traverse his escapades while pursued by nemesis-type Tatsuzo (the Viper); also brushing up against our hero, and thereby us, are a swag of conflicted personalities tethered to tangents of betrayal, suicide and love.

There's certainly death and mayhem here, as sometimes an entire room full of people is laid to waste, and the lead is played by Tetsuya Watari — later a veteran of Kinji Fukusaku's '70s yakuza offerings like *Graveyard of Honour*.

But what's really at play is Suzuki's canny appreciation of interior shots, a striking use of the colour palette, and innovative lighting — which border on the surreal and take the viewer into a terrain way, way out there. His shot of a large room that swings wildly from black (with a splash of scarlet) to snow white with alabaster pianos, is something British director Peter Greenaway would toy with 23 years later in *The Cook, the Thief, His Wife & Her Lover*.

The following year the director unleashed *Branded to Kill* (*Koroshi no Rakuin*, 1967) starring regular Suzuki player Joe Shishido as contract killer Goro and Annu Mari as Suzuki's most memorable *femme fatale* Misako, who dreams of death.

Apparently edited in just one day, Suzuki riotously mixes satire with the surreal, offbeat with the abstruse. Our hero sniffs boiling rice to get his erotic kicks, there are bulletproof belts and headbands, Misako's interior decorating bent involves dead butterflies, and one assassination involves camouflage within an animatronic cigarette lighter.

On top of this there's bizarre cartoon imagery in certain scenes, and a gloriously eclectic sound score by Naozumi Yamamoto, who — oddly enough — also did soundtracks for the homogenized *Tora-san* movies.

Influences seem plucked from things as diverse as kabuki theatre and the Sean Connery James Bond films, pop artists like Roy Lichtenstein, and with a heavy nod (or three) in the direction of film noir, gothic cinema, and Japanese New Wave.

Gloriously violent, revelling in a theme that later directors like John Woo and Takashi Miike would extend upon, it's since shaped up as a cult favourite regularly cited by the likes of Woo, Quentin Tarantino, Wong Kar-wai and Jim Jarmusch.

The movie proved pivotal in other ways as well — after the film fizzed at the box office and he was fired, Seijun Suzuki sued the studio, Nikkatsu, in a legal battle that took more than three years; in return he was blacklisted for a decade at the height of his filmmaking prowess.

Just in case you were wondering, the director's enforced vacation from cinematic excess didn't faze him upon his return to the clapboard.

Although obviously older, he's been chameleon-like in the years following on from his heyday in the '60s, yet no less essential. At one stage Suzuki even ventured into anime — helming one of the movies in the long-running Lupin III franchise, *Lupin III: Legend of the Gold of Babylon* (1985).

Other nuggets include *Pistol Opera* (2001), which is either (a) a femme fatale remake of or (b) a sequel to *Branded to Kill*, and the disarming musical romp *Princess Raccoon* (*Operetta Tanuki Goten*, 2005), which featured Ziyi Zhang, Joe Odagiri (*Azumi*) and Taro Yamamoto — better known as the mysterious transfer student Kawada in *Battle Royale* (2000).

I also like to write about music — having started my hack journalism career reviewing and waxing critical about electronica in Melbourne at a local street press publication called Zebra, *along with* 3D World *in Sydney and* Onion *in Adelaide.*

Most of the older articles were tossed out, burned or stored away in boxes now ridden with snails when I left Australia in 2001, but I've continued to keep on top of the trick, occasionally for local English language magazine Metropolis *here in Tokyo.*

I hope the next two tiny articles, pushed through that outlet in 2009-10, give you a marginally better understanding of the depth and breadth of Japanese music, and in fact Sayuri Ishikawa makes a guest appearance (hummed by Kohana) in One Hundred Years of Vicissitude.

'Fuyu' (winter) is Floyd's tattoo in Tobacco-Stained Mountain Goat, *and mine.*

Yamataka Eye from Boredoms

With scraggly hair awry in most of the press-shots I've glimpsed, Tetsuro Yamatsuka's not the best candidate to hustle home and greet sheltered parents.

Yet while appearances-wise this 47-year-old is nowhere near Keith Flint from The Prodigy, he's in fact far more raucous. Yamatsuka may have a predilection toward changing his DJ and production names but he's best known as Yamataka Eye, and as such a member of Boredom — one of the greatest noise rock bands from Japan, a country equally renowned for Melt-Banana and Merzbow.

Formed between 1982-86 and likely inspired by The Birthday Party and Einstürzende Neubauten, Boredoms have wildly rotated their membership while keeping Yamatsuka in the role of front man. Known for his atypical vocal workouts and post-production prowess, Yamatsuka was a pivotal player in the band's most enduring album *Pop Tarti* (1993), which still stands strong 18 years on.

Beyond Boredoms, Yamatsuka's also recorded an EP — *TV*

Shit, 1993 — with Sonic Youth, worked with Bill Laswell's band Praxis and John Zorn's Naked City, and released two absolutely brilliant live LPs in 1995 with experimental composer Yoshihide Otomo...under the underplayed alias of MC Hellshit & DJ Carhouse.

Thrown together in disseminated ways Yamatsuka would probably appreciate, he's a rock *kami* unto himself — hair awry and all.

'Tsugaru Kaikyo Fuyugeshiki' by Sayuri Ishikawa

When local kids deride enka, I try to nudge them in the direction of singer Sayuri Ishikawa's classic 1977 outing.

Literally translated as 'Winter View of Tsuguru Straits' (the moniker given to the ocean between Honshu and Hokkaido), this is the '70s and Japan at their best. Mournful and kitsch, grandiose yet poignant, the music here sublimely infuses a funky orchestral backdrop with graceful power vocals by Ishikawa drifting toward Gloria Gaynor.

The song was conjured up by lyricist Yu Aku with composer Takashi Miki (a.k.a. Tadashi Watanabe) who passed away earlier this year [2009] — and was also responsible for the insanely catchy 'Anpanman no Machi' theme song for the kids' anime series *Anpanman*.

The '77 effort, rather than that Anpanman ditty, is the first and only enka number I've actually fallen in love with.

There's *fuyu* (winter) in the title — my favorite season; I have a silly tattoo of the *kanji* to prove it — and as a hack DJ I've dropped this song between techno and hip-hop tunes in clubs as far afield as Beijing and Melbourne…and it's (somehow) worked.

It's also the one song I coerce my Japanese mates to sing at karaoke; they're never quite Ishikawa, of course, and they grimace a bit, but they always give it their best.

Since we're on a musical bender here, I'm going to unveil a soapbox rant I made in 1999, when I was the editor of street press publication Zebra *in Melbourne.*

I found a copy of this on the 'net, so it's one of the few bona fide archival pieces I'm able to include. Yes, it's a pretentious, dictatorial diatribe — but I did my uni thesis on industrial music in Britain in the 1970s, and I remember being annoyed about something.

Problem was I had to squeeze it all up into one printed newspaper page.

I ought to give this a go-through, edit, shake, update and double-check the accuracy, but that wouldn't be honest to the archival nature of the beast...would it?

Besides, I'm a lazy sod and no George Lucas.

From Dada to Disco: a (Brief) History of Electronic Music

Too often lately I've read the simplifications, the blanket statements, the outrageously inaccurate assumptions — that techno was started in Detroit, and that Kraftwerk are the godfathers of electronica.

Sure, both that American city and the German band made vital inroads and helped to steer electronic-based music along a certain course, but the fact is that the foundations had already been laid decades before; a break from traditional instrumentation was engineered by the Dadaists as far back as 1916 and over the years since there's been an undercurrent determined to push the perimeters of sound iconoclasm and to invent new means through which to generate these sounds themselves.

So there's always been an inexplicable link between electronic and experimental music, but the problem remains: how far back can we trace the ancestry of the machine-based sounds we take for granted towards the end of the 20th century?

Let's flashback here to the First World War, to Zurich in 1916, where a fledgling artistic group who got together at the Cabaret Voltaire formulated an ideal called 'Dada' to identify their activities; the movement's spirit was best captured by Andre Breton who declared that "Dada is a state of mind... Dada is artistic free-thinking."

As such, the Dadaists set about turning 'normal' artistic conventions on their head and severed links with traditional concepts of art, including music, in order to create new and often anarchic forms. During the early 1920s in the USSR physicist Lev Sergeyevich Termen — a.k.a. Léon Theremin — developed the synthetic music instrument that became known by his name, and in 1922 performed the world's first 'official' concert of electronic music at the Kremlin before an enthusiastic Lenin. The instrument Theremin developed has been called the first synthesizer — it operated by using electrical fields which were tuned by the changes in distance between an antenna and the performer's hand — but his own life was just as remarkable, reading like a trippy episode of *Melrose Place* intercut with *The Maltese Falcon*.

Over the next 15 years he taught Lenin how to use the instrument, he worked in the same studio with Einstein, and reportedly spied on the Americans while living in New York City; after being abducted by the KGB and returned to his homeland, he spent time exiled in Siberia before returning for 'special duties' and developing the first wireless bug that was installed in the US embassy in Berlin during the Cold War.

The Theremin instrument he originally developed so long ago has continued to be used here in the West, ingratiating itself with its eerie sound effects in B-grade horror and sci-fi films like *Forbidden Planet* (1956) in Hitchcock's *Spellbound* (1945), in television themes for *Doctor Who* and *Dark Shadows*, and in songs like 'Good Vibrations' by the Beach Boys and Led Zeppelin's 'Whole Lotta Love'.

Now rewind three decades.

It's 1939, and the eve of the Second World War. While working with broadcast radio John Cage uses test records of pure frequency tones, which he plays on variable-speed turntables, in his early piece 'Imaginary Landscape No. 1'. In his subsequent effort, titled 'Imaginary Landscape No. 2', Cage pioneers live electronic music by using among his sound sources an amplified coil of wire.

But it was the arrival of the tape recorder, invented in 1935 yet not widely available until 1950, that transformed the practice of working with sounds in the studio.

Tape presented the composer with a flexible, versatile means of recording and storing sounds; of changing them in pitch and rhythm by altering the playback speed, of superimposing them, and of rearranging them in any order. Tape was, in effect, the first sampler.

In 1948 Pierre Schaeffer, a sound technician working for Radiodiffusion Télévision Française, extended earlier work with discs to produce several short studies in what he called 'musique concrète', and here tape came to the forefront. Each of his compositions was based upon sounds from a particular source, such as railway trains or the piano, and the recordings were transformed by playing them at different speeds, forwards or in reverse, isolating fragments and superimposing one sound over another, with the intention to free his material from its native associations.

Concurrently, in Germany, Herbert Eimert established the leading European studio for electronic music in Cologne and was soon joined by Karlheinz Stockhausen. In opposition to the principles of musique concrete, Eimert and Stockhausen set out to create what they called 'Elektronische Musik': music generated exclusively by electronic means, without using natural sources of sound. Stockhausen's 'Studien' (1953-54), for example, was an attempt to mimic the sounds of an existing source, such as a piano, by superimposing the requisite pure frequencies obtained from oscillators, and alternatively by composing entirely new sounds by creating combinations different from those emitted by any natural instrument.

Stockhausen's next venture was one of reconciliation. Composed in 1955-56, his 'Gesang der Jünglinge' (Song of the Youths) sought to bring together Elektronische Musik and musique concrète by combining purely electronic sounds with natural ones — those of a child's singing voice — and the result was a fusion of electronic music with language.

Concurrently in the United States the film industry encouraged the new electronic music medium.

Louis and Bebe Barron had set up a private electronic music studio in New York to provide suitably strange and eerie soundtracks for science fiction films like *Forbidden Planet*, and it was in this studio that John Cage composed his 'Williams Mix' (1952) — a collage of all kinds of material, from purely electronic sounds to pre-existing music; from amplified "small sounds" (Cage's own term for the barely audible) to city noises.

From 1948 to 1954, therefore, the technical and aesthetic foundations of electronic music had been firmly established. In particular the advancing technology and experiments by people such as Cage, Schaeffer and Stockhausen had opened up four new approaches to musical composition: using natural and machine-made sounds, altering the sounds of traditional musical instruments, creating new sound material, and constructing overlaid collages.

The concept of the collage harks back to the Dadaists, and it was only natural that electronic music coming from the experimental community would have a leaning towards similar theatrics and mixed media orientations.

This collage, or synthesis as it became known, was developed into the 1960s; mostly it was an attempt to bring together diverse styles within a single work, often using references — or samples — of music from the past to bring an ironic accentuation to the modern condition of abundant variety.

It was also the means for some Dada-inspired experiments with sound. The recordings of Cage's 'Variations IV' (1964) includes scraps of sampled music and speeches of different kinds, all willingly admitted in a free-for-all montage. Cage himself declared that the work was his own personification of the fact that "Nowadays everything happens at once." Yet in spite of the technological and artistic advances of this time, by the first half of the 1960s it was apparent that electronic music had reach limitations.

Stockhausen's 'Kontakte' (Contacts, 1958-60) — which was composed for four-channel tape and generated a whole new world of sound from the simple basic material of electronic pulses — was symptomatic of the restrictions faced. It took two years to complete. Too many hours were necessarily spent in the studio, experimenting by trial and error with equipment never intended for musical composition.

Many of these affected composers and electronic technicians therefore concerned themselves in the search for their own Holy Grail of the time: an effective electronic music synthesizer.

The first such functional instrument was the RCA Synthesizer built by Harry Olsen and Herbert Belar — a gargantuan assembly installed at Columbia University in 1957 and capable of producing and altering a wide variety of sounds — but an invention of far wider significance came in 1964 when Robert Moog constructed the first sound devices responsive to control voltages.

Moog had developed the twin elements of a voltage-control oscillator and a voltage-control amplifier.

Whereas previously it had been necessary for a composer to 'tune' his equipment by hand in order to obtain the desired pitch, volume, and so on, it was now possible for this to be done by electronic signals, thus increasing the speed and precision with which sounds could be created.

This in turn paved the way for the development of an

instrument for sound synthesis, and with the simultaneous miniaturization of electronics and the evolution of modular systems, a synthesizer could finally be produced.

In 1966 synthesizers developed by Moog and Donald Buchla became commercially available, and in 1968 the release of Walter Carlos's *Switched-On Bach* — an album of music by Johann Sebastian Bach performed entirely on a Moog synthesizer — brought the innovation to global public attention. Carlos went on to produce the music for Stanley Kubrick's film *A Clockwork Orange* (1971) which, along with the electronic-inspired soundtrack to Kubrick's other film *2001: A Space Odyssey*, confirmed the synthesizer's place and electronic music in general as an increasingly accessible and relevant medium.

Until the mid '60s, however, electronic music experiments had been confined to the studio; as the decade drew to a close it began its fractious assimilation into popular culture and progressive music styles.

Influenced by Stockhausen's work with his own ensemble on such compositions as 'Kurzwellen' (1968), rock musicians like Frank Zappa, Pink Floyd, the Velvet Underground and the Beatles began to make use of live electronic techniques and more experimental sound nuances, while with their album *Anthem Of The Sun* (1967-68) the Grateful Dead played on the development of electronic rock by drawing on references of musique concrète in between songs.

However, in the first half of the 1970s there was a conscious shift away from the abstraction, discontinuity and non-harmoniousness that hallmarked the 1960s. Assured, often sophisticated techniques of recording, and of integrating electronic music into this process, was the hallmark of British bands Yes, Roxy Music, the Matching Moles and Emerson, Lake & Palmer, yet in general the use of synthesizer was often relegated to instrumental imitation and nothing definitive.

Aside from the more adventurous offerings of Brian Eno and

the German-based dabbling of Tangerine Dream, Neu, Can, and Kraftwerk, music in general had relegated machine-based sounds to a more subservient position.

While punk's arrival in the mid '70s was a subversive way in which to combat the excesses of pomp-rock, there was an equally defining and vital underground that surfaced in Britain under the moniker of "industrial music".

The principle protagonists in this movement were Cabaret Voltaire and Throbbing Gristle, bands as much influenced by Dada and the Beat generation writers as they were by Stockhausen, Schaeffer, Brian Eno, basic sound iconoclasm, the new electronic music technology coming through...and James Brown.

These bands had more in common with Germans Kraftwerk, Can and Karlheinz Stockhausen than they did with anyone else in the UK, but they made an enormous impact upon the emerging 'hip' new British media cartel that included fledgling magazines like *The Face* and *NME*.

What made Cabaret Voltaire unique in their early records — in particular *Mix-Up* (1979) and *The Voice Of America* (1980) — was the manner in which band members Richard H. Kirk, Stephen Mallinder and Chris Watson created unique, sometimes obscure soundscapes and grooves through the use of a collage of effected sound-sources and spliced-up tape loops; for their live shows the band integrated a multi-media approach that included slide-shows and political imagery, for an all-encompassing effect and an often deliberately heavy-handed message.

There was a reason behind this, apart from basic visual aesthetics: in 1983 Mallinder reflected that "People react a lot more immediately to a visual image than to an audio one. Audio can be far more subconscious, more subliminal, but audio doesn't have the immediacy of the sense of sight."

Industrial music as an autonomous artistic *putsch* effectively sputtered to a halt around 1982, and bears very little resemblance to the music style calling itself 'industrial' that emerged later that decade and continues to be flogged like a dead horse.

But the short-lived movement has had a phenomenal impact on the electronic music we take for granted twenty years later. Its impact on young British musicians, artists, designers and music journalists at the time was integral in the development of a better understanding and appreciation of experimental music and underground culture in general; its use of sampling techniques and an untraditional approach to composition, along with the integration of new technology to do so, is a practice that has continued.

You can hear its legacy in the soundscapes of artists like Coldcut, Jeff Mills, DJ Krush, Optical, Little Nobody, Steve Law, Aphex Twin, Black Lung, Atari Teenage Riot and Voiteck.

Many of industrial's principle protagonists also helped to develop techno in its formative stages, and some still continue to make vital contributions.

Although Throbbing Gristle split in 1981, founding member Genesis P-Orridge went on to form Psychic TV just as his cohorts Cosey Fanni Tutti and Peter Christopherson formed Chris & Cosey. Cabaret Voltaire, while still ostensibly together 25 years after they were formed, has seen Richard Kirk join up with Sheffield's Warp label to create some poignant electronic muzak albums and Stephen Mallinder — who now lives in Perth — moonlighting as a member of Sassi & Loco as well as the Ku-ling Brothers.

Ollie Olsen, who was a member of pioneering local synthe-sizer outfit Whirlywirld in the late '70s then worked with exper-imental band Orchestra Of Skin & Bone in the first few years of the 1980s, went on to push the perimeters with No, found pop success with Max Q, and set himself up as one of Melbourne's first purist techno musicians as Third Eye; these days he still produces electronic sounds, he DJs around the traps, and he runs Psy-Harmonics.

So, what exactly is this music we call techno as the new millennium kicks into gear?

It's a hybrid creature, a fusion of influences and interests, ideas and ideals, that has no specific original source; in its time it's drawn upon previous movements such as industrial, hip hop, house, funk, disco, soul, blues, punk, rock, salsa and Dada. It's been influenced not just by the cerebral experimental studio work crafted from the 1940s through to the 1960s, but also by B-grade '50s sci-fi film soundtracks.

Meaningful monologues from *The Twilight Zone* sit comfortably beside news broadcasts appropriated from CNN; inane vocal samples are shaped to become just as pivotal a part of the music as the TB-303 bassline beneath.

Contemporary electronic music is a realm in which culture, politics, history, entertainment, humour and technology can all sit alongside literally hundreds of diverse musical influences jammed together to create the whole; it takes stock from the world we live in and flashbacks to the past in order to create a new and ever-changing futurist entity. It's electronic music that derives its sounds from machines and its ideas from the environment, and it has the potential to restrict itself less than any other musical style in history.

Amen to that.

Occasionally I do get these bees in my wee bonnet (shhh!). At one stage, since I was an electronic muso and music journalist (at the same time) I trumpeted the joys of local indie electronica in Melbourne, along with the vitality of sampling and a sense of humour in music.

I think anyone who's read my writing will have noticed that I sample from myself (and pop culture) just as much there as I do in the music I make under silly aliases like Little Nobody and Funk Gadget. I remember reading that Raymond Chandler did a similar thing, so — while I'm hardly comparing myself to the great man — I can hang onto the coattails of his habits.

Anyway, living in Tokyo over the past 12 years has allowed me to watch the rapidly developing skyline, which is a joy to see — but I do pine for the history that is lost, for the little old weatherboard numbers with the sliding doors that you'll see in post-war domestic flicks by Kurosawa and Ozu.

So I had another soapbox-moment in Geek *magazine in 2009.*

I pinched some of this for one of Floyd's rants in **Tobacco-Stained Mountain Goat.**

Tokyo's Post-Modern Purge

One of my preferred sci-fi flicks from the early '50s is *The Thing from Another World*, with James Arness menacing a crew of American military trapped on an Arctic base.

The direction, while credited to Christian Nyby, smacked more of Howard Hawks's style — and while Hawks is listed in the credits just as a producer, people do have their doubts.

Anyway, my lasting memory of the movie is the final paranoid riposte, "Watch the skies, everywhere! Keep looking. Keep watching the skies!", and the truth is that in Tokyo, you really do always have to look heavenward.

It's a lesson I thought I'd learned after I first arrived in this city and cottoned on that some of the coolest cafes and record shops are tucked away on the sixth or seventh floors of inconsequential skyscrapers.

But I think a recurrent crick in the neck negated Ned Scott's warning in recent years, and my gaze had fallen back to ground-floor level — that is, until I stumbled across an article, in the oft indispensable, Tokyo-based English-language lifestyle magazine, *Metropolis* (metropolis.co.jp), that reported on buildings slated to be condemned in this self-reinventing city of flux.

As it was, I already knew about Minoru Takeyama.

He's one of Japan's more famous architects, a Waseda and Harvard graduate, as well as a professor, author, and innovatory thinker; the man even worked at one stage in the early '60s with Arne Jacobsen, deviser of the seriously pricey Series 7 chair.

Takeyama is best known here for the landmark Ichi-maru-kyu (109) building in Shibuya, erected in the late '70s — but a decade before, in his mid-30s, he'd conjured up a couple of far more iconic towers in Kabukicho, a few minutes' walk from Shinjuku Station, and thereby created some of the earliest examples of Japanese architectural postmodernism.

It's these, rather than the 109, that give Takeyama kudos in architectural circles in the West, and what I didn't know was that I'd passed these buildings by on several occasions, without ever noticing. It wasn't until the *Metropolis* piece that I got the heads-up, realized my error, and started watching the skies again.

Once you do raise your eyes from the garish thrall of the surrounding men's host clubs, you get to see the pop-art colours of 'Nibankan' (Number Two Building, 1970), which looks like Roy Lichtenstein had a hand in the palette, and the monochrome, superbly *Gigantor*-styled 'Ichibankan' (Number One Building, 1969).

Both buildings have, however, seen far better days.

They're now bereft of tenants (Ichibankan completely so) and in disrepair, while the owners — love hotel and business accommodation operators, Sankei Hotel — act suitably indifferent.

One senses Sankei are biding their time, and the buildings themselves are just waiting to be demolished — as is the Nakagin Capsule Tower in Ginza, right near Shinbashi.

A mesmerizing structure that deigns to juggle some 140 boxes (modified containers that vary in size, depending on the source material you check, but around 4 x 2.5 meters), stacked at angles on 14 tottering floors, this was the first "capsule hotel" per se — designed by architect Kisho Kurokawa, and constructed between 1970-72.

Kurokawa had previously helped to found the Japanese Metabolism Movement in 1959, an architectural group equally philosophical in tone, with an eye on technological advances; they envisaged a futurist city whose principle structures would be flexible and encourage an organic growth potential.

10 years later, Kurokawa apparently conceived of the Nakagin Capsule Tower while abiding by the maxim of "metabolism, exchangeability, and recyclability". Truth is, though, that I'm not quite sure what two of these ideas entail, nor how they relate to this rather cool building that's slowly crumbling away due to overt lack of maintenance.

Apparently the designer was into the idea of replacing the capsules where necessary (hence the 'exchangeability', which is the bit I'm blessedly able to nut out), but nobody's ever bothered to follow through, and the structure is now quite visibly on its last legs.

Ironically, while the Nakagin Capsule Tower was originally under construction, Minoru Takeyama was busy setting up the group ArchiteXt (long before the founders of Excite started using the same moniker — sans the big 'X' — for their new-fangled Internet portal in 1994) — to counter the Metabolist ideals that Kurokawa espoused; they instead they cited equally dizzying concepts like contradiction, discontinuity, individualism, and pluralism.

Funnily enough, the fate of both divergent schools of thought seems to have been pretty much the same.

Like Ichibankan and Nibankan, the Nakagin Capsule Tower is overdue for demolition — in this case due to reported fears of use of asbestos in the construction, as well as concerns that it's not an earthquake-proof building.

Coupled with the costs of making structures seismically-sound and attractive to an ageing clientele forever interested in things new, developers in Tokyo place precedence on the wrecking ball rather than on landmark properties that're getting a wee bit long in the tooth.

You get the impression that all three buildings are blocking the path of funkier, newfangled residential crystal palaces — while the government certainly hasn't wasted a lot of time considering notions like artistic architectural heritage and its preservation for future generations.

So, when that mindset takes its natural course, I might as well ditch the sage advice from *The Thing from Another World*, and stop watching those skies after all.

The other thing I've indulged in over the past few years here in Japan has been acting out (literally) as a bit-player and extra in local cinema. I wrote about my first brush with the industry in an article published in Geek *in 2008.*

I Was an MP in Post-WWII Japan*
(*...in a new Japanese movie, anyway)

Ever feel like you've been thrust into a '60s revisionist version of World War II?

Not so much *Catch-22*.

I'm thinking instead of 1965's *The Battle of the Bulge*, helmed by regular Disney director Ken Annakin, starring journeymen soldier actors Henry Fonda and Robert Shaw.

Far be it for me to tart up the battle itself, but I'd like to draw your attention to a subplot in that movie. It was one that related to the real-life, duelling-scar bearing German Waffen-SS commando, Otto Skorzeny, who assembled a unit of English-speaking German soldiers, dressed them up in American and British uniforms and dog tags snatched from corpses and POWs, and operated behind enemy lines (here read our side) to misdirect traffic and generally cause disruptions aplenty.

Operation Greif was nicknamed the Trojan Horse Brigade, as the Allies mistakenly believed Skorzeny & Co. were planning to kidnap or kill their commander, General Dwight D. Eisenhower.

The general was subsequently assigned a lookalike in Paris, while thousands of American MPs were waylaid from more important chores, and put to work instead trying to hunt down Skorzeny's men.

The American MP bit is vaguely ironic, because this February I got tapped on the shoulder to play an extra in a Japanese movie set just after WW2 — as an American MP.

And I'm Australian.

None of the other 12 *gaijin* roped into the movie to play American MPs were from the USA, either. Russian, sure. French, German, Brazilian, British, another Australian. The closest we got was one Canadian.

Which brings me to the *Battle of the Bulge* reference.

Weird as it may have been to see so many people wearing WW2-era American GI and MP uniforms, more surreal was the fact that the majority of these "soldiers" didn't speak English without a heavy accent, and they preferred rattling on in Russian, French and — yes — German between takes.

It was like those phony enemy infiltrators from the Bulge all over again.

Oh yeah, but we each had tags to prove our international flavour. These read "Gaikokujin", which is basically another reference to *gaijin*, or foreigners — as if it wasn't already obvious that we (collectively) stood out on the set like sore thumbs or dismembered left feet, with our white helmets, wooden truncheons, faux M1 Carbines, and menacing scowls.

One of the reasons for these scowls was the cold weather; another the God-awful coffee on offer. A third was the title of the movie itself. It's one that a lot of people here seem to have trouble translating into English: *Watashi wa Kai ni Naritai*. The title has been variously interpreted, but seems to shape up best as *I Want to be a Shellfish*, and is listed on imdb.com under this moniker.

Due for a theatrical release early next year, the movie stars actress Yukie Nakama (*Trick, Shinobi*, and one of the hottest faces

in Japanese advertizing right now), alongside Masahiro Nakai —
a member of domestically famous J-pop band, SMAP.

Unfortunately, in my two days on set doing the MP rounds, I
didn't get to see either of these people, but it was February, a
particularly cold winter, and the shoot was outdoors. No doubt
they were somewhere cushy and warm with their feet up,
laughing at the outtakes.

Instead I got to push and pull heavy prison gates, and
wandered dusty streets with an actress dolled-up as a particularly unattractive prostitute. Going by this movie, all post-war
hookers in Japan were hideous creatures, and American MPs six
decades ago must've had remarkably open taste.

My only aspiration in this wasteland of extras was to ride
about in the white on-set military jeep, which the Brazilian and
the Canadian MPs got to do on both days. Lucky bastards.

They were the escorts for the military bus, on which rode
Nakai's character, Toyomatsu Shimizu, who's been abruptly
arrested as a war criminal following the cessation of hostilities in
World War II, and is now being tried for murder even though he
believes he's not guilty of any wrongdoing.

This story was also made as a TV drama last year, for NTV
(ntv.co.jp/watakai/), starring Shido Nakamura from *Letters from
Iwo Jima* and *Death Note*.

It's based on autobiographical notes by Tetsutaro Kato —
during the war years, reputed to be one of the more brutal
commandants of Niigata 5B POW camp, located 160 miles
northwest of Tokyo — under the pen-name Ikuo Shimura.

During the subsequent occupation, Kato was tried and found
guilty of an array of sordid activities, including beatings which
left some POWs permanently disabled, and was sentenced to
death by hanging for the bayonet execution of an American
prison escapee named Frank Spears.

In 1959, Kato's yarn was adapted into a screenplay, drama-
tized, and directed by Shinobu Hashimoto — a man better known

as the co-writer, with Akira Kurosawa, of *The Seven Samurai* (1954) — and the movie starred Frankie Sakai, of *Ghost Story of Funny Act in Front of Train Station* (1964), and *Mothra* (1961).

The ending was also vamped up to tweak the tragic.

Whereas Kato's sentence was conveniently commuted by Douglas MacArthur, thanks to family connections, and he left Tokyo's Sugamo Prison on good behavior in 1952, the fictional Toyomatsu Shimizu goes all the way to the noose.

Prior to his execution, Shimizu writes a longwinded farewell letter to his wife and son, the gist of which says that if ever he were to be reincarnated, he would hate to come back as a human being, and would prefer instead to be a shellfish living on the bottom of the sea.

Hence the strange title of this affair.

While Kato no doubt had a lot of time on his hands during his initial interment for war crimes, Sugamo Prison was an interesting place for the conjuring up of the original tale.

Built in the '20s to a European blueprint, the prison was located in Ikebukuro in Tokyo, on the site that the 60-storey Sunshine 60 building now stands, erected in the '70s as part of the Sunshine City shopping metropolis.

It's confided that the ghost of wartime Prime Minister, Hideki Tojo — himself an executed Class A war crim — haunts the retailers there, but in amenably Japanese style: after closing time.

So it came as some surprise to find myself dressed in that American MP uniform, standing beneath a huge sign that read "Sugamo Prison", with a big blue back-screen that'll no doubt be used to superimpose the CG ring-in for the prison complex itself.

My VIP job in this all-encompassing human drama? Ceremonial gatekeeper. Sure, I got the helmet, the gun, and the girl. But I also had to drag two huge prison gates open and closed again, open and closed again, ad infinitum, as the director and his extensive crew shot and reshot that white jeep (with the Brazilian and the Canadian) and a military bus driving through, for about eight hours all up.

Even more interesting, it seemed, was that the other gate-keeping sentry doing this manual labour was also an Aussie.

60 years on, Americans are, it seems, too busy for such mundane chores in Japan — as are the British, French, Brazilians, Germans and Russians.

Give the job instead to the newer kids on the block. It's a job that may in fact suit our talents, if you take into account that 220 years ago Australia started out as a penal colony.

Bah; humbug.

In November 2005, our daughter Cocoa was born — hard to believe this was going on eight years ago. What a life-changing experience, clichés be damned. Never looked back. Thank you, C-chan. Simple as that.

This article was written for **VICE** *magazine in the weeks leading up to Cocoa's birth, but some of the VICE-ish changes done thereafter were not so much my cuppa — 'Japanese' changed to 'Japs', and the main title appended with a subber saying 'Being Pregnant in Japan is Weird' — so I removed those things here.*

Gaijin, Baby

There are somewhere in the vicinity of 34 million people living and working in the Greater Tokyo area, of which 691,000 (two percent, according to my rough calculations) are non-Japanese.

About three percent of these *gaijin* freeloaders (i.e. over 20,000) get married to a local and/or have kids.

I know a bit about this because, well, I am one of them. In fact, by the time this article is published I will be the first-time father of a half-Japanese baby girl and it is totally freaking me out. In a good way. I have basically gone, in a really short space of time, from someone who would stop calling friends who had kids to someone who knows tonnes of inane facts about everything to do with miniature humans.

I have also prepared myself for the likelihood that I am probably also going to lose most of my more exciting friends. That's cool though because I'm not really going to have time for them either.

The Japanese have some pretty out-there customs and when it comes to something like having a baby, they turn them on big time. Here's a bit of a diary I've kept of the experience.

Thursday Sept. 1st

According to the Japanese, a pregnancy takes ten months, not the predictable nine cited by the rest of the known world. This is because the Japanese count lunar months instead of calendar months. So, today, at the Japanese nine months, Yoko visited her midwife and found out some pretty disturbing news.

The ultrasound, or "echo" as it's known here, revealed that the baby was the wrong way around. The midwife told her that she was going to have to do upside-down exercises, stick bizarre adhesive incense sticks to various pressure points on her legs, and have her belly tightly bound in a 10-odd-meter cloth called an *iwata-obi* for the rest of the pregnancy which, at the height of a particularly hot Tokyo summer, is pretty heavy.

Thursday Sept. 8th

We found out today that Yoko was also an upside-down baby and that her parents turned a picture of a hen upside down to rectify the problem — which apparently did the trick. As stupid as this sounds and as un-superstitious as we are, we will spend the next couple of days upending everything in our apartment — books, furniture, posters and anything else that we physically can.

One traditional belief states that Japanese women are not allowed to eat any seafood with claws such as crabs or lobsters, as it causes the child to become a thief. Yoko doesn't rate this. Another belief is that pregnant women should clean their toilet daily for a healthy and good-looking baby.

Again, it's totally ridiculous, but imagine if we didn't do it and happened to have an ugly kid. Let's just say Yoko is cleaning the toilet daily.

Thursday Sept. 15th

It's pretty difficult to afford everything associated with having a baby in Japan as the insurance system doesn't seem to cover anything that we actually need. Instead, they pay the mother a "congratulations" fee after the baby is born.

I feel like all I've been doing is working, but I took today off so we started reading a book which detailed all the horrendous things that can happen to babies during pregnancy, from toxic-shock to dissolving fetuses. After hearing myriad number of horror stories from this tome, everything starts to seem really ominous and I am basically reduced to a nervous, quivering mess.

Friday Sept. 16th

Today I got an SMS on my mobile phone, from Yoko. It says "Baby's upside-down has been fixed. Girl. I'll buy princess blanket."

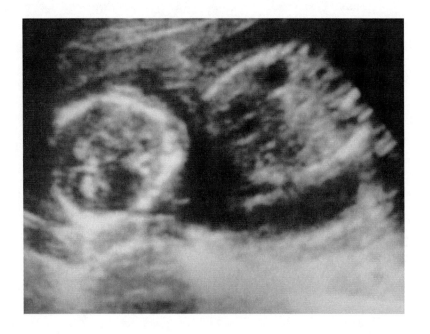

While we're on the subject of Cocoa's birth, this movie review was published in the Daily Yomiuri *newspaper the day she was born.*

I vividly remember an hour or so later celebrating and being somewhat overawed (about the birth, not the review I'd written) as I chugged away at a genuine Cuban cigar, Ozeki One Cup saké in hand, outside a shrine somewhere in Tokyo on a cold November afternoon in 2005.

Artistic Shoot-out in Takeshis' House of Mirrors

Two years after dusting off Shintaro Katsu's blind Zatoichi persona for his quirky period-drama rejig, Takeshi Kitano is back in his own original territory — with a somewhat intriguing inclination toward double vision.

Takeshis', which debuted at this year's Venice International Film Festival and subsequently screened at the celluloid festas in Vancouver, Toronto and London, has thus far traversed a bumpy course, with critical mauling riding shotgun up there alongside the more expected superlatives.

On one level a homage to the yakuza gangster flicks Kitano helped define (since taken to the violent extreme by Takashi Miike in *Ichi the Killer*), this movie also doubles as a parody of the style and might just be Kitano's farewell kiss to same.

The 58-year-old writer-director has quipped that this is a funeral for the genres he explored over his last dozen movies, in particular the gangster premise. Die he apparently does — several times over — as do more than half the cast and extras in a series of grandiose shoot-outs. The yakuza die. The samurai and the sumo wrestlers die. Heck, even the deejay in the club scene dies.

In the process, Takeshis' throws together a smattering of melancholia, a whacked-out sense of humour, tap-dancing musical interludes, a Bonnie and Clyde twist, and more guns than a John Woo slugfest. The fractured narrative structure peppers the screen like a spray of bullets from an Uzi.

The gist of the story is a shakedown of two characters played by Kitano himself: one the "real life" movie star and director, and the other a shy, deadbeat convenience-store clerk who aspires to be an actor. But there's a third overwhelming id here, and that's Kitano's own on-screen alter ego from those earlier yakuza romps. The question — which one of these three is the real McCoy? — disintegrates as proceedings reach out on a surreal, metaphysical limb in which dreams interplay with reality, night-mares become farce, and then it all swings violently back into an unsure version of the here and now. This makes for a sublime visual feast that's as baffling as it is refreshing.

Kitano's trinity of parts aside, there's a bevy of other doppel-gangers, mirror images and dead ringers running through this movie. Kotomi Kyono, while a tad dull as the girlfriend of movie star Takeshi, shows more than just costume jewellery sparkle in her ulterior role as a glitzy, ditzy yakuza girlfriend who happens to be the deadbeat Takeshi's tormenting neighbour.

Kitano certainly isn't afraid to poke fun at himself or the genres he's looked at more seriously in the past. But, after teasing with some mischievous insights, he then skirts the issues. And the weak moments in Kitano's earlier film *Dolls* (2002) — self-conscious "artistic" references — are stitched into *Takeshis'* with abandon. A recurring clown motif, a bullets-as-star-constellations riff, and heavy-handed symbolism (in this case a caterpillar) almost bludgeon the viewer, as if Monty Python had taken a blunt instrument to David Lynch, rendering it all a bit like

Eraserhead on a bad hair day.

Not that this is such a bad thing; at times, it's brilliant. In some bizarre manner — don't bother asking how — Kitano pulls off the slapstick Mothra-sized larva pantomime that appears at various stages throughout proceedings.

But on the whole it's these asides that make the movie lurch, and offshoots like the World War II scenes that bookend the film come off as just plain obscure.

Takeshis' could have been a stronger movie. As it stands, in spite of (or because of) the pointed vignettes, the tap-dancing, and the associated meanderings-within-daydreams, it's a minor masterpiece. Just.

Movie reviews were my secondary niche (after music-related interviews) in the mid-2000s, and I do miss tweaking them — but now (again) I get to kick back and enjoy a cinematic romp without taking notes or trying to conjure up uncatchy one-liners.

One of my favourite comedies of all time is The Producers *(1968), and I was asked to view and review the remake in 2006. So, yeah, I was biased from scratch.*

A Gay Old Time for The Producers

Arguably Mel Brooks' most rib-tickling movie, the 1968 production of *The Producers* showcased Gene Wilder and Zero Mostel at their comedic best. Then it lay dormant in the vault, before being dusted off in the form of a Broadway show at the beginning of this decade with a few bonus song-and-dance numbers penned by Brooks.

In the polished renewal, Matthew Broderick and Nathan Lane filled the formidable boots of Wilder's Leo Bloom and Mostel's Max Bialystock and, according to most reports, their shoe sizes were compatible. Lane in fact won a Tony award.

This movie, based in turn on the Broadway rejig, reveals just how much the whole shebang relies on the '68 original. Everything is the same. Well, almost — aside from the tunes and one or two plot changes.

It's 1960s New York. Max, a failed theatrical producer who's lost his musical shtick as the architect of a string of Broadway flops, crosses paths with the meek, anxiety-ridden accountant Leo — who just happens to conjure up an ingenious plan for raking in millions of bucks on the back of a bona fide Broadway bomb.

First they have to raise the funds from Max's aged female financial backers, to whom Max acts out the role of toy boy, offering to sell the old dears a stairway to the stars with half the steps missing.

Step two? Locating the worst play ever written: *Springtime For Hitler*, penned by German helmet aficionado Franz Liebkind, whose lasting memory of the Führer is that he was "a good dancer." Add to this an egocentrically self-preoccupied director and an utterly incompetent cast, and all that's left for Max and Leo to collect are their plane tickets to Rio. Or so the plan goes...

While Broderick's interpretation of Leo is occasionally (high) pitch-perfect, he isn't up to the persona that Gene Wilder so effectively nurtured 28 years ago. By contrast, Lane genuinely excels as Max, the double-dealing slimeball impresario with a heart buried somewhere deep beneath his hefty production money belt.

It's a similar story with the rest of the cast. Uma Thurman positively smoulders in the role of the sexy Swedish blonde bombshell Ulla, but Will Ferrell — who strangely was nominated for a Golden Globe for this performance — fumbles his take on playwright Liebkind, a part that equally off-the-wall comedian Kenneth Mars had down pat back in 1968.

And absent here is one of the more hilarious characters from the earlier celluloid production, that of Dick Shawn's flower-tossing Lorenzo St. DuBois, known as just plain 'L.S.D.' to his friends, who took on the stage role of Adolf Hitler and rendered him a hip-jive flower child with a swastika armband.

This time around the honour to goose-step the boards for Germany goes to cross-dressing director Roger DeBris (debris, get it?), played by actor Gary Beach, who also camped it up in TV series like *Queer As Folk* and *Will & Grace*.

Gay, it seems, has replaced flower power in the mind of Mel

Brooks some three decades after he originally wrote and directed the yarn, this time with emphasis on the characters of DeBris and his catty, posturing partner, Carmen Ghia (Roger Bart), along with supporting characters modelled on the Village People.

Brooks' script is loaded with high-school-level sexual innuendo, vulgarity, occasionally offensive racial stereotypes, ageism and anything else he wants to bludgeon with a blunt instrument — all delivered with such banal exuberance and gusto it somehow works.

Great for a bit of toe-tapping and a mild guffaw or three, *The Producers* may be set in the 1960s — but the superior 1968 version it's not.

I don't know about you, but I'm a big fan of the majority of the stuff that's been pushed through by Pixar, in particular The Incredibles, Monsters, Inc. *and the* Toy Story *series.*

Cars, *however, left me cold.*

This is the review I did in the Daily Yomiuri *in 2006. Steve Jobs was still alive and kicking, Pixar was relatively independent of Disney, and* Cars 2 *nowhere near the horizon.*

Pixar's Cars Stalls Mid-Race

Ever since Steve Jobs rather presciently snapped up the former computer graphics division of Lucasfilm, Ltd., for a measly ten million dollars back in '86, Pixar has accelerated its winning streak in Hollywood animation stakes, against inconsistent competitors like DreamWorks.

Last year was the studio's most profitable to date, raking in fifteen times Jobs' original investment — mostly on the back of *The Incredibles* (2004) and *Finding Nemo* (2003). This January, Pixar also scored the keys to the Magic Kingdom, via its merger with Disney.

It's been a mesmerizing ride.

Throughout its twenty-year jaunt, through earlier hits like *Toy Story* (1995) and *Monsters, Inc.* (2001), Pixar's strength has been not just its über-progressive eye for CG detailing, but the team's sense of humour and flexibility with its intended target-audiences — an animated sortie by Pixar can appeal equally to preschool whippersnappers and grouchy retirees' laugh quotas.

The versatility of the studio's subject matter over the years has also been enviable, Pixar proving itself as adept at lampooning cultural icons as it has been at unfurling cool characters for kids' lunchboxes.

On first impressions, with Pixar's founding father, John Lasseter, back in the driver's seat after a seven-year directorial hiatus, *Cars* has all the essential ingredients to create another sure-fire winner, chequered flag, lunchbox and all.

But scrape beneath its waxed and polished exterior, and you may walk away a tad disappointed.

Let's start with the plot premise: Churlish, high-octane motor-racing rookie Lightning McQueen (Owen Wilson) sets the track afire and is all set to take the national championship before an accidental detour off Route 66 sets him in the slow-lane in a sleepy little hick town called Radiator Springs.

There he realizes the error of his ways and becomes best buddies with a multicultural cross-section of motor vehicles bearing engines of gold; he also gets the chance to fall in love with someone aside from himself, and saves said town from obscurity.

All in all, it's a bit like *Toy Story* on wheels, filtered through a homogenized host of celluloid predecessors including *City Slickers*, *U-Turn* and *Petticoat Junction*.

While at times quirky, mostly this yarn borders on pedestrian. Chances are it's all the backseat drivers involved — Lasseter may have written and directed with Joe Ranft (who was tragically, if ironically, killed last year in an automobile accident), but there was scripting input from at least nine other people.

The cast also struggles to turn over. *Cars* plunks 81-year-old veteran actor Paul Newman alongside the more comic-inclined Wilson, Michael Keaton, Cheech Marin, and Pixar regular John Ratzenberger (Hamm the Piggy Bank in *Toy Story*).

Ratzenberger is side-tracked (as Mack the transport truck) until the final credits, Marin fills out a tired Latino stereotype, Keaton isn't allowed driving time to develop his surly take on

McQueen's chief racing rival, and Wilson is unusually flat as the stock-car enfant terrible.

It's left to Newman to save the (spoken-word) day, but even his gravelly intonations — as Doc Hudson, the 1951 Hudson Hornet M.D. with a mysterious, racy past — aren't quite up to the Herculean task here.

Lasseter has confirmed that the character name of Lightning McQueen is in part a homage to the late, great Steve McQueen, the actor who pushed the driving envelope in movies like *Bullitt* and *Le Mans*; Newman himself has been a renowned car racing nut for years on end. Classic Pixar would've tweaked this angle for more than it was worth, yet all we get here is Lightning McQueen's racing number (95) that is a mundane reference to the year *Toy Story* was released.

There are some genuinely funny sequences here, like the tractor tipping, the closing-credits Ratzenberger rant, and the flying bugs which are, yes, VW Beetles. But these moments are fleeting and spaced far apart.

Most surprising is the lack of depth in the personas — particularly since Pixar usually renders insightful character designs and personalities. This may be just animation, but colouring between the lines is essential.

Luigi, the 1959 Fiat 500, and Fillmore, the 1960 Volkswagen Kombi van, offer cute asides, but visualizing central character Sally (voiced by Bonnie Hunt) as a 2002 Porsche 911 is a bland choice for the love interest. Wouldn't a 1969 VW Karmann Ghia or a 1960 Volvo P1800S Sports qualify as far more sexy options, if we're going to get all auto-erotic?

For a studio following up on its two most internationally successful films, in its 20th anniversary year, *Cars* is Pixar's least satisfying outing.

Unless you reside in the heartland of the American Midwest, twiddle with V8 engines, listen to country music, smash the odd mailbox, vote for George W., have secret hankerings for reruns of

The Beverley Hillbillies, or adore NASCAR racing — as Lasseter does — your attention span may start sputtering before you've completed the first lap.

I'll throw in one final movie review here, for a movie by Satoshi Kon.

Kon was one of my favourite anime directors, a creative genius and lovely guy I had the opportunity to once interview. He died far too young at age 46.

The man had a cheeky sense of humour undercutting an impressive vision and equally influenced fellow filmmakers Darren Aronofsky and Christopher Nolan.

Kon's Millennium Actress *(2001) remains one of my favourite movies, holding quite the amount of sway over my novel* One Hundred Years of Vicissitude, *and in 2006 — four years before Kon passed away — I reviewed his last movie for the* Daily Yomiuri.

I loved the romp, even though I went to a screening here in Tokyo that was in Japanese, without the benefit of subtitles, and my grasp of the lingo was tenuous at best.

Sometimes there is no language barrier.

Sometimes.

Paprika Spices Up the Anime Aesthetic

The opening minutes of *Paprika* introduce the pivotal character of police detective Konakawa (voiced by Akio Otuska), and his recurring nightmare, which revolves around the spliced-and-looped discovery of a homicide victim.

Director Satoshi Kon then undercuts this traumatic vignette with references to a roll call of Hollywood standards, like *Roman Holiday*, Cecil B. DeMille's *The Greatest Show on Earth*, *Tarzan the Ape Man*, and Hitchcock's *Strangers on a Train*, all rolled up into one sweet dream-sequence.

It additionally ushers in the titular character of this exposition.

Paprika is exotic, super-powered, and a femme fatale with a Peter Pan streak. She also doesn't exist.

She's the cerebral flip side of Dr. Atsuko Chiba (Megumi Hayashibara), the cold and austere head-honcho of a research team that's developed a new gadget called the 'DC Mini'.

It's a headset that enables Chiba to free-fall into patient's psyche, hack into their dreams, and record the encounter; she does so under the guise of her far more liberated alter ego, and while the psychotherapeutic medicinal possibilities are an enticement, there's obviously a more alluring impetus in Chiba's case.

Then, stage left, a bunch of DC Mini prototypes are stolen by a mysterious psycho-terrorist, and the unravelling of a sinister tangle of events leaves the fate of the world suspended in the balance.

The movie dips precariously, not only between Chiba's contradictory personas, but also between the twin realms of conscious reality, with its natural laws, and that of dreams — where those rules are remoulded or rejected entirely.

There are moments here where you could misconstrue this yarn as a remake of Jennifer Lopez's patchy turn-of-the-millennium vehicle *The Cell*, except that the original story for *Paprika* was penned in 1993 by Yasutaka Tsutsui, who created that other recent anime hit, *Toki o Kakeru Shojo* (aka *The Girl Who Leapt Through Time*).

Kon himself previously helmed the anime movies *Perfect Blue* (1997), *Millennium Actress* (2001), and *Tokyo Godfathers* (2003); he worked closely with Koji Morimoto on the remarkable 'Magnetic Rose' segment of Katsuhiro Otomo's anime omnibus *Memories* in 1995, and co-wrote the screenplay here.

Kon and Tsutsui themselves voice two of the more enigmatic characters — the bartenders Mr. Jinnai and Mr. Kuga — and, even by anime standards, this one's completely out there.

Anybody familiar with outings by Kon, Morimoto, Hayao Miyazaki or Mamoru Oshii, would appreciate that anime bends the rules of moviemaking, and in *Paprika* it's like Dr. Seuss has reworked the script and tweaked the visuals for Oshii's thought-provoking *Ghost in the Shell* (1995).

The film rates as the most mesmerizing animation long-player since Miyazaki's *Spirited Away* five years ago, and Kon exhibits an equally playful willingness to pitchfork the texture of the more dramatic moments.

Am I gushing yet?

They're not skimping in the voice actor stakes here — Hayashibara and Koichi Yamadera (Dr. Morio Osanai) previously lent their dulcet tones to two of the most iconographic of recent anime characters, Faye Valentine and Spike Spiegel, in *Cowboy Bebop*, while Otsuka voiced Batou in the *Ghost in the Shell* franchise.

Add to this some stunning background art, peerless integration of 2-D and 3-D animation, and some wonderful character designs by Studio Ghibli regular Masashi Ando.

But it's obvious that Kon's forte is in the surreal interaction of reality and dreams — which all too often drift into nightmares.

The recurring motif of a parade of Japanese cultural knick-knacks (some traditional, and others kitsch, from dancing Kewpie dolls and tin toys to marching sets of samurai armor, *torii* gates yanked right out of shrines, and the disturbing scaled-down Statue of Liberty from Odaiba) is downright superb.

Next up, food.

Like Homer J. Simpson, I seriously do love my fugu (blow fish). Simple as that. I don't care if it can kill you, painfully.

Probably why I devoted an entire chapter to the cuisine in One Hundred Years of Vicissitude.

This genuflection was published in Geek *magazine in 2009. And I just looked up genuflection in my thesaurus. Nice.*

I Want My Fugu!

There's a question on my mind, and it's one I've mulled over for years, ever since Homer Simpson demanded *fugu* at a Japanese restaurant, that time when the sushi chef was out canoodling Ms. Krabappel on the backseat of her car.

Cue assistant chef's stressful splicing and dicing of the deflating delicacy.

For those precious insular types without an operational TV who may've missed this episode, and double-up on the offence by having no access to Wikipedia or even a moth-eaten edition of the *Encylopædia Britannica*, fugu is the Japanese name for blowfish, and the majority of these fish have extremely high levels of a neurotoxin called tetrodotoxin in their ovaries, liver, intestines, gonads and skin.

These little fellas, with a penchant for getting sizeable relatively quickly, in fact get honourable mention on both Wikipedia and in the *Britannica* for being the second most-poisonous vertebrates in the world. There's also no antidote. That doesn't seem to faze the Japanese, though — apparently some

10,000 tons are consumed here each year.

When I first came over from Australia, I really had no choice but to play Homer and indulge in the expensive dish, and the best way to have fugu is sashimi-style, sliced exceptionally thin and raw, and served with a special dipping sauce called *ponzu* (a canny blend of citrus juice and soy sauce).

You can also have it deep fried or conjured up in a *nabe* (hot pot), but for me it's sensational as sashimi, combined with *fugu hirezake*: toasted fugu fin served in hot saké. It smells a wee bit fishy, but has quite the celebratory kick to it

You can usually tell the fugu eateries by the huge storefront tanks full of the fish: Swimming, carousing, looking a little the worse-for-wear, and occasionally floating listlessly upside down.

The allusion of those bottom-up types runs a little close to home when it comes to fugu.

Both in fiction and reality the fish has had a huge impact on the culture of this country. While it's the foodstuff of kings (but not the emperor, apparently), lauded in *haiku*, and all Japanese office workers with big annual bonuses aspire to tuck into the aquatic delight, there's a hint of the morbid and suicidal involved, along with some mention of egos quashed. Fugu, while outrageously priced, is the Russian roulette of the wining and dining set — and fatality is, after all, the great leveller.

Theatrical rumour has it that the flamboyant Chairman Kaga (played by actor Takeshi Kaga), of *Iron Chef* notoriety, died of fugu poisoning after the series ended in Japan, but kabuki star Bando Mitsugoro VIII really did die (of paralysis and asphyxiation) just hours after a stint in a Kyoto restaurant in 1975 — having thrown care to the winds, boasting invulnerability, and tossed down four of the fish's highly-toxic livers.

And then there's that question I hinted at earlier, the one that's followed me ever since I saw Homer carted off to hospital with suspected fugu poisoning.

The origin of the fish's consumption in Japan remains unclear

— it definitely goes back centuries, and there've been possible fugu table scraps found in burial mounds that date back to the Jomon period, over 2,400 years ago.

The question for me is this: Who were the very first people who decided to snack on this exceptionally unattractive fish, and how on earth did they work out which bits were OK for consumption, and which other parts would grant them slow, excruciating death?

Were short straws involved? Furry dice? Some kind of class-system pecking order? Or just manic rounds of *jan-ken-pon* (rock-paper-scissors)?

Personally, every time I eat fugu (which has actually been only twice), I canonize the experience — then spend the rest of the night fretting that I'll die in my sleep, much like the unluckier pioneers of aquatic vertebratic cuisine before me.

Back in February 2011, I worked with Francesco Prandoni at anime studio Production I.G, the people who did Ghost in the Shell *and the anime sequence in Quentin Tarantino's* Kill Bill: Vol. 1.

Endeavouring to avoid the stilted, unnatural English subtitles that typically come with Japanese anime, they asked me to get on board and make them unnatural in my own special way, 'ready' to hit the festival circuit that year.

This was for their new pet project Drawer Hobs.

Fortunately for me, as this can be a painstaking process to get the timing right and the correct number of words on-screen at any particular time — without overloading the viewer — I loved the film.

It was directed by Kazuchika Kise, who may not be so well known, but has a sensational CV — think senior animator at I.G's Studio 1, with credits including the two Patlabor *movies helmed by Mamoru Oshii, along with* Ghost in the Shell *and its sequel* Innocence.

Kise was also involved in the production of Blood: The Last Vampire, Musashi: The Dream of the Last Samurai, *and all the* xxxHOLiC *animated adaptations and he did character designs for the* Blood: The Last Vampire *spin-off,* Blood-C.

For Drawer Hobs, *Kise conjured up the original story concept, which was then touched up by Daishiro Tanimura (*Ghost Hound*), and even the supercute character designs are also by Kise — in collaboration with Ryo Hirata (*Oblivion Island*).*

*The surprising background art, which is often simple yet surprisingly effective, has been rendered by Hiromasa Ogura (*Ghost in the Shell, Jin-Roh, Ghost Hound*), and spot-on voice acting work comes from Mamiko Noto (*Rin in* Inuyasha*) and Etsuko Kozakura (*Tamama in* Sgt. Frog*).*

I decided to insert here a snippet of the to-and-fro email process that Francesco and I went through in order to get the subtitles done. Not sure it makes sense, but basically we tackled each subtitle according to the time-code.

If you can locate this 24-minute joy, take a squizz.

Subtitling The Drawer Hobs

0021 01:02:12:05/01:02:15:07

"Drawer" can't be used singularly since there's more than one drawer here, so we'd always have to use the plural. If you really prefer to keep it singular, we could go with "dresser" instead – but personally I don't love the word, and I think it's better to use "drawers" to match up with the title of the movie itself!

0067 01:05:56:12/01:06:00:03

"Furniture is not fixed with spurs" – unfortunately I thought straight away about cowboy spurs (wikipedia.org/wiki/Spur), and I think a lot of people might. I tried checking if "spur" is commonly used in America for earthquake safety, but only came up with a sharp, thorny growth on some animals' legs.

So...changed the line to "Not a single furniture bracket", which is a similar length, rolls better here, and brackets are apparently what people use to fix furniture so it's safe in earthquakes. (worksafetech.com/pages/SeismaFlex.html)

0083 01:06:49:12/01:06:51:20
"Hell" is a bit serious; "heck" is more playful — suits nature that this is aimed at all ages.

0101 01:08:19:15/01:08:22:10
"Meet Hanpei. He's always messing things around" comes a little soon after Noeru says "who made this mess", so how about we change this to "He's always creating chaos".

0113 01:09:05:07/01:09:08:21
"What are you cooking" — more natural using "what're" for spoken word.

"I'm consulting the ingredients" — I almost left this in because it works like he's a mystic, and I liked your explanation, but I'm not sure this conveys what you want to here.

Possible change: "I'm contemplating my options" works better in English, and sounds equally wise, as he's planning what do for dinner with limited resources.

But if you want to keep the original, I'm fine with that too! ;)

The fun part of publishing novels is trying out new tangents to help promote them, rather than retreading the same boards (and dull lines) over and over.

With the proliferation of websites and blogs, the opportunity to diversify the approach has increased — like this one I put together in September last year for Lori Hettler at The Next Best Book Blog.

Cheers, mate!

I'll Drink to That

In my first book *Tobacco-Stained Mountain Goat*, it was "any drink goes" — basically, our hero Floyd Maquina would guzzle anything with a smidgeon of alcoholic content.

He rises high at times, when straight Johnnie Walker whisky is in the offering, along with a bottle of Moët & Chandon champagne. Otherwise Floyd scrapes the barrel with synthetic brandy (this is an apocalyptic, dystopic future world we're talking up) and rotgut liquor of various kinds.

Floyd does, however, draw the line at Siamese vodka.

"I'd owned two bottles of Siamese vodka in my life, drunkenly bought one night from the back room of a seedy bar I used to regular," Floyd confesses. "The first bottle left me without a voice for a week, like the Devil himself pissed down my throat. The other has gathered dust for years — even at my drunkest I knew better than to touch the stuff."

James Bond also can't abide by Siamese vodka. If you watch the 1967 movie *You Only Live Twice*, you'll see Sean Connery's horrified reaction to the drink.

My second novel *One Hundred Years of Vicissitude*, coming out in October, has a more even-keel, shall we say sophisticated approach to the drinking thing. While Japanese moonshine — called *katsutori* — does enter the picture, mostly we're blessed with quality saké. And the two people towing the story, Wolram and Kohana, have expensive palates.

At one point, in a swinging '60s Tokyo bar, Kohana orders for Wolram a Vesper, the classic 007 martini.

"Three measures of Gordon's, one of shōchū, half a measure of Kina Lillet," she tells the bartender. "Shake it very well until it's ice-cold, then add a large thin slice of lemon peel. Got it?" It's Ian Fleming's original recipe to a tee, except that vodka is replaced with Japanese shōchū.

Of course.

But the truly original drink in *One Hundred Years of Vicissitude* is the one that Kohana, our former geisha, orders for herself. While I have no idea what's in the thing, I do dig the name.

The passage reads thus:

Kohana held up her drink. It had a blood-coloured cocktail in it, with shards of ice arranged like sharp teeth around the top.

"It's a house specialty: The Piranha."

"Ahh, of course. Well, bon appétit!"

"Kanpai."

We clicked glasses.

And now we come to a close.

I wrote the next story ten days after the big earthquake and tsunami on March 11, 2011, now known on Wikipedia variously as the 2011 Tohoku earthquake, the Great East Japan Earthquake, and Higashi nihon daishin-sai in Japanese.

Whatever the moniker, it was one of the five most powerful earthquakes in the world since record keeping began in 1900, nearly 16,000 people died — and the temblor brought with it a tsunami that tipped 40 metres.

Afterwards, things were fairly stressful, as you can probably imagine, even though we lived a considerable distance from the epicentre. Being a journalist in Japan, I got asked to write a couple of opinion pieces on life immediately thereafter, and this was one of them.

This article was published in Sydney magazine 3D World *as well as in* Impact *in the UK.*

I debated with myself whether or not to include the piece, but the disaster had a profound impact on my personal psyche at the time, and still holds some sway.

I'm not saying it changed my life, but moments like this make you look at things afresh — in this case being a major motivation behind the writing my second novel One Hundred Years of Vicissitude, *which is dedicated to this country and these wonderful people.*

Two years later the effects of the earthquake and tsunami continue to reverberate.

Japan's economy is struggling to cope with the costs, rebuilding is in flux, and radiation tips worrying levels even here in Tokyo.

Japan Shakes

Unless you've had your head buried deep inside some obscure sandbox in a place a thousand miles from the nearest social network or wireless connection, you'd already know about the eye-opening series of events that have been taking place in Japan, and continue to spiral in a realm hopefully a wee bit more under control as I write this waffle here in Tokyo.

But Tokyo was fortunate compared with other places in this country up north, like Miyagi (think tsunami) and Fukushima (where the nuclear reactors sit).

Thus far we've been lucky enough in this city to have survived the fourth or fifth biggest earthquake in recorded history in one of the world's most seismically active nations, and I guess we're keeping fingers crossed regarding those darned elusive huffing-and-puffing reactors.

What's been more exhausting are the recently implanted foreign journalists strolling the streets of Tokyo, a city they barely know, and making blanket proclamations like "Although there's not quite panic yet, there's definitely a sense of nervousness and edge."

Whatever.

These are strange times here, for all too obvious reasons, and sometimes it feels like we're collectively treading water awaiting the next Big Thing to transpire. Meanwhile the reactors still belch scary looking clouds and we get shaken by dozens of aftershocks every day.

The last few days in the supermarkets around our place, almost half the shelves have been empty as people are stocking up in case of another emergency. Or three.

But the local residents have been astoundingly resolute — not here the looting and general mayhem on the streets you see in other lesser disasters elsewhere in the world — and it's nowhere near desperate, at least in Tokyo.

People are getting on with their lives and are quick to share a smile; there's a stunning sense of camaraderie that prevails. My respect for these people has increased ten-fold over the past week.

And there are the lighter moments: the primary school kids wearing their pointy silver radiation hats that make them look like Gandalf; the fact that I've never seen Tokyo so quiet and sedate and it's actually quite a nice change to its usual hectic nature — it's like a Sunday morning in Melbourne.

Almost.

That quietness, however, along with the power cuts and the continuous aftershocks are choking the local clubbing scene.

A high percentage of events and parties have been cancelled, and attendance is lower than usual at the places that are still open. A lot of the DJ/producers I know are spending most of their time at home, creating tunes — or putting together worthy benefit compilations, like the ones coming out through Shin Nishimura's Plus Tokyo label and another called *Kibou* that's being put together by Japanophile DJ Hi-Shock through his Elektrax label — which features contributions from a wad of

Japan's finest techno bods.

It's been mad timing for my new novel to come out; teaches me to write a yarn that's been described as "post-apocalyptic noir." I'm supposed to have the Tokyo book launch this Friday, but the postal service is all screwed up so I probably won't be getting the books themselves in time from the U.S. We're doing it anyway, regardless of earthquakes and/or radiation levels.

Still, it does give us nice fodder for silly jokes about glowing in the dark at the party (and therefore no need for lighting), plus going tree-friendly "green" at a book launch.

It's the humour-in-adversity thing that really does get you through.

The situation seems to be on the mend at the moment, which is a relief, and cautious jocularity and a touch of optimism help to clear the shoals.

Then again, the other morning when I first woke up I was partially hungover and parched so indulged in a sizable glass of tap water; straight after I switched on the computer and found a big headline that declared that radiation had infiltrated the Tokyo water supply — just before reading the fine-print that the level itself was negligible and within safety standards.

Ye gods.

And OK, I'll 'fess up here — I've seen my fair share of Japanese disaster flicks and in fact have always been a bit of a fan.

I loved Godzilla movies when I was a kid — the way in which he walloped little balsa-wood versions of Tokyo and Osaka — and I still DJ out the awesome theme song to 1961 monster flick *Mothra*, written by Yuji Koseki and sung by The Peanuts.

But these past 12 days have been a little too close to home, and I say that not just because I currently live in Tokyo and my balcony partition is busted.

The quakes and shakes this time were real, not cheap FX on celluloid with high-definition surround sound. It's eerily like the plot in Sakyo Komatsu's novel *Japan Sinks* — made into a B-movie classic in 1973 and a lesser creature in 2006 — but defies the page or the artificial set seen via a viewfinder.

Real people have died, and thousands of other bona fide human beings have lost loved ones and friends. Hundreds of thousands are destitute, lacking basic provisions, and braving zero-degree temperatures up north.

The fact is that this is going to take a long time to clean up, let alone forget.

And to be honest, while all along there's been this unshakable urge inside me to pursue some quixotic gonzo journalistic trail, sticking it all out no matter what — and thereby see the situation right through to the other side — my mind has been on those nuclear reactors melting down up north. I've therefore had an eye on self-extraction if irradiated push came to likewise shove.

As I said, fingers are crossed for everyone here that we've stepped beyond the multiple-disaster abyss for now...and for a long time to come.

Acknowledgements

My writing wouldn't be 'my' writing at all without the input of
family and friends, editors, fellow authors, artists, critics and
people who bother to read my stuff — and let me know how they
felt about it.

I specifically want to thank my mum Fée, dad Des, wife Yoko
and most of all, my daughter Cocoa — who continues to fire up
my imagination with her own hijinks — along with Peter Bergin,
mates Briony, Tim, Brian, Seb, Luke, Alby, Dames, Scott, Chloe,
Trish, the IF? crew, cuz Zoe, Pete, Camille, Kristina, Danielle,
Nikki, Jason, Wolfgang, Devin, Marcus, Neil, Baz, Steve, Lee,
Yoshiko, Toshie, Hashimoto-san, Tsukako, Yumiko, Nonaka-san,
Hiroko, and the high-school kids I've taught at Chiyoda here in
Tokyo.

Similarly, I wouldn't be hammering together this acknowl-
edgements section of a published book without the belief and
support of people like Kristopher and Christine Young at
Another Sky Press, giving me my first big break with *Tobacco-
Stained Mountain Goat*, and Phil Jourdan and everyone else at
Perfect Edge Books — who gave me my next. Phil in particular
has proven himself as much a buddy as he is an ally, publisher
and emotional arbiter. Hats off to my editors Dominic C. James
and Trevor Greenfield, along with cover designer Nick Welch.

Other editor/publishers who've offered engaging hands of
support have included Chris Rhatigan, Nigel Bird, Paul D.
Brazill, Luca Veste, K.A. Laity, Liam José, Cameron Ashley,
Andrew Nette, Ron Earl Phillips, Martin Garrity, Nathan
Pettigrew, Paul Jackson, Jeff Bond, Stefan Blitz, 'Big' Mike Leeder
and Andrew Hudson.

Respect to Reviews by Elizabeth A. White, the Booked
Podcast, Forces Of Geek, Books and Booze, Bare*Bones, The
Thrilling Detective, The Momus Report, Alwaysunmended,

Fantasy Book Review, Steampunk Magazine, Dark Wolf's Fantasy Reviews, SF Book Reviews, Solarcide, OzNoir, A Fantastical Librarian, Verbicide, Warmed & Bound, Drying Ink, Permission To Kill, Crime Fiction Lover, Madman, Angry Robot, Geek Girls, Dirty Noir, The Jack Kirby Museum, Bleeding Cool, Sons Of Spade, Fox Spirit, The Ink Shot, Comic Bastards, TNBBC, Pulp Pusher and LitReactor, Shotgun Honey, Crime Factory, Pulp Ink, Solarcide, Weird Noir, Off the Record, All Due Respect, Slit Your Wrists, the Writing Cult and Snubnose Press.

Extra special kudos must go to supportive (and more talented) types like Fiona Johnson (aka McDroll), Elizabeth White, Marcus Baumgart, Renee Asher Pickup, Mckay Williams, Joe Clifford, Lloyd Paige, Heath Lowrance, Josh Stallings, Gordon Highland, Craig Wallwork, Jeff Shear, Mihai Adascalitei, Dakota Taylor, Benoit Lelièvre, Zoe Kingsley, Julie Morrigan, Caleb J. Ross, Tony Black, Katy O'Dowd, Raymond Embrack, Chad Eagleton, Richard Thomas, Olivia Wakey, Susi Holliday, Sean Cregan, Eva Dolan, Christopher TM, Travis Haydon, Laramore Black, Guy Salvidge, Jay Slayton-Joslin, Sabrina Ogden, Gerard Brennan, Jonny Gibbings, Tony Pacitti, A.B. Riddle, Mitzi Akaha, Damien G. Walter, Chad Rohrbacher, Patti Abbott, Michael J. Riser, N.E. White, Eric Beetner, Richard Godwin, Alan Herrick, A.M. Harte, Michael Gonzalez, Lee Sibbald, Emlyn Rees, Ryan K. Lindsay and Pete Goutis.

Gratitude here also to the comic artists I've worked with over the past 12 months — you'll find the contributions from Marcos Vergara, Nicolas Gomes, Andrew Chiu and Maan House inside this tome, but others have included Cocoa Bergen (of course!), Drezz Rodriguez, Nathan St. John, Harvey Finch, Michael Grills, Paul Mason, Dave Acosta, Carlos E. Gómez, Yoko Umehara, Saint Yak, JGMiranda, Rodolfo Reyes, Fred Rambaud, Juan Saavedra and Giovanni Ballati. Some of these guys crop up in *The Tobacco-Stained Sky*, others in *Who is Killing the Great Capes of Heropa?*

At Production I.G over the past couple of years it was a joy to get to work with anime and live-action material by Mamoru Oshii, Kazuchika Kise and Naoyoshi Shiotani (thanks, Francesco!).

Filmmakers equally deserving a pat on the back? In no particular order: Oshii-san, the late (great) Satoshi Kon, Akira Kurosawa, John Huston, Seijun Suzuki, Christopher Nolan, Howard Hawks, David Lynch, Terry Gilliam, Joss Whedon, Quentin Tarantino, Kon Ichikawa, Sam Raimi, Don Siegel, John Woo, Ronald D. Moore, Sergio Leone, Gerry Anderson, Darren Aronofsky, Terrence Malick, Norman Jewison, David Peoples, Zack Snyder, Dario Argento, Martin Scorsese, Tim Burton, Gene Kelly, Bill Bennett, Koji Morimoto, Peter Yates, Bruce Beresford, Billy Wilder, Stanley Kubrick, Lewis Gilbert, Wong Kar-wai, John Ford, Kinji Fukusaku, Andrey Tarkovskiy, Nicolas Roeg, Peters Weir, Greenaway & Jackson, Ridley Scott, Gregor Jordan, Pixar, David Michôd, Tarsem Singh, Takashi Miike, Charles Chauvel, Robert Rodriguez, 99% of old film noir, and Hammer movies and American International flicks from the 1960s.

Essential writers would easily include, over the years, Philip K. Dick, Haruki Murakami, Graham Geene, Nicholas Christopher, Hunter S. Thompson, Katsuhiro Otomo, Eugene O'Neill, Michael Chabon, A. A. Milne, Ryu Murakami, Edith Wharton, Dr. Seuss, Akira Yoshimura, Norman Lindsay, Hergé, Carson McCullers — and especially Raymond Chandler and Dashiell Hammett (of course) along with the 1930s-40s Hollywood big screen versions of their books.

Music? Produced by way too many people to mention here. Food of the gods.

Other things/people I must pay debts of gratitude to would be the 1960s Marvel Comics put together by Stan Lee, Jack Kirby, Roy Thomas, Jim Steranko, Barry Windsor-Smith, John Buscema and their cohorts, and ballet (especially the pairing of Massimo Murru opposite Alessandra Ferri in Roland Petit's version of *El Murciélago* ~ *La Chauve-souris*, aka *The Bat*).

About the Author

Andrez Bergen is an expat Australian writer, journalist, DJ, and ad hoc saké connoisseur who's been entrenched in Tokyo, Japan, for the past decade. He makes music as Little Nobody and ran groundbreaking Melbourne record label IF? for 15 years.

Bergen has also written for newspapers such as *The Age* and the *Yomiuri Shinbun*, as well as magazines like *Mixmag*, *Anime Insider*, *Australian Style*, *Remix*, *Impact*, *Beat*, *3D World* and *Geek Magazine*.

He published noir/sci-fi novel *Tobacco-Stained Mountain Goat* in 2011 through Another Sky Press and the surreal fantasy *One Hundred Years of Vicissitude* via Perfect Edge Books in 2012.

He's recently finished a third novel, titled *Who is Killing the Great Capes of Heropa?*, and is plowing into #4 (*The Mercury Drinkers*).

Bergen has published short stories via Crime Factory, Shotgun Honey, Snubnose Press, Solarcide, Weird Noir, Big Pulp, Full Dark City Press and All Due Respect, and worked on translating and adapting the scripts for feature films by Mamoru Oshii,

Kazuchika Kise and Naoyoshi Shiotani with Production I.G.

He married artist Yoko Umehara in 2005 and they have one child, Cocoa.

http://andrezbergen.wordpress.com

PHOTO BY YOKO UMEHARA BERGEN

PERFECT
EDGE
BOOKS

"There are many who dare not kill themselves for fear of what
the neighbours will say," Cyril Connolly wrote, and we believe
he was right.
Perfect Edge seeks books that take on the crippling fear of other
people, the question of what's correct and normal, of how life
works, of what art is.
Our authors disagree with each other; their styles vary as widely as
their concerns. What matters is the will to create books that won't be
easy to assimilate. We take risks, not for the sake of risk-taking, but for
the things that might come out of it.